Other Novels by Kate Bailey

Rising Flock Series

1) Flight of the Flock
2) Shifting of the Shadows
3) Warnings of the Wind

WARNINGS OF THE WIND

RISING FLOCK: BOOK 3

KATE BAILEY

LifeRich PUBLISHING

This is a work of fiction. All of the characters, names, incidents, organizations, and dialogue in this novel are either the products of the author's imagination or are used fictitiously.

LifeRich Publishing is a registered trademark of The Reader's Digest Association, Inc.

LifeRich Publishing books may be ordered through booksellers or by contacting:

LifeRich Publishing
1663 Liberty Drive
Bloomington, IN 47403
www.liferichpublishing.com
844-686-9607

Because of the dynamic nature of the Internet, any web addresses or links contained in this book may have changed since publication and may no longer be valid. The views expressed in this work are solely those of the author and do not necessarily reflect the views of the publisher, and the publisher hereby disclaims any responsibility for them.

ISBN: 978-1-4897-3527-0 (sc)
ISBN: 978-1-4897-3526-3 (e)

Library of Congress Control Number: 2021907582

Print information available on the last page.

LifeRich Publishing rev. date: 06/11/2021

CONTENTS

Background and Characters ix
Previously in the Rising Flock xiii
Chapter 1 The Chase 1
Chapter 2 Back to HQ 5
Chapter 3 Threat of War 14
Chapter 4 Always be Prepared 22
Chapter 5 Pride Before Fall 27
Chapter 6 Strike One 32
Chapter 7 Well Laid Plans 41
Chapter 8 The Hated Plan C 47
Chapter 9 Counting the Cost 56
Chapter 10 Promises 69
Chapter 11 House of Death 78
Chapter 12 You Need Us 85
Chapter 13 The Walk 95
Chapter 14 Falling Apart 110
Chapter 15 Setbacks 117
Chapter 16 Connect the Dots 122
Chapter 17 Interrogation 126
Chapter 18 Balance of Life 135
Chapter 19 Coloring Outside the Lines 143
Chapter 20 Room 22B 150
Chapter 21 Clues 156
Chapter 22 Escape 160
Chapter 23 Running Intel 166

Chapter 24 Tick, Tick 176
Chapter 25 Power 185
Chapter 26 Hearts of Men 194
Chapter 27 Into the Fire 203
Chapter 28 The Star-Gem 209
Chapter 29 Risky Maneuvers 216
Chapter 30 Lighting the Fuse 223
Chapter 31 Travel Plans 236
Chapter 32 Fortress of Darkness 241
Chapter 33 Spinning the Truth 253
Epilogue 265
About the Author 267
Discussion Questions 269

This story is dedicated to my family, my roommate, and my team for giving me the strength and kindness it takes to make it through life. With your help and God's, I am able to write and sing and show love.

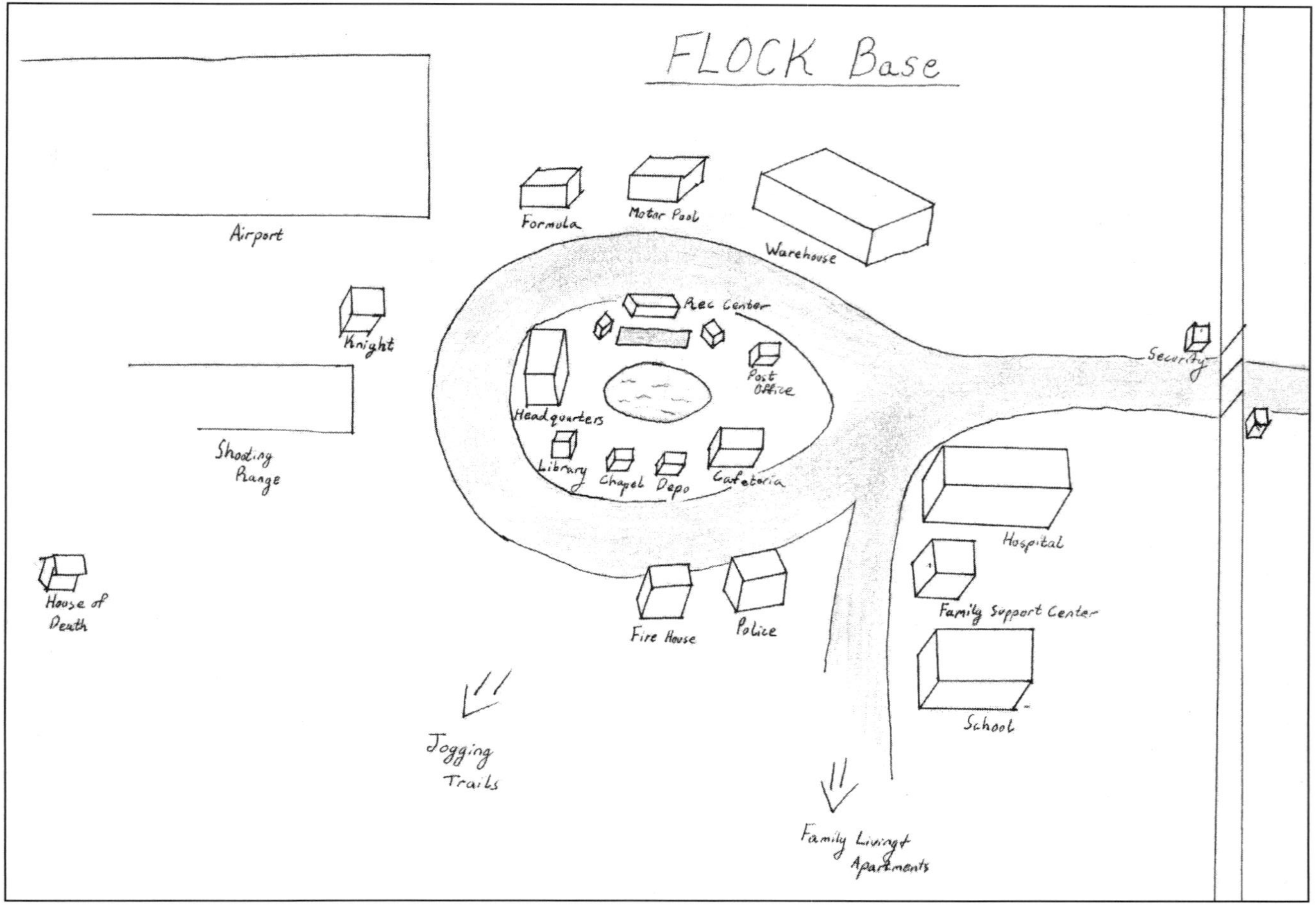
FLOCK Base
Airport
Formula
Motor Pool
Warehouse
Knight
Rec Center
Post Office
Headquarters
Shooting Range
Library
Chapel
Depo
Cafeteria
Security
Hospital
House of Death
Fire House
Police
Family Support Center
School
Jogging Trails
Family Living & Apartments

BACKGROUND AND CHARACTERS

The Flock is made up of five divisions which work together to accomplish major goals: Formula, Light, Omega, Coordinate, and Knight.

Formula- the team that designs and builds new technology, weapons, and other gadgets, and is also responsible for building projects in disaster torn regions of the globe.

Light- the team that gathers and monitors intelligence

Omega- the team that devises strategies, leads the individual teams, and holds the organization together

Coordinate- the team that works with other groups (FBI, INTERPOL, local police) as well as disaster relief agencies and working press releases

Knight- the team that runs operations

Rising Flock Team (alphabetical order)

Brooke Castleberry: twenty-year-old librarian from Texas working with the Light division, code name "Sparrow"

Max Davis: twenty-year-old architect from California working with the Formula division, code name "Blackbird"

Lukas Dekker: twenty-four-year-old mechanic from Germany working with the Knight division, code name "Falcon"

Tonya Miller: twenty-four-year-old counselor from Arizona working with the Coordinate division, code name "Hummingbird"

Emily Moore: twenty-year-old forensic scientist from England working with the Knight division, code name "Nightingale"

Ryan Murphy: twenty-three-year-old actor from New York working with the Coordinate division, code name "Hawk"

Sam Rogers: twenty-year-old archeologist from California working with Light division, code name "Osprey"

Collin Scott: twenty-five-year-old pilot from Ireland, leader of the Rising Flock, working with Omega division, code name "Eagle"

Nichole Thomas: twenty-three-year-old journalist from France working with the Coordinate division, code name "Mockingbird"

Other Cast (in order of appearance)

Michael Seaward: member of the Flock, Director of Knight division

Reid Whitmore: member of the Flock, Director of Light division

Tatiana Petrikov: member of the Flock, responsible for the training of the Rising Flock

Juan: member of the Flock, specialist in South America for Light division

Bob: Department of Defense agent stationed in Chicago

Caleb: Department of Defense agent stationed in New York

Kelli: member of the Flock, an analyst for the Flock in Light division

Brady: member of the Flock, based in Chicago

Cynthia Lombard: member of the Flock, Director of Coordinate division

Stephon Taylor: member of the Flock, Director of Formula division

Felix St. James: executive director of the Flock

Benji Martinez: high school friend of Tonya, firefighter in Houston

Jasmine: social worker in Houston, friend of Tonya, organizer of the Walk to End Human Trafficking.

Sarai: Jasmine's daughter

Lilly Castleberry: Brooke's younger sister

Zane Tennison: Member of the Shifting Shadows captured in Chicago

José "Reaper" Garcia: the Flock's head interrogator

Tadi Miller: Tonya's younger brother

Agent Lionel Smith: FBI agent from New York

Officer Nelson: police officer in Indianapolis

Rick Peabody: nuclear scientist

Hunter Drake: the new Radenie, leader of the Shifting Shadows

Pedro Ramon: Shifting Shadow pretending to be Matias Gonzales from Argentina

Professor Sinclair: professor of astronomy at the University of Colorado

Colonel Brice Fulton: Air Force colonel targeted by the Shifting Shadows

Susan Ammons: nuclear scientist taken by the Shifting Shadows

PREVIOUSLY IN THE RISING FLOCK

Collin Scott left his life in Ireland to work for the University of BLITS, but the secrets of his family quickly caught up to him when he joined the Flock, an organization focused on bringing down the bad guys and helping those hurt by them. His father, Andrew Scott, had been the leader of the Flock before he was killed by Radenie, the very man who had kidnapped Tonya.

There are two things everyone knew about Tonya Miller. One, she was the kindest soul to ever get her master's in counseling, and two, she loved her family. But Peter Seaward, the leader of the Flock, gave her a wooden bear before he died, telling her to keep it safe because in it was the last piece to the treasure of the Shifting Shadows and proof of their crimes. Because of her possession of this map, Radenie, the leader of the Shifting Shadows, kidnapped her.

Lukas Dekker was a fixer of broken things. When Tonya was taken, he was one of the first, along with his girlfriend Emily, to go undercover and rescue her. They succeeded in rescuing her and stayed in Nepal to stop the Shifting Shadows from carrying out an assassination, but the only way to do that was to pretend to kill the target themselves.

Emily Moore not only succeeded in "killing" their target and gaining the respect of Radenie, but she also succeeded in proving a threat to his wife and nephew, Hunter, who were planning a coup. In an attempt to take over the Shifting Shadows, Radenie's wife poisoned Radenie with Emily's poison and shot Emily after framing her for his death.

When Tonya was kidnapped, the Shifting Shadows didn't find the bear with the map because Tonya gave it to Nichole Thomas. As a journalist, Nichole loved a good story, and nothing made a better story than finding a hidden treasure. After finding the map hidden in the bear, she made her way to Egypt to work with Sam and follow the clues to the treasure of the Shifting Shadows.

Sam Rogers was completing his internship in Egypt as an archeologist. When Nichole arrived with the map, they followed it to the next clue, but the Shifting Shadows burned down the site and chased them out of Egypt to France where they joined up with the rest of the team and deciphered the map that led them to the treasure hidden in Brazil.

Years before this, Sam moved from Los Angeles leaving behind his best friend Max Davis only to be reunited with him at the University of BLITS. When Max was young his father disappeared. Max didn't think of that often until he found himself in Brazil at the end of the treasure hunt face to face with a man who looked just like him. His father, Mark, had been working with the Flock while Andrew Scott was the leader, but when Andrew was killed, Mark switched sides and worked with the Shifting Shadows as a thief. When Radenie sent him to the treasure, he blackmailed the Shadows and sold back the treasure map a piece at a time, which Peter Seaward, the leader of the Flock, got to before Radenie. And that was how the map ended up in Alaska.

Ryan Murphy was accustomed to traveling with his father, an international business man, but his first time to Alaska was with Michael Seaward, the one who created their team and son of Peter Seaward. There they pieced the map together, and Ryan practiced his high school Latin in translating it. After Sam deciphered where the key led, they picked up Max and Brooke and left for Brazil.

While Ryan was no stranger to travelling, Brooke Castleberry was content to stay at home. But her luck would never let her. When she was in high school, she witnessed Hunter, the nephew of

Radenie, kill someone and was relocated by the police. She was safe for four years until Hunter found her at the University of BLITS. Winter break, he snuck into her house to kill her, but ended up being shot by her sister, Lilly, and hauled away by Michael Seaward. That Summer, the Shifting Shadows came after her again, but this time for a ring called the star-gem. Inscribed in it was a constellation which, if read as a map, lead to the Fortress of DARKNESS.

CHAPTER 1
THE CHASE

Undisclosed Location

"We're losin' him!" Collin's voice yelled, his Irish tenor barely audible over the blare of horns and screech of tires.

The black sedan sped ahead of them, running the red light and disappearing down an alley. Lukas pressed the horn on his red charger and slowed only enough to ensure the intersection was clear.

Sliding past the street, Lukas hit the brakes and jerked his wheel to make the alley.

"No! Go straight!" Nichole's voice came through over the Bluetooth speaker in his car. Normally Lukas liked the sound of her French accent, but not when she was late in giving him directions.

The car lurched back on the road. Collin reached for the grab bar and yelled over the acceleration so Nichole could hear him. "Why'd ye do that?"

"The road he is on dead ends on 23rd. If he is trying to leave the city, you can cut him off by taking a right at the second light."

"How's backup coming?"

"Right now, it looks like I'm it. I will be your eyes in the skies."

Lukas laid onto his horn again as he slid back and forth between vehicles, swapping paint with several, and came to a stand-still as all three lanes of traffic stopped at the light.

Lukas stole a look at his friend Collin, whose green eyes darted in every direction, looking for an exit. The two friends had been through worse, but that was only if they succeeded today.

The light turned from red to green, giving Lukas a little more maneuvering room. His charger was not a small car, but he made the most of it.

"Uh oh." Nichole's voice came through again.

"What's wrong now?" Lukas shouted as he slipped through an incredibly small gap.

"The police have a call in of a reckless driver on 21st."

"I think that would be us," Collin quipped.

"No kidding." Lukas stepped on the gas, hearing the Hemi squeal in response. "We're almost to the second intersection! Where is our target?"

"Running almost parallel to you."

"Perfect. Hang on!"

The leather steering wheel slipped through Lukas's hands with ease. He tapped the emergency break with precision, causing the back wheels to cut loose with a squeal and pull them through the tight turn. Releasing the brake and stomping the throttle, the charger jerked forward.

The street was wide and clear, and visibility was perfect. The black sedan sped past the intersection, and Lukas spun around the corner, coming up directly behind him.

There was too much traffic here to do anything dangerous without putting others at risk. "Nichole! I need an open stretch to take him down. Where is the closest?" The flash of red and blue out of the rearview mirror caught Lukas's eye. "Now would be greatly appreciated!"

"If you want to bottle-neck him, Avenue Q has construction and is being diverted so only workers are there."

"Pedestrians and car chases do not mix well."

"Then try Avenue P. Force him right."

Lukas maneuvered through the traffic, dodging in and out as he crept up on the sedan's driver's side quarter-panel, then rear door, then front door, then front bumper. With a few encouraging nudges, the sedan pulled into the right lane with Lukas blocking him in.

The next light, Avenue P, was green, which only meant he didn't have to worry about stopped cars.

Staying slightly in front of the sedan, Lukas turned his wheel to the right. Either the car would turn the way he wanted, or they would be in for a heck of a ride.

The sedan jerked left, ramming into the charger's front bumper. Lukas managed to keep it from sliding out of control, but the sedan gained distance. Not only had he not gotten the car to turn, but now the police were gaining on him fast.

At least with the police on their heels, most of the traffic was pulling over and staying out of their way.

"Heads up," Nichole said. "Only two more blocks until he's out of town and on the motorway."

"I assume the traffic is clearer up there."

"Yes, but we cannot let him leave the city."

"That may not be possible."

Any offensive move he made now would put people at risk. The six-lane road separated the traffic by a cement barrier. They were officially out of town, but the city limits probably extended a couple of miles.

Lukas eased up on the sedan's quarter-panel and took a deep breath. This would be the first time he pulled this maneuver, but there was always a first time for everything. Ideally, he would brush his nose against the rear of the other car with enough force to spin it out of control in either a sharp ninety-degree or one-eighty-degree turn.

With the only approaching vehicles being police, Lukas pulled his nose right into the sedan's tail with the sound of crashing metal. The car spun out perfectly, but instead of speeding past him, the charger's right wheel blew out, pulling them hard right. So much for getting away.

The black sedan backed up, turned around, and raced off again followed by two police cars.

"Looks like you are in trouble." Nichole's voice came through again.

"No duh," Collin answered.

Lukas hit the steering wheel with his fist. A third police car rolled up behind them, a single officer stepping out. Instead of drawing his weapon, he simply walked over and leaned in Lukas's window. Ryan's recognizable curls stuck out from under his helmet. Although his last name was Murphy, his mother's Italian genes had a prominent display in her son's hair.

"You boys better come back with me to the station."

Lukas stepped out and looked at his car, running his hand through his thick dark blond hair. "And what should we do with the car?"

"I don't know. Call a mechanic? Oh, wait, you're already here."

Leaning down, Lukas hit the button that opened the trunk. "Collin, I think we busted that front tire."

The black sedan and two police cars came back toward them. Stepping out of the sedan, Michael shook his head. "If this would've been real, I would've let you sit and rot in jail for a couple of days before coming to rescue your hides."

The heat of frustration burned Lukas's cheeks, but his boss was right. Opening the trunk, he handed Collin the jack and lug wrench and pulled out the spare tire.

"Be thankful we had this 'town' set up and enough volunteers to make this realistic. Because of your reckless driving, your car is now recognizable and stuck on the side of the road. Not only did you let me go, but you got yourselves caught."

Silence answered the reprimand. Lukas hauled the tire out and brought it around to the passenger's side. Collin already had three of the five lug-nuts out and was working on the fourth. "We learn from our failures," Collin muttered just loud enough to be overheard.

"Yes," Michael answered. "But in our business, failure can mean death. I'm trying to keep you alive." Turning back to his car, Michael got on the radio. "Okay everyone, the last of the exercises are over. Let's pack up and leave this city for the military's next training."

Lukas took the flat tire from Collin, who rolled the spare on and started tightening the lug-nuts. The cars began to pass by, leaving them on the side of the road in obvious defeat. So much for the newest team who single handedly took down the head of the Shifting Shadows.

CHAPTER 2
BACK TO HQ

Flock Headquarters

Brooke looked out the window of the company's SUV, watching the open farmland go by. Another semester at the University of BLITS had ended, and she and the rest of the team were on their way back to base. A year had passed since they had worked together to take out Radenie, the leader of the Shifting Shadows. Half of the team had stayed with the Flock while the other half had gone back to the university to finish their degrees.

Max drove while Sam flipped through the radio stations. They were childhood friends and their personalities were as contrasted as their appearance. Beneath Sam's fair hair was a dark tan from years out in the sun exploring, while Max's dark spiked hair spoke to his thinly veiled genius which sometimes bordered on manic.

Behind Brooke, Emily slept with her head against her chest. She was fearless. If anything needed to be done, she was the first to volunteer, except for killing spiders. Everyone had to have one fear.

But when it came to people, Brooke would trust the woman sitting beside her, Tonya. A counselor just graduating with her master's. If Emily couldn't fix it by beating it into submission, Tonya would talk it to death.

The usual smile on Tonya's face, however, had disappeared, replaced with concern.

"What's wrong?"

"Nothing." Tonya looked up and shook her head, plastering on a fake smile. "I just got a text from Jasmine."

"Your classmate?"

"Yeah, she graduated last year. Anyway, she just texted me that she's hosting an event in two weeks to stop human trafficking."

"That's great."

"Yeah." Tonya paused again. "It's in Houston two weeks from now, which barely gives me enough time to ask off."

"That's good news, right?"

"Yes." Her answer was delayed and distracted.

"But it's not?"

"It's…" Tonya took a deep breath and turned back to Brooke. "I wanted to use my time off to see my family."

"How is Tadi?" Tonya's youngest brother had been sick since Brooke knew her.

"The doctors still don't know."

"The seizures?"

"Yeah, the medicine helped for a time, but…"

They sat in silence for a minute before Brooke continued. "So, what are you going to do?"

"For now, settle in at headquarters, take it day by day, ask the days off, and… I'll decide where I'm going closer to the time."

"One day at a time," Brooke said.

"One day at a time," Tonya repeated.

Pulling up to the Flock's base, Max rolled down the window of the SUV and held out his ID for security to check. The base was larger than Max had originally expected, but now it made sense when Michael had told them it housed all five hundred employed by the Flock and their families.

Rolling past security, they turned left. Going straight would have led them around the circular drive around the operational base.

Along the outside was the warehouse, motor pool, airplane hangar, shooting range, and Formula and Knight buildings.

Each of the divisions of the Flock (Formula, Light, Omega, Coordinate, and Knight) had their own places. Formula and Knight had separate buildings on the far side because of the experimental testing done by the scientists and the downright dangerous exercises performed by the operatives.

The inside of the drive was the mail room and the recreational center, which was made of three buildings surrounding an obstacle course. From there was the headquarters, which housed the Coordinate, Light, and Omega divisions. It was rumored to have a separate entrance to bring in CIs and anyone who didn't need to be seen.

Past headquarters was the library, the chapel, the depo where they got any supplies they might need, and the cafeteria.

Following the road left, as they were doing, took them past the hospital, family support center, school, police station, and fire department, and straight to the living section which consisted of three apartment complexes and thirty-five individual homes for the bigger families.

Max stopped the car outside of Adams apartments and popped the trunk so the girls could get their bags. Each of the complexes were named after the first three U.S. presidents: Washington, Adams, and Jefferson.

Adams was a quaint complex with individual buildings spread around and eight apartments per building. The grass was green and there were a few trees shading the sidewalks that lead around. He had helped them move in, and the neighbors seemed friendly, some even having dogs. Tonya and Brooke chose to share a two-bedroom, while Emily opted for the single bedroom to herself. She could have roomed with Nichole, but with Nichole's life-of-the-party lifestyle and Emily's tendency to keep to herself, chances were that situation was not ideal.

After watching to make sure the girls made their way in safely, Max worked his way through to Jefferson. It wasn't much different than the dorms at the university, except there were no resident mentors and no dorm meetings at ten o'clock on Tuesday nights.

Max pulled out his suitcases and followed Sam in. The apartments all faced in to an open common area where a game of flag-football was going on with some of the younger men.

He unlocked the door and kicked it open. It was just as they had left it. The double studio apartment had identical furnishings on either side, but they looked nothing alike. Max's room was filled with posters of Marvel movies, a Spiderman bed cover, and a giant television screen. The only decoration in Sam's room was a squared-away bed with a hat from Egypt and random papers strewn across the side table.

Their phones chirped at the same time with a message from Collin.

Welcome back. We're currently on our way back from a training and won't make it back in time for supper. We'll meet at 2000 at the club in the rec center.

Collin sat at the table in the back of the club watching the people come in and out and sipping his second coke. This was the unofficial meeting place of the Rising Flock. It had everything his team needed: food, drinks, darts, billiards, and music loud enough to appreciate but soft enough to still hear and be heard in conversation.

The reason he called this meeting was Felix St. James (the Executive Director of the Flock) and Michael (the one who had formed his team) had offered him the position of team leader. Collin was honored but wasn't sure how his team would respond. He wished they had asked his team first, but the decision was made and he had accepted.

The last year had gone smoothly for his team, as far as he knew. Those who had graduated trained, while the others finished their education. But with the news he kept hearing in morning meetings, he doubted it would be smooth for long.

The first of his people walked in, and Collin raised his hand to motion Ryan over. He had changed out of the police uniform and was now wearing a t-shirt and some faded jeans. He sat down heavily and ordered some hot wings. Out of all the team, Ryan was the best at improvising and rolling with the punches, but for what they were going to face, they would need a plan.

"Hey, Ryan. How was your day?"

"Better than yours." He paused and considered his words. "Just glad the team's back."

"Yeah." Collin took another sip of his coke before continuing. "I just wanted to warn you before the rest of them show that the bosses want me to be the person of contact."

"Good with me. I'd rather be out fighting bad guys than doing paperwork."

Collin nodded. "You do realize this makes me team leader. And what I say is final."

"Yeah," Ryan winked at the waitress as she set down the hot wings with a drink. "No big deal. As long as you're not a jerk about it."

Collin rolled his eyes but saw Brooke approaching and waved her forward. "I won't."

Within ten minutes all the members of the Rising Flock sat around the table. It was good to be together again, but he only wished they could enjoy their time and not just jump into the next assignment.

Once everyone settled into their seats and seemed to be loosening up, Collin took the envelope he had tucked away and set it on the table. The conversations quieted down as all eyes focused on the envelope.

Collin took one last sip of his coke and set it aside. "I'm glad you all made it here safely."

Ryan raised his glass in a toast. "To safe returns."

"To safe returns." Most around the table answered.

Collin waited until the glasses were set back down before continuing. "The last time everyone was here, we took our written exams to become active members of the Flock. In this envelope are your badges and card keys to the Flock in its various divisions. We are still a team, and as such we will be given assignments to complete as a team, but each of your skill sets are also useful to the greater good."

Opening the envelope, Collin passed their name tags and key cards around. "Just a recap, the Flock is made up of five different divisions, making it an acronym. Formula, Light, Omega, Coordination, and Knight. Max, you will be assigned to the Formula division working on designing and building homes that have been destroyed by natural disasters, war, or other calamities. Your final schooling will be supervised here, under our Master Architect who will sign off on your degree."

Max tapped his plastic key card to the Formula workshop against the table and nodded.

"Sam," Collin continued, "you will be working with the Light division in Egypt, finishing up your archeological studies, and keeping an eye on the Shifting Shadow division there. Even though we beheaded the organization, it was big enough that we know aspects of it still exist and there was a major sect where you were working in Egypt."

"But they know who I am."

Collin had the same trepidation but repeated what his bosses told him. "After the fire, the original team split up. Based on your description and the evidence they left behind, we were able to arrange for their imprisonment, so no one should recognize you."

Sam shook his head, tapping his fingers on the table. "As comforting as that's supposed to sound, you don't know them or what they're capable of."

"*I* don't know them?" Collin had to focus to take a deep breath before his temper got the better of him. "Sam, each of us have had a run in with the Shifting Shadows. Each of us have had some experience with these monsters. No, I didn't see the site burned to the ground, but a bounty was never put on your head to see how far their influence was. I know it's dangerous, and you don't have to go if you don't want to. But each of us has a skill set that we can use to help this organization as a whole."

"Who made you the boss of us?"

"Michael Seaward," Collin answered. "We as the Rising Flock needed a person of contact or team leader. Michael chose me, so unless we make a different decision as a team, I'm the one that makes the tough decisions."

He looked around the room at his team. Tonya gave him a supportive smile. Brooke flashed a thumbs up. Lukas nodded his approval. Only Sam seemed reluctant to accept his position. And that would be something the two of them would have to work out.

"I am part of the Omega division, which means I'm your point. If you have any problems or anything you want moved on, let me know."

Collin then turned to Brooke and her light, innocent smile. "Brooke, you will also be part of the Light division."

"How would I gain the bad guys' trust?"

"The Light division also works with uncovering our enemies' schemes, and you will be taking point on the star-gem."

"Okay," Brooke nodded. "I can do research." Since she had worked as a librarian, she was used to diving into the depths of research.

"Ryan, Nichole, Tonya, you will be with the Coordinate division. Ryan, because of your connection with the FBI and your father's business connections."

"My father's business connections are with the Shifting Shadows," Ryan said. "But like I told you earlier, I'm not much use with that."

"That's why I assigned you to Coordinate instead of Light."

Turning next to Nichole whose naturally blond hair was complimented with a new set of red highlights, Collin continued. "Nichole, you'll be with Coordinate because of your connection to Agent De' Angelo with INTERPOL and your experience as a journalist. You will be working with media outlets on what information to give them and doing press releases for major investigations."

"Press releases? I thought we didn't exist."

"We don't, but people will notice our involvement. You make sure we continue to be invisible."

Collin turned to Tonya who sat beside him and paused. It had been almost six months since he'd seen her, and now that she'd graduated, she would be working with him permanently. Since the moment he first saw her standing over him after he was half-drowned and beaten, the compassion flowing from her eyes captured him, but he hadn't told her. He had thought she was a bronze angel, but she was much more than that. Then he had rescued her from the Shifting Shadows and the Leviathans, and they had found the treasure together. They made a good team. But there was something about her, something angelic, that made him almost hesitant to approach her about that.

Confusion over his pause brought Tonya's brows together, and Collin blinked back into what was happening then. Handing her the ID, he continued. "You'll be working with Coordinate, focusing on the wellbeing of members of the Flock. Our physical wellbeing is checked and monitored by the doctors at the hospital on base, but our psychological wellbeing is under the care of Becky, our onsite counselor. She and her team also do trauma care and go with our action team to take care of the mental and emotional wellbeing of those we help after natural or manmade disasters."

Handing the final IDs to Lukas and Emily, Collin smiled at his friends. They had grown so much since the first day at the shooting range. Two competitors constantly challenging each other. In the months that Emily had been gone, Lukas had kept their promise of going on a run together every day. Although Collin would never admit as much, it warmed his heart watching Lukas run with his headset connected to his phone, talking with Emily or just running in silence, knowing they were doing the same thing hundreds of miles apart.

"Lukas, Emily, you are assigned to the Knight division because of your work in Nepal and your skills. You will be on the front lines, and although it will be dangerous, I have confidence you two will be excellent."

Collin paused again before addressing the group as a whole. "Although we are each assigned to different divisions, we are still a team. We will be taking on missions together. To go over the current threats, we'll meet at 8:30 in the Life meeting room."

Brooke raised her hand. "I don't know where that is."

"Ground floor of the headquarters building. Ask the receptionist and she'll show you the way."

"And it's called Life?"

"Yes, the three meeting rooms on the ground floor are Life, Liberty, and Pursuit."

Ryan rolled his eyes. "Life, liberty, and the pursuit of happiness. How original."

Shrugging a shoulder, Brooke smiled, "I kind of like it."

"Of course you would."

Collin folded the now empty envelope and stuffed it in his pocket. "That's all I had tonight."

"Then who's up for some bowling?" Sam asked, a little too quickly for Collin's liking, but he was done.

The table clamored with taunts and sounds of chairs sliding back. Collin looked to Tonya, wanting to catch up from the last four months, but she was already up, following behind Nichole to the bowling alley. Looking to his right, Collin caught the last glimpse of Lukas and Emily heading off together. If he wanted any conversation or good time, he'd have to follow the group downstairs to the bowling alley.

CHAPTER 3
THREAT OF WAR

The sun was just rising when Emily's alarm woke her. Why she had ever agreed to the idea of a morning run was beyond her. Opening her eyes, it took her a minute to remember where she was. Right, apartment with the Flock.

The red numbers on her clock read 6:00. The late night and the time zone difference begged her to go back to sleep. Maybe just today.

Her phone chimed at twenty after, jerking her from the clutches of sleep. Squinting at it with unfocused eyes, she could just make out the text from Lukas. *Good morning, beautiful. See you in five.*

Throwing off the covers, Emily flipped on the light and rummaged through her clothes still in her suitcase. Finding a pair of running shorts and a t-shirt, she changed quickly and clumsily.

A knock sounded at the door as she was pulling her dark hair into a ponytail. "One minute!"

Her socks were mis-matched, one bright pink and the other lime green. One sneaker lay in front of the dresser, while the other was MIA. The mission lasted longer than she liked to locate and extract it from the recesses of her closet.

With both shoes on, she made her way down the stairs and opened the door. Leaning against the doorframe was the man who had occupied her dreams for the last two years. The German mechanic with smudges on his face and stains on his jeans had grown into the man wearing cargo shorts and a t-shirt that barely concealed his bulging muscles.

Her heart thrummed against her chest, trying to make its way toward him. Oh, silly heart.

Lukas's chocolate eyes pulled her like a magnet, but she could not be pulled in... not yet.

Closing the door and locking it, they made their way down the street to the jogging paths. The morning air was crisp with the lingering scent of the evening showers. A perfect day for a run.

Sam followed Max to the conference room where they were to meet. He was running on less than five hours of sleep. He usually didn't take his coffee black, but this morning it was his second cup, and the stronger the better.

The door opened to a room filled with overlapping conversations. Ryan sat on the counter along the side of the room, waving his arms emphatically as he told a story. Nichole reached over to push him to which Brooke laughed. Tonya sat alone at the oval table staring at her phone, her shoulders slouched, and her head dipped. At the front of the room, Collin stood in front of a large flat screen with a man Sam hadn't seen before. He wore a short-sleeved plaid shirt with his long brown hair tied back in a ponytail.

Sam moved to sit across from Tonya, spinning the chair around as he drained the last drops of his coffee.

"Everyone, find a seat." Collin sat down at the head of the table with the other guy beside him.

Ryan jumped off the counter and took a step closer to the table. "I found one."

Nichole rolled her eyes. "Now sit."

"It's 8:35, so we better get started." Collin looked around the room, counting off who was there. Lukas and Emily were nowhere in sight. "This is Reid Whitmore. He is the director of the Light division. Take it away."

Light division. That would be Sam's division. The reason he had tossed and turned most of the night. Could he go back to Egypt and work alongside the men who had burned down the site and shot Omar? Was his cover blown? The Shadows obviously knew he worked with the Flock, but with the names they got from the treasure hunt, the Flock was able to work with the Egyptian government to arrest those responsible. But did they get everyone?

"As Collin said, I'm Director Whitmore. Excuse the casual attire, I've been on the floor for the past two hours assisting with a server issue. Now, as director of Light, I will be the one debriefing you before and after missions." He reached down beside him and pulled out a black folder. "Some of you will be working directly for me and my team, and I look forward to getting to know you, but today's reason for our meeting is more of an update.

"Last year, your team was responsible for the arrest of Radenie and his top lieutenants. While this was good and ensured justice for Tonya's capture, it is by no means the end of the Shifting Shadows. Our primary informant has lost contact with the group, but our other CIs have reported a splintering in the organization. Hunter Drake, Radenie's nephew and heir, has tried to unite the Shadows, but in order to gain the trust of the different factions, he needs to pull off something big."

"What are you expecting?" Sam asked. Although the Shifting Shadows had been powerful as an organization, this disorder would result in unpredictable chaos.

"The chatter we've been picking up indicates–"

The door slammed open against the wall, cutting off Director Whitmore. Emily and Lukas walked in, both covered in dust and sweat.

Collin simply motioned for them to sit in a couple of empty chairs.

"As I was saying," Whitmore continued, pulling his eyes from the latecomers. "The chatter we've been picking up indicates a decrease in their operation as contractors and an increase in the purchase of guns and sale of drugs."

Lukas drummed his fingers against the table. "They are raising money and arms. They are planning action not business. What about movement at port cities? What have you heard from the fences?"

"No movement at the border or major airports, but of course we can't monitor everywhere."

"Of course, but the movements you are monitoring, is it specified to one country or one region?"

"As I said before, if you would have come on time, the Shifting Shadows have scattered."

"I'm not so sure about that."

The vein on Director Whitmore's forehead bulged and his jaw tensed. "Who are you to question the research of our division?"

"I am not questioning you. I am simply stating that is what the Shadows want you to think. I have been to their headquarters. I have seen the layout of their organization. Even with the capture of Radenie, Hunter is more than capable of taking up the organization's mantel. In fact, he was plotting to do just that before we took Radenie down."

Whitmore's chin was still clenched, but his eyebrows raised from anger to curiosity. "Who are you?"

"Lukas Dekker and this is Emily Moore."

The tension lining Whitmore's face dropped in surprise. "You are the Lukas and Emily that successfully infiltrated the Shifting Shadows and took down Radenie last summer? I apologize for my hasty assumption. We would value your opinion of this circumstance. Why do you think they aren't scattered?"

"Radenie was a man of contingency. This may not be the case with Hunter, but Hunter would be a fool not to follow his uncle's plan. I was not privy to the specifics of these, but I know the next Radenie would have to prove himself in a major way. The rough outline of the plan I was able to get consists of four points: guns, people, medicine, and propaganda, not necessarily in that order."

Medicine? Sam could see how guns would be needed for a major attack. People could be used to fight. And propaganda could influence the masses. But medicine?

Collin was the first to fill the silence. "They want to start a war." His words were barely audible over the air conditioning.

War.

Guns to shoot people. People to kill people. Propaganda to make them do it. And medicine to patch them up.

"Where?" Whitmore scribbled notes across a blank paper.

Lukas shrugged. "That's all I know. Their outline on some scale or another could create war in any country if done correctly."

"Okay, I'll have my team run the data again, this time looking for those specific factors. Sam, Brooke, when would you be able to start?"

Brooke cast a quick look at Collin. "Whenever you need me."

Heat surged up Sam's chest and to the base of his ears as the doubts he felt that night threatened his composure. "I'm not needed in Egypt?" He tried not to let the fear clench his throat. If that was where he would be of the most help, that's where he'd go.

"No. Considering the scale of what we might be facing, I need anyone that can find a pattern up on the second floor with me."

"Then I should go too," Lukas volunteered. "After I have changed."

"And I think a shower is in order." Emily nudged him with her elbow.

"That too."

Whitmore nodded. "Having your eyes will be good since we don't have any actionable leads yet. But once we do, you'll be needed in the field. You proved yourselves in Nepal. With a threat of this scale, we need every able-bodied man and woman out there stopping this."

He and half the team stood to leave, but Collin stopped them. "Wait. Everyone needs to pass their field training. Lukas, Nichole, and Ryan passed last week. The other five need to finish their training before I send them anywhere."

"Collin, going up one flight of stairs does not constitute going into the field. Since you assigned Sam and Brooke with me, they are analysists."

"No. The Rising Flock is a field unit first. Their individual assignments are for times when they are not needed. You will get my people if and when they are not working as part of my team."

"You would rather them waste their time in training than saving the world?"

Collin stood to match Whitmore's intensity. "They are my people, and they are under my protection. In our line of work, they could be called out at any minute. They need to be able to protect themselves. They will help you when they are ready but not until then. So, Whitmore, you are dismissed."

"You think you're so high and mighty because your father-"

"No, Reid. If you have a problem, take it up with Michael. I am this team's leader. You will respect my authority as it comes to my team, goodbye."

Five seconds, later Director Whitmore was out the door. Collin set his hands against the table.

The night before Sam had challenged Collin's right to be team leader, but watching that play out, Sam would be more than happy to leave the people and politics to Collin.

Collin kept his hands pressed against the table so no one could see them shake. Ever since Michael had asked him to take leadership of this team, he had been faced with doubt and disrespect. But no one would respect him or his team until they had proven themselves.

Might as well start with the task at hand. "Lukas, you said you'd help. Would you-?"

The hint of Lukas's crooked smile made Collin breathe easier. "Yeah, I will after I shower and change."

Lukas left but when Emily turned to follow Collin caught her arm. He hated to ask her this question. She was his friend, but they had to work as a team. A team that worked with precision. "Why were you and Lukas late?"

"That was my fault." She dipped her chin a fraction but kept eye contact. "We went for our morning run on the trails. Lukas warned me to go on one of the easier trails, but I wanted a challenge."

"So, you went on a hike instead of a jog."

"How was I to know?"

"Listen to Lukas. I know you push each other, and that's a good thing. But if he asks you to do something, I urge you to listen. He respects you too much to push you to make a decision. He is my friend. Honor him. You don't need to prove you are strong to him. He already knows."

Emily ran her fingers through her black hair. The roots were blonde, the dye having grown out. "I… training starts soon, and I need to make my way over to the rec center."

Collin simply nodded and watched her leave. "The rest of you should follow her. No use being late for the first day." He then turned his attention to the two who already passed their training. "Ryan, Nichole, I know you have a conference on interrogation this week. Go ahead and pack up and head out. If anything major develops, I'll let you know."

Everyone left except Tonya who stared blankly at her phone. Something was wrong. She hadn't said a word this morning, and that was unusual for her. "What's going on?"

Without looking up from the phone, she shook her head. "I'm stuck."

"Stuck?" Collin sat down in the chair next to her.

"My phone's been blowing up with texts from my mom and Jasmine and you."

"Hey, I only texted you once." Her glare stopped his defense. "Why are you stuck?"

"Jasmine needs my help in Houston in two weeks. She is a social worker and trauma counselor for those affected by human trafficking. She is hosting a walk and her assistant quit this morning."

"Go, help your friend."

"If it was only that easy. My mom texted me they are moving. She wants me to help."

"Okay…" Collin prompted.

"But it's the same weekend."

"Oh."

"And, with this new development *you* want me to stay." Her anger had turned to frustration and she buried her head in her hands. "I don't know what to do."

Collin put a hand on her shoulder, hesitant of the contact but wanting to reassure her. "You'll do the right thing. You always do."

"But each decision I make would leave someone in the lurch. If I go to Houston, that would leave my mom in need, and if something happened here, I wouldn't be able to help. If I go to Arizona, that would leave Jasmine without help and the team possibly vulnerable. If I stay, I might stay for naught. My family and Jasmine would need help and chances are nothing would actually happen here. What is the point of all this?"

"Does your mom have people who can help?"

"Yeah, but-"

"Chances are, things will be okay here. Call Jasmine. Tell her you can come, but you're on call."

"You can't just make the decision for me."

"Just take it as advice then." Collin stood and extended a hand. "Let's get moving. Maybe hitting something will clear your thoughts."

CHAPTER 4
ALWAYS BE PREPARED

When Emily had mentioned the rec center, Max immediately thought of the university. Darts and billiards, basketball and the sand volleyball court outside where they played every evening unless it was snowing. But this was so much bigger.

The complex had three buildings that surrounded an assortment of objects. As Max got closer, he saw they ranged from monkey bars and a pit with mesh over it, to a single rope bridge and a thirty-foot rock wall.

A woman with long braided blonde hair dropped from the monkey bars and approached him. "You are late." Her tone was curt. She spoke with an exotic accent Max couldn't quite place.

Max was the first of his friends to leave the meeting and looking behind him, the rest of them were just catching up. "Well, considering I was told five minutes ago, I thought I made good time." He extended his hand in greeting. "My name's Max."

She looked at his hand for a moment before turning and motioning for him to follow. "Let us begin."

The woman led them past the rock wall and to the building to the right. As Max passed the wall, he turned back. His feet stuck to the ground in shock. On the other side of the thirty-foot rock wall were three ropes. Normally heights didn't scare him, but the thought of repelling down from such a height made his stomach plummet to his toes. Hopefully, he wouldn't have to face that today.

The rest of the team had caught up, and Max followed them inside. The blonde woman led them up the stairs and to a classroom. "My name is Tatiana Petrikov. It is my job to train you into assets. This will not be easy, but you will be better for it."

Russian. The accent made sense with a name like that.

"Before we begin the physical aspect, I need to make sure you come home alive. First aid is your last defense in any self-defense. It doesn't matter if you are the best fighter, all it takes is one lucky shot and you're gone. Am I right, Emily?"

Max turned in time to see Emily blush and give a slow nod.

More studying, just great. As a rule, he enjoyed learning, but at the moment punching something seemed much more enjoyable.

New York

Ryan looked out the window of the private jet as it taxied to a stop. This would be his first time to come home in a year, but with this conference he wasn't really coming home. He talked with his mom when she called, every couple of weeks or so. But he and his father had shared only a handful of words. How could he tell his dad that one of the corporations he dealt with was responsible for him being shot at and Jake being killed?

So, he had simply moved on, pretended that didn't happen, but the Flock took him on. The Flock took him on because of his father's connection to the Shifting Shadows. Originally, they wanted him to be a spy in his father's company, but after much persuasion, Ryan convinced them that a kid who had run to the stage instead of the boardroom would look suspicious now trying to get in.

The plane stopped, and Ryan pulled his carry-on bag out of the overhead bin. The conference center was on the same side of town as his favorite pub. Maybe he could take Nichole and the guys out that night.

"Hey, Ryan. I need a favor." Ryan turned, catching sight of his co-worker Liam. "I need you and your girlfriend to get us coffees.

Since you're from here, you know where to get the best. Two cream and two sugars for me. I know Al likes black. Tiffany–"

Beside Ryan, Nichole spun around so fast her hair hit his cheek. "We may be new, but we do not answer to you. Get your own coffee. And I am not his girlfriend."

A smirk crept across Ryan's face at the shock on Liam's. It was obvious Liam was used to having his way, but that would not be the way with him and would never be the way with Nichole.

The trek to the conference was uneventful, and Ryan was glad the Flock had been able to book them rooms in the same hotel.

Registration included a lanyard with the words National Security and Defense Seminar written in bold across the top, his name printed in the middle and Seaward Security Firm on the bottom. Right, the Flock was a *secret* organization. They could go to public events but only under a fake name.

The conference would include guest speakers from agencies around the world revolving around the theme of truth. There were classes on interrogation techniques, non-verbal cues, what not to say, and the legality of approaches.

While Ryan knew this would be helpful, he couldn't help but feel he'd be of more help back home coordinating with other departments to identify possible targets. All they currently had was a rumor of a plan and no solid evidence.

In the year he had worked with the Flock, most of his job was cleaning up and investigating after major events happened. It was rewarding to catch the bad guys, but it always left his stomach turning with what ifs. How could they stop them *before* something happened? But that was not his job, and this conference should help them crack someone they caught and prevent further damage.

Ryan waited at the elevator, the rest of his co-workers already going ahead of him. The elevator chimed, Ryan stepped in and pressed five. The elevator was empty except for a teenager in shorts and a t-shirt, holding onto the straps of her backpack.

"Your name is Ryan Murphy, right?" she whispered as the doors shut.

Studying her face, he knew he didn't recognize her. "Yes, why?"

"Your father is Sean Murphy?"

Although his father was well-known in the world of international business, no one had ever approached Ryan like this before. Everything in him told him to use caution. "Why?"

She licked her lips, clearly nervous, and continued. "Tell him to look into Chile's copper exports."

"What is this about?"

"If he has any stock in it, dump it. If he's buying supplies from them, get new contractors."

Ryan could feel his pulse raising. Something bad was going to happen. "Do you know something?"

The teenager shook her head and licked her lips again, clearly hiding something. The elevator opened before he could question her further. "Your floor," she whispered before reaching over and hitting the first floor button.

He picked up his suitcase and walked to his room. What was all that about? Without saying much, she certainly made implications. Was his dad involved in insider trading? What was going to happen in Chile? Did this have to do with the Shifting Shadows? And how did she recognize him?

Flock Headquarters

Collin stood in front of the world map that took up an entire wall in the Light division's floor. He ran his hand through his thick red hair and tried to piece together the information Ryan had given him in a phone call about Chile. This map had sticky notes posted on it for any attack that could be related to the Shifting Shadows and when it took place.

Looking at the map, he was inclined to agree with Whitmore's assessment that these were random attacks and no longer coordinated. They took place on every continent, with the exception of Antarctica, and had no particular timeline.

Juan stood beside him studying the map with his arms crossed in front of him. He was the Flock's specialist in South America and spoke with a thick Brazilian accent, occasionally slipping back into Portuguese. "Of course, there are the conflicts in Cambodia and Venezuela, which mask the Shadows' movements down there, but as we go farther south, there is very little of interest. Argentina has been a hot spot for them in the past, but after the arrests, they seem to have abandoned their base there."

"What about weather?" Collin asked. "Anything to indicate we may have a natural disaster heading their way?"

Searching through his phone, Juan pulled up a NOAA weather map. "No, and why would someone give Ryan this tip if it was something everyone could see coming?"

Collin nodded and looked back at the map. Questions raced through his mind, but most of them weren't even relevant. What was so important about Chile? Why would a stranger approach Ryan? Did this have to do with the Shifting Shadows? Were they still together? Would his team remain together with them all assigned to different divisions? Would he be able to ask Tonya out? Was she even interested in him? No, back on topic.

"So, we've got nothing?"

"Nothing, right now, which is a good thing. Even if this has nothing to do with the Shifting Shadows, we'll be one step ahead all the way."

"Sounds good."

Juan headed back to his desk, but Collin couldn't help but wonder if the Shadows were thinking the same thing—that they were one step ahead of the Flock.

CHAPTER 5

PRIDE BEFORE FALL

"Today, I will introduce you to pieces of our challenge course," Tatiana said, leading them out in the evening breeze. Max followed her to the place they met, staring at the thirty-foot rock wall on the far side.

They had spent the morning working on physical fitness, starting with a three-mile hike. After breakfast was two hours at the shooting range followed by survival preparation in the classroom during the heat of the day. It was astounding, the amount of stuff needed to survive any long period of time. Trying to balance a light pack with everything that was needed was the hardest part.

Max turned his attention back to Tatiana and the challenge course in front of him. "If any of you are familiar with the military challenge courses, this is not it. We based several of our obstacles on theirs and added a few of our own. A successful completion of this course will mark the end of phase two of your training."

"What about phase one?" Max asked.

"That was the written test you took before you got here."

"So, we're already half-way through training?"

"No." Her answer was immediate and sharp. Obviously, a response to what she thought was a foolish assumption. "It is a three-phase training, and you are nowhere near ready."

Three phases. Looking again at the thirty-foot rock wall, Max wondered what the final for the last phase would be.

Before he had a chance to ask, Tatiana read his mind. "And before you ask, the end of phase three will be marked by a four-day wilderness challenge. Pass; fail. If you survive you pass."

What she left unsaid was if you don't pass, you die.

Tatiana turned back to the challenge course. "Today, we will be going over the first obstacle." She led them to an eight-foot wall with three ropes attached to one side, swinging slightly with the breeze. "Use the ropes to get up the wall and jump down."

"Jump down?" Brooke repeated. She was the shortest of them all and had struggled the most with the morning workouts.

Ignoring Brooke's comment, Tatiana continued. "The best can scale this without a rope. This may be a good goal for some of you." Her eyes slid to Max. As the tallest of the group, he stood at just over six foot two inches. He could reach the top, but his strength was speed. He made a mental note to add weightlifting to his workout routine.

"Once you are comfortable with that, you can move on to the next obstacle: the parallel bars." Max walked around the wall to see what she was talking about. Eight hurtle-like-bars which were approximately two and a half feet tall spanned to the next obstacle. "The purpose of this," Tatiana said while moving through the obstacle sideways, "is to get over the bars without using your hands. Throw one leg over, shift your weight, then throw the other leg over."

Tatiana left, and Max and his friends spent the next hour throwing themselves at a brick wall, or more accurately over a brick wall. Other than a few skinned knees and rope burns, they made it through the first two obstacles until they had confidence and speed.

"What a bunch of lollygaggers!" A man's voice called from the road.

Max spun to see Michael coming toward them with Collin and Lukas behind him. It was strange to see him in a tie, as if he had just come from a meeting.

"I thought you were supposed to be training!"

"We are!" Sam defended.

"Then why has no one tried to climb the wall?" Michael motioned to the rock wall at the end of the course.

"Because I told them to focus on these two." Tatiana appeared by his side. Max hadn't seen her coming.

"The slow approach."

"The practiced approach."

Silence lingered between the instructor and Michael, the director of the Knight division. Tatiana flipped her hair over her shoulder. "Then you wouldn't mind racing me?"

Michael considered her for a moment before shaking his head. "That would be a test of experience not training. How about at the end of training, the best of yours goes against the best of mine?"

"Fair enough. But I think you are afraid to face me."

"Miss Petrikov, I can assure you that is not the case."

"You can assure me all you want, *Mister* Seaward, but..." she leaned in closer and whispered something Max couldn't hear. Michael's face flushed, and he jerked off his tie, handing it to Collin.

Tatiana bounced on her toes at the starting line, rolling her neck. Michael unbuttoned his dress shirt revealing a white undershirt, before joining her.

"Count us off," he said to Collin.

The team cleared the course and stood off to the side. Collin laid Michael's dress shirt over his arm and counted down. "Three! Two! One! Go!"

Both went off at a run. Tatiana jumped to reach the top of the wall, hooked her elbow over the edge, threw her legs over the side and dropped down.

Michael grabbed the rope, scaled the wall, and jumped from the top.

"I've got ten that Tatiana wins," Max said to Lukas.

"Make it twenty."

"Deal. Anyone else in on the action?"

Both contestants were out of the parallel bars and to the monkey bars.

"Yeah," Sam said, reaching into his pocket. "I'll put twenty on Michael."

Michael and Tatiana flew through the monkey bars, Tatiana pulled ahead by half a second.

The team ran alongside them, cheering them on.

The contestants ran for the logs, which lay at an incline. Scrambling up them, they then balanced across three more elevated logs before coming to the rope bridges.

Bridge was the only word Max could think of to describe it, but in reality, it was a single rope on either side spanning a mud pit. The contestants grabbed the rope with their hands and swung around so that they were upside down with their legs giving additional support.

With Michael's long arms, he pulled alongside then passed Tatiana. They both fell to the ground and dropped to their stomachs.

A net lay suspended above the ground, giving them half a foot of clearance as they army-crawled through. Inch by painful inch Tatiana caught up to Michael.

Standing up at the end, both were breathing hard. There was only one obstacle left. The thirty-foot rock wall and rappelling down on the other side.

Tatiana started up immediately. Michael took five seconds to fasten on the safety belt and made sure it was secure. Thirty feet was a long way to fall.

With Tatiana's shorter stature, she worked her balance dangerously as she stretched for the next foothold. It was clear that she needed the five second head start, and though she was cautious, it never came across as hesitation.

The team shouted their support, but the contestants remained quiet, focused on the task at hand.

Foot by foot they climbed. Half-way up, Tatiana reached for a hand hold but overextended. Her right foot slipped. She reacted by throwing her weight left and to the wall, slamming her head into a rock.

Max grabbed the safety harness and started up.

"No!" Tatiana shouted. She settled her right foot on its hold and continued up.

"If you fall from that height, I can't catch you!" He shouted back.

"I won't fall!"

The shouts from the team had quieted for the rest of the climb, Brooke was the only one cheering them on. "Go Michael, you've got this! Come on Tatiana, just a little more!"

Michael's long limbs gave him the advantage, and even with the five-second delay, Michael was pulling ahead.

He hooked his fingers over the edge, used his elbow to prop himself up, and swung his left leg up to roll his body to the edge before starting his descent.

The rest of the team ran around the wall to watch Michael's descent, while Max stayed to watch Tatiana as she climbed the final few feet.

Aside from the one slip, she scaled the rest of the wall with no problems. It made no sense to Max that she would put herself in that kind of danger for a meaningless race. He remembered reading somewhere that a fall from over twenty-five feet would most likely be fatal. He had resigned himself to the fact they may be risking their lives out in the field hunting bad guys, but during training?

Max ran around to the other side as Tatiana rappelled down. Michael landed and the team cheered, but his face showed frustration and anger not celebration.

When Tatiana landed, the team cheered again. Michael set a hand on her back but not in congratulations. He led her over to talk privately, but their conversation was heated enough that Max could make out most of what they said.

"Are you really so short sighted as to risk your life for pride?"

"For pride? Is that all you think of me? Every time I do this challenge, I push myself to my limit so it becomes instinct when I need it."

"When you take unnecessary risks, you endanger the rest of your team."

"Sometimes you don't have time for safety!"

Michael's voice softened. "Do you want me to tell your loved ones that?"

Silence lingered uncomfortably.

Michael turned back to the team. "You are dismissed for the rest of the evening. I will see all of you tomorrow at seven o'clock sharp for drills."

"Yes, sir," the team voiced in unison.

CHAPTER 6

STRIKE ONE

New York

Ryan swept off his conference lanyard and shrugged off his suit coat, laying it on the bed of his hotel room. He had learned a lot in the last two days, but his head pounded from the bright fluorescent lights in the meeting rooms.

Pulling the mostly empty water bottle from his bag, he downed a couple of aspirin. The rest of the Flock team had gone for dinner and drinks at a local tourist trap, but he had other plans.

Most of his life, Ryan was known to be quick to make friends, and this conference had been no exception. These last two days, he had met people from major departments that had the words *defense, security, or intelligence* in them, along with some, like himself, that were registered with alias companies.

In the last couple of classes, he befriended a couple of men from the DOD, who had invited him out for drinks to watch the Yankees and Cubs game.

Digging around in his suitcase, Ryan found his Yankee's cap. It was a little worn, but fit comfortably and helped him blend in at the bar.

While the conference had been interesting, he was still trying to figure out how that girl in the elevator recognized him. His father was known well enough in his circles, which involved multi-national business. But other than the companies, he kept a low profile. Knowing his name meant knowing the international market. Or...

The other angle was she recognized him as Ryan Murphy. Before going to the University of BLITS, Ryan had spent several years on the stage. His face had been on the cover of a couple of posters, and in his bio, he included the names of his parents: Sean and Francesca Murphy. With those names it was feasible to find out their occupations. But why would someone want to know that?

His mind raced with a multitude of questions, but he simply shook his head and took the last swig of the water. It was time to relax and watch his team annihilate the Cubs.

Making sure he had his hotel key and wallet; he went downstairs to join Bob and Caleb.

The two men stood in stark contrast to each other. Bob was a short white man that could have passed for Santa if it wasn't the middle of the summer. And instead of a red fur suit, he wore a blue Cubs jersey. Caleb looked to be of middle eastern descent with dark curly hair, a deep tan, and a black and white Yankees jersey.

"Bob," Caleb was saying as Ryan approached. "Wearing that around here today is a good way to get mugged."

"Yeah, but remember that next year when we meet in Chicago." Bob turned to greet Ryan. "Are you ready?"

"Of course. Do you two always watch this game together?"

"Baseball season is conference season." Caleb shrugged. "We've been doing this since '98."

"But the Yankees didn't play the Cubs in '98."

Caleb poked Bob in the arm as they made their way out to the bar only a couple of blocks away. "I was a Red Sox fan then."

"You switched your loyalties."

"Yeah, and that's not something I'll admit to just anyone."

"Was this after the world series in '16?"

"I'm not a bandwagoner if that's what you're implying."

They ambled down the sidewalk and discussed different teams and players until they reached the bar. It wasn't overly crowded for a

Friday night and the three of them easily found seats at the bar facing the flat screen to watch their game.

Ryan ordered up hot wings and a drink. The vibe in the room was electric. After the fifth inning, Ryan had to make sure some random guy with too many beers didn't take a shot at Bob after an impeccable home run by the Cubs.

He had turned away to use the restroom when the bar went silent. And silence in the middle of the game meant something very bad happened. Most likely a player got injured. But what really happened was much worse than Ryan could ever have expected.

The heavy silence turned to curses and shouts. All attention was fixed on the main tv.

When Ryan saw it, his stomach dropped, his ears rang, his palms grew slick with sweat. The camera was no longer focused on the game and the rivalry that caused Bob and Caleb to come together every year. Instead, it was sweeping the crowd. People were running in a panic, climbing over one another to get to some cover. What had happened?

The screen blurred for a moment as the camera re-focused, coming in for a close shot. The field was clear except for the pitcher who lay over the pitcher's mound, the ball having rolled a few feet away from where he dropped.

Above the dug-out, the seats were mostly abandoned, but those left behind lay deathly still. The camera continued to pan up, showing again the panicking crowd and security officers trying to make their way down to the wounded. Above was the VIP lounge, or what was left of it. The camera couldn't make out much except the shattered glass.

By the time Ryan made it up to his friends, they were both on their phones to their respective bosses, on their way out the door.

Caleb covered his phone and made a quick apology to Ryan, who waved it off and wished him luck.

He pulled out his phone to call Michael or Collin, but then a reporter was on the screen with the mic set over his head inaudible over the roar of the crowd.

"Quiet!" someone shouted, and the entire bar hushed.

The screen was split with the nightly news-anchor on the left and the sports-anchor on the right. "Tell us what's happening out there."

"As you just saw, the utter carnage left here is horrific. We are told by the police that the shooter has been apprehended and the threat secured. But we are still waiting for the first responders to get here and help the wounded. As of yet, we have no knowledge of how many are injured and how many…" The reporter blanched.

"Any word on Senator Barbara Wynn?"

"No. No word on anyone yet. Her lounge area was hit, but we have no reason to think she was specifically targeted."

The sound of the tv was drowned out by the grumbling chatter of the bar crowd as the reporter had nothing more to report. Images of destruction filled the screen again.

"It was probably an automated rifle."

"He was probably crazy."

"It wouldn't have happened if we just banned all guns."

"Don't you know that Chicago has the most gun restrictions? It has nothing to do with laws."

"But if he was crazy, we could've stopped him by evaluating gun owners every year."

"That wouldn't have stopped him. Once the insane get their minds on something, you can't stop them."

Ryan looked back up at the screen, blocking out the conversations around him. They were assuming it was just random violence, something the United States had been seeing a steady increase in over the last years. But something told him this was not random.

If the shooter had been going for body count, he would have raked the escaping populous. And why would he shoot for the senator? The windows were tinted, so he would have to shoot the window out to get a clear target before shooting her, wasting bullets if the real goal was body count like the recent attacks.

Pushing his way through the crowd, Ryan dialed Collin and stepped out into the street, away from the noise.

"Collin, are you watching this?"

"Watching what?"

"Turn on the tv."

"Which channel?"

Ryan paused. "Any. And get Michael."

Flock Headquarters

Collin raced across the second floor, or the first floor above ground, which housed the Light division. Six televisions were mounted on the wall of the main meeting room. Most of the time they worked as one giant flatscreen, but today Collin had filled the different screens with different news stations.

"Are you sure this is related?" Michael asked as Collin tried to catch his breath.

"What Ryan said makes sense. Just look at the scene. I mean, I don't know if it's related to the Shifting Shadows, but it doesn't look random."

Michael walked with him to the meeting room. Each screen showed different pictures of devastation. Both stood speechless watching the coverage. "We'll coordinate with local law enforcement and help with the investigation if needed."

"And what about the senator? She looked to be more than a target of opportunity."

"Yes, Senator Wynn. We already have a couple of people from Light working on that information. We should have some news before the hour."

Collin looked at his watch, noting ten minutes until seven o'clock. "Okay. Anything I can do in the meantime?"

The ding of the elevator sounded. Collin turned to see Lukas and Emily coming toward them, the looks on their faces grim.

"You've heard about the attack?"

Emily shook her head. "What attack?"

Collin motioned toward the monitors. The four of them stood

in silence. Lukas fidgeted with the phone in his hand, but it wasn't his phone. Instead of his black smart phone, it was a small red flip phone. What was that about?

"We-" Lukas started, but Michael cut him off.

"Hold that thought for a second."

One of the analysts, Kelli, came through the door and handed a folder to Michael.

"All the positions Senator Wynn was taking."

"Was?"

Kelli nodded, the pixie cut of her raven hair bouncing. "Yes, my sources say she was dead by the time the paramedics found her."

Michael nodded and she turned to leave. "Where are you going?"

"I gave you the information. I usually leave after that."

"No, the rest of the team leaders will be here in a few minutes. I need you to share the brief version of this with them."

Kelli hesitated. "Wouldn't that be a breach of-"

"No. I would just be reading off this paper. You spent the last half hour collecting this and know what highlights we need to share."

"Collin," Lukas said quietly, pulling Collin from the conversation. "We got a call."

"Yeah."

"No." Lukas held up the red flip phone. "We got a *call.*"

There was something about this he should remember. Something from their time in Nepal with the Shifting Shadows.

"Is that the phone that-?"

"Yes," Emily responded quickly. "And if this attack wasn't the beginning move of the Shifting Shadows, this call is."

Michael turned, hearing the Shifting Shadows. "What did they say?"

"A gun deal is going down in Chicago tomorrow," Lukas said, "and they want extra protection. They want us to protect the buyer."

"Chicago," Collin muttered. "Too much of a coincidence."

"So, the Shadows are buying guns," Michael continued.

Lukas nodded. "But I know they have an arsenal. There are only three reasons I could see as to why they would be on the receiving end of a gun deal. One, their weapon stores were destroyed last year during the raids. Two, they want to transport the weapons inside the country's borders and cannot bring them in. Or three, they need specialized weapons for a specific job."

"We need to know what they're planning," Collin thought out loud. "But we can't let them get those guns."

Emily nodded. "Precisely. And we need to keep our cover if at all possible."

Several team leaders were starting to enter the room with mixed looks of shock over the attack and curiosity over the conversation.

Once all the team leaders and division directors were seated, Michael began the debrief. "Thirty minutes ago, there was a shooting at Wrigley Field. From what we know, the numbers are twenty-seven wounded and thirteen dead including Senator Wynn. We don't know if she was specifically targeted, but if she was, I had Kelli put together some information on the senator and why someone would want her dead." Michael nodded to Kelli and sat down.

Kelli stood and opened the folder, her fingers shaking with nerves. "Senator Wynn, like any other senator, has… or had many stances that criminals would oppose. Her main stance was gun control. She was aggressive in her approach and had a task force created specifically targeting the Chicago Outfit, the mob."

"Was she successful?" Brady, a team leader and native of Chicago, asked.

"Enough that there are several newspaper stories about this, and the arrest rates have risen."

"So, it is a serious possibility she was the target."

Kelli gave a small shrug. "It could be."

"That is what we believe," Collin threw in. "Look at the carnage. Out of the press boxes and VIP lounges, hers was the only one destroyed. If they were going for numbers, why shoot at a target through tinted windows as opposed to the hundreds out in the open?"

"Are there any other names that stand out among the dead or injured?" Michael asked.

Director Whitmore scratched his chin while scrolling on his

phone. "None that my team have found so far, except the obvious. A couple of lawyers, a teacher, the pitcher, some businessmen, and two children."

The weight of his words threatened to crush Collin's chest. He felt sick to his stomach and his eyes couldn't focus. *Children.*

The heaviness of silence hung in the air as each turned to his or her own thoughts. Finally, Michael spoke. "Anything connecting this attack to the Shifting Shadows?"

Around the table, team leaders and directors shook their heads. Lukas tapped his phone on the table. "I received a call from Hunter Drake." All eyes turned to Lukas. "He wants Emily and myself to go to Chicago tomorrow to be security for a gun deal. I think this is a little more than coincidence after hearing this information."

"What's your plan?" Director Cynthia Lombard asked. Her long green fingernails clicked against the table. Collin wasn't sure how she managed to always look like she could step out of the war room and onto a set in Hollywood and no one would give her a second glance. She was the head of the Coordinate division, responsible for working with other organizations.

Before Collin could respond, Brady stood up. "I already have a team-member there who is working with the local law enforcement and has been a part of this since the bad guy opened fire."

That was the missing piece Collin was looking for. He cast a glance at Lukas and Emily. He hadn't had time to discuss his idea with them. Heck, he'd only just figured out part of it. But Lukas nodded his encouragement, reading his mind, and Collin continued. "Lukas and Emily were called to be security for the buyer, the Shifting Shadows. Now, we know we can't supply them weapons, but we also need to know what their plan is to use these weapons."

People were nodding, but he had only given them their problem, not his solution. His hopeful solution.

"I propose a ruse. A two-team mission." Collin turned to Brady. "And I would like to enlist you and your team's help since your team has contacts in the city." Brady gave a slow nod, and Collin continued. "Your team will take care of the guns. With Senator

Wynn dead, the Chicago Outfit will expect the police to focus their efforts on today's shooting, giving them a small window of time for the exchange. Brady's team will work with law enforcement for the sting and take the weapons."

"Did the Shifting Shadows tell you the Outfit is the dealer?" Brady asked Lukas.

"No."

"Then-"

"But it makes sense. Like I said, I do not believe in coincidence. The Shadows must be getting a large shipment or they would not have requested Emily and myself. The Chicago Outfit is the largest organization in Chicago. If this attack-" Lukas gestured to the monitors- "was the Shifting Shadows, they were taking out the Outfit's enemy to free them up for the exchange."

Lukas looked at the other leaders gathered, focusing on Director Whitmore. "As I mentioned earlier, the Shadows' plan revolves around four major points: guns, people, medicine, and propaganda. Step one is guns."

He nodded to Collin who took it from there. "After Brady's team takes the guns, my team will come in to take the Shifting Shadows. Lukas and Emily have an invite and will be security for the event. Three of my people will pose as the dealers and four as officers."

"Sounds like it could get dangerous," Michael voiced.

"Not if we use some of Stephon's magic." Collin turned to Stephon, a burly man with a thick beard and a full belly. He was the director of Formula division in charge of unique weapons and other gadgets.

Stephon ran his hand through his silver hair. "I'll see what I can do."

CHAPTER 7

WELL LAID PLANS

Chicago

The Chicago safe house was beside a run-down motel, where a few more cars wouldn't draw attention. Inside, the team met to prepare and go over final details before the mission.

Tonya released the magazine on her Glock and checked her ammunition again. "I don't like the idea of shooting at our friends, even with rubber bullets."

Brooke tied her hair back in a tight bun. "I know. It goes against everything my dad ever told me."

Looking back at her, Tonya smiled as Brooke struggled to get her body armor in place. The bright white POLICE letters did little to make her intimidating. "Did you go shooting with your dad?"

"No, and I never wanted to. But my sister, Lilly, did, and she's a good shot."

Over a year before when Hunter tried to kill Brooke, Lilly had shot him in the shoulder and saved both of their lives. Although Tonya had never met Lilly, Brooke talked about her often, and Tonya knew she would recognize her on sight.

"You will be a good shot too once you're done with training," Nichole commented, coming over to help her secure her armor. "Or once it is done with you."

"Enough." Tonya moved to stand between her and Brooke.

"Oh, Tonya. You talk a good game, but I see that bruise under your eye. No amount of makeup can hide that from me. Who were you sparring with? What mission was that from? Oh wait, it was the wall, wasn't it? And not even the thirty-foot one."

From across the room, Ryan yelled, "If I remember correctly, Nichole. You had a trip to the hospital our first day."

"You said you'd never-"

Ryan cut her off with a wave of his hand.

"Okay, listen up, everyone!" Collin waved for them to gather around. "Brady's team just called in and we're a go. Lukas and Emily are already on site, and the rest of us are wheels up in ten. If some of you could help Ryan load the van, that would be appreciated. Otherwise, triple check your weapons and load up."

Lukas pulled to a stop behind the fifth warehouse. The directions had been detailed and left nothing up for misinterpretation. Emily stepped out of the car and Lukas popped the trunk before getting out himself.

They both wore their weapons in the holsters on their hips out in the open. Though open carry was not legal in Illinois, he was no longer Lukas Dekker. He was Lukas Keller who was hired to do a job without letting the law get in the way.

He had paid special attention to the detail of his appearance, from the polish on his shoes to the part of his hair. He usually kept his dark blond hair long enough to run his fingers through, but for this, he cut it in the way he had a year ago, buzzed on the sides and the top just long enough to feel when the wind picked up.

Emily had undergone a similar but more dramatic makeover. In the year since Nepal, she had let her blonde roots show and her hair lengthen. Her makeup was softer with more natural hues. She thought he didn't notice, and though it took him a while and Brooke outright saying something for him to know what it was, she looked more herself, like she wasn't trying to hide from the past. But today, her hair was black, cut again to her shoulders, with red lips and bright eye shadow.

When he first saw her, he thought it made her look attractive, but now with her body armor and old scowl, the only word to describe her was outright intimidating.

The trunk closed with a loud *thunk*, and Emily hefted the tac bag over her shoulders. If things went according to plan, they wouldn't need it, but things rarely went according to plan.

They walked around the warehouse, and another vehicle came into view. As they approached, the driver got out, pulling a briefcase from the backseat. He was a short man with glasses and a jumpy predisposition. "You're the Kellers, I assume. I'm Victor." He stuck out his hand to shake, but Lukas simply gave a nod of acknowledgement.

The man tried to smile, but fear radiated off him in waves. "Well, since we're all here, let's go in."

Lukas placed a hand on his shoulder to stop him. "Let me scout the perimeter." He gave a nod to Emily to stay with the man before moving off.

After a thorough search of the warehouse and the surrounding area, Lukas determined it was safe to enter. It wouldn't do to walk into a trap on their first day as security, and something about this man set Lukas ill at ease. Perhaps it was the way he couldn't stand still, or the bite of his lip when he thought they weren't looking, or the fact he wouldn't shut up. Why would the Shadows send him to make the exchange when this was clearly his first time?

"The Kellers are killers they said. He said, 'If anything goes wrong, the Kellers will clean it up.'"

Lukas stood stoic and on guard while Victor rambled on, but Emily stepped forward, standing close enough to fog his glasses. "If you say our names one more time," her voice was a whisper, but the type that sent a chill down his back, "I swear you will not live to tell anyone else. You would be wise to keep your mouth shut."

He nodded vigorously. "Okay, whatever you say Mrs.-" He caught himself before saying *Keller*. "Whatever you say."

But Victor was as incapable of controlling his mouth as the rest of his body. He paced and fidgeted and babbled on. If they were meeting with the real mafia, Lukas would have sent anyone but this man. What were the Shifting Shadows thinking?

Victor looked at his watch. "Here they come. They come now. Any minute."

Sure enough, a black van pulled in front of the building and three men stepped out. But something was off. These were not Lukas's friends. Where was his team?

One held a briefcase identical to Victor's, set it on the table, opened it, and turned it so they could see the contents: stacks of hundred-dollar bills.

Something was definitely wrong. This wasn't about a gun deal.

Victor set his briefcase down and opened it, revealing a thin stack of papers.

Information.

The buyer stepped forward. "Radenie and the commanders of DARKNESS send their regards."

Wait. Radenie was the title of the leader of the Shifting Shadows. Which meant they weren't guarding for the Shifting Shadows but rather against it.

Another puzzle shifted around in Lukas's mind. They said Radenie. Did they mean William Drake who was known as Radenie and taken captive at the end of their adventure the previous summer? Or did they mean someone had successfully taken the title of Radenie? In that case it would be Hunter Drake, William Drake's nephew.

But that puzzle didn't matter at the moment, as the men Lukas identified as the Shifting Shadows read through the files Victor brought.

"It's all there," Victor said, breaking the silence. Lukas wanted to keep him quiet, but his job was to keep the man alive. Or at least that's what he thought his job was.

"Are we supposed to take your word for that?" the buyer asked.

"You don't trust the seal at the top? Those are the official copies."

"Yes, but are they the only copies?"

Victor hesitated. "Yes."

The buyer looked up at him before looking back down. "No."

"Insurance. I know who I'm dealing with. You didn't hire me bodyguards but killers."

The buyer rolled his eyes and put the papers back in the briefcase. "Where is the other copy?"

Victor put his hands in his pockets but not before Lukas could see how badly they were shaking.

The man next to the buyer leaned over and whispered something in his ear. Out of his peripheral, Lukas saw Emily shift her weight and pull her hand closer to her weapon.

"Very well, Victor," the buyer said his name for the first time. "We don't have time to play, so I just have to call your bluff."

A simple nod from the buyer. A swift draw from the second. A loud crack of the bullet. A heavy thud of the body. A pool of blood from his head.

A second later, Lukas and Emily drew their guns, but it was a second too late. Their charge was dead.

The buyer, who Lukas identified as the lead Shadow, motioned for his man to holster his gun. "We need to move." He inclined his head, indicating for Lukas and Emily to follow him.

Lukas looked back at Victor's body before following them out. "Why did you kill him?"

"Would you rather we kill you?"

"No, but what about his secret file? You could have taken him and gotten the information out of him later."

"Ah, but we don't actually care about the file."

"Then why all this?" Lukas spread his arms to what just happened.

"You ask too many questions. Get in the van and shut up."

Sliding into the back of the minivan, Lukas counted heads and was glad the three at the meeting were the only Shadows. Or the only Shadows for this part of the plan.

The lead Shadow got into the passenger seat and turned to face them. "Now, what you need to know about this next part is simple. We are meeting with the Outfit."

Lukas let out a small breath. At least they were correct about who they were meeting and would be back to plan A.

"We told them we would each bring two guards for the exchange."

That was a lucky guess by Collin since he was sending a three-man team in as the sellers. This was a good sign.

"So, the three of us will go in, while you two perch up there and take them out if anything goes wrong."

Emily spoke for the first time. "We came armed as bodyguards not snipers."

The barest hint of a smile pulled at the man's cheeks. "We brought the adequate materials. Your preference is the SIG SSG 3000, right?"

How could he even pretend to know her preferred weapon? When they were in Nepal, Emily's choice of weapon was poison. They must have looked at the file the Flock had backstopped them with.

After returning from Nepal, she and Lukas studied the Flock's entire backstop, including preferred weapons.

"I prefer the Steyr SSG 69." Because the backstop had been for Lukas from Austria, they had chosen the Austrian military rifle for the two of them. While the rest of the team trained on M24s, the two of them had to be proficient in both.

"Yes," the Shadow said, continuing the conversation. "Of course. But an Englishwoman using an Austrian gun?"

"I am beholden to no country."

"And no organization I see. We haven't had contact with you for a year."

"We went dark," Lukas answered. "The last thing Radenie told us was to answer the phone when it rang. Other than that, we went home to heal." He glanced over at Emily, imagining that scar on her left shoulder where she was shot. "We have been working contract with some other organizations and biding our time."

"But we would've heard about you."

"No, you would not. Not if we did not want to be found."

The driver pulled over and killed the engine.

"This is where you get out. Set up in a place where you can see the yellow building. If anything goes south, shoot to kill."

Lukas nodded. "Affirmative." And he would.

CHAPTER 8

THE HATED PLAN C

Ryan stood with Max and Sam on either side of him waiting at the second location, a warehouse a couple of miles from the original meeting place. They had left to meet Emily and Lukas when Collin called them off. They met with Brady's team to collect the weapons and learned the meet would happen at this new location. But so far, all Ryan saw was the deserted street in front of them.

Had the meeting time changed too? Where were Lukas and Emily? What if this was a trap?

A van rolled up, and Ryan shared a look with Max. Lukas and Emily were driving a car for the getaway part of the plan. This van was unexpected.

"Hawk," Lukas's voice came over his watch in a whisper. "I'm set up in the building across. Real fire in play. Payment changed. Leave keys in Sam's right pocket."

He knew better than to say anything back. The Shadows were already incoming, and Ryan trusted Lukas enough to roll with whatever he had up his sleeve.

Three men got out of the van. Ryan hoped they could pull this off. He, Max, and Sam were chosen because they were the American men, and he took lead. He got his surname Murphy from his father's Irish heritage, but his curly brown hair and long nose he got from his mother's Italian genetics. And though his voice was normally laced with a New York accent, his acting career gave him control over his voice, and with some prep work, he switched his inflection to mid-west.

When the men stepped in the shadow of the building they paused. "You are not Frank."

Shoot. They had met before. Ryan was counting on this being a first meeting, but there wasn't anything he could do about that now.

"No. He was caught up. He sends his regards."

"Then send my regards because that is all you will get from this meeting."

The buyer turned, and Ryan stepped forward. "With the senator's death, the police-"

"That was your idea. We executed it perfectly, just as you ordered. That is why we chose now to meet."

This was not going well. If they walked away… Ryan realized he was on the defense and needed a switch in tactics.

"I'm here. The guns are here. Do you want them or not?" He motioned for Max to open one of the cases they brought so the buyers could see the weapons. "Now, the payment." Ryan was careful not to say money, since Lukas indicated there might be a change.

One of the men stepped forward with a briefcase, and Ryan looked through its contents. Names and numbered accounts. Legislative bills. This information was taken from the government.

But that wasn't it. While the buyer looked composed, his two sidekicks were nervous. Ryan handed the briefcase to Sam. "And?"

"And the information is verified and secured. This is the only copy."

One of the henchmen swallowed visibly, meaning that was probably a lie.

"And the money." Ryan risked to say.

"What money? This is a straight trade."

Ryan pointed to two of the containers and jerked his thumb over his shoulder. Sam picked them up and started toward their SUV. "Then what you see is what you get. And you don't get a glance at the big toys in the back."

The buyer stood for a moment, watching Sam walk away. "Wait, I'm sure we can come to some sort of agreement."

"And I am sure this will be a continuation of a fine partnership."

The other man just nodded.

Sam brought the cases back over and opened one, revealing a Barrett .50 cal. It was clearly the primary weapon of the deal as they had looked through the cases and inventoried what the Shifting Shadows thought they were getting.

It weighed close to thirty pounds, with a considerable amount of weight at the front end, reducing the recoil to regain the target quicker between shots.

Ryan handed it to the buyer, who inspected it closely.

That was when the police sirens sounded. The cavalry had arrived. And in about thirty seconds this would turn into a war zone.

In anticipation of this, Ryan had made sure all of the guns in their deal were unloaded, and Collin waited to lead the team in until the focus was on the deal, and the buyer's hands were occupied with the empty gun.

This was supposed to go smoothly with everyone in the room armed with rubber bullets, but the fact that Emily and Lukas weren't there meant there were three with real deadly ammunition.

All of this went through Ryan's head in the five seconds between the sirens sounding to seeing the police car pulling around front. The six of them involved in the trade pulled their weapons and turned to face the door.

"Drop your weapons and come out slowly with your arms up!" Tonya's voice came over the loudspeaker. Although Collin was leading this group, an American police officer wouldn't have an Irish accent.

Ryan fired off two rounds in their general direction as he ran to cover. Behind him he heard Sam and Max doing the same.

He couldn't see the police car from where he was, but he heard when the window shattered. He heard Tonya's yelp, and came around to let off a few more rounds.

In front of him, the three Shadows approached the police car together.

Collin poked his head up and let off a burst of rounds.

One of the Shadows fell to the ground, clutching at his chest, blood escaping through his fingers.

Sam, who stood beside the fallen man, fell seconds later with a dark red substance pooling beneath him.

An object sailed over the car. Ryan managed to cover his ears and open his mouth against the concussive pressure of the explosive. The noise inside the warehouse was deafening, and all he heard for the rest of the firefight was a loud ringing.

Looking beside him, Ryan saw what was left of the second Shadow. His face was covered with a maroon mask of blood, hiding the extent of his terminal injuries. Ryan's own leg was covered with a sticky substance of the same color.

Max gave a triumphant last run before being cut down by Collin. His body jerked as the bullets hit him, and he tumbled to the ground.

Over the ringing in his head, Ryan heard two distinct cracks from a handgun followed by Collin and Brooke falling to the ground.

Emily stood over them for a second, but what Ryan saw was nothing like his friend. The hardness in her eyes looked like she just killed two people, and her usual playful smile on the edge of her lips was replaced with a scowl.

She turned and reached into Sam's right pocket, pulling out the keys to their SUV. "Hurry," she said to the remaining Shadow. "Follow me."

As she moved closer to Ryan, she paused. Her eyes flicked as if making a decision. Then she raised her pistol and Ryan felt before he heard the bullets hit his chest.

He gasped for breath as the oxygen was forced from his lungs. He reached up and brought his hand back slick and red before he toppled over.

Emily knew she had four rounds left. She knew the police were on their way. And she knew she had less than three minutes to get out.

She bolted toward the black SUV parked out back and hit the fob to unlock it. On instinct, she went to the right side to drive, but this was the United States where the Yanks drove on the wrong side of the car.

The Shadow jumped into the car and took the keys from her, turning over the ignition. He threw it into gear and jerked forward, speeding away from the meet now covered with bodies.

"Why did you shoot him?" the Shadow asked.

Emily reached for the seat belt. "He saw our faces. Go straight and make a right."

"Where are we going?"

She dug her phone out of her pocket. "Somewhere safe." She sent a quick text before pulling up a map.

The car bounced as they jumped over the curb. "And your husband?"

"He knows where we're going." They swerved to pass a car and ran through a four-way stop. "Take the second left."

"You left the weapons."

"Would you rather have spent the rest of your life in jail? Besides, they only brought out the big guns. The rest of the product is in our boot."

He spun left around a corner. The vehicle rocked and threatened to end this chase before it began. But it stabilized and they raced back down the road.

"Where do you intend to use these things anyway?" Emily knew she was risking suspicion by asking the question, but they were running short on time.

"Why do you want to know?"

"I'm taking a holiday. Anywhere I shouldn't be?"

"Texas. Don't go to Houston."

They were heading out of town, and the buildings on either side were slowly becoming residential when the hit came.

Emily's head jerked as their SUV was thrown to the left. The seatbelt cut across her neck at the sudden deceleration. She could feel the vehicle spinning as it came to a stop, and her stomach roiled. Her vision filled with the white of the air bags in front and on the side of her. Then she slipped into the darkness of unconsciousness.

Everything about this deal had gone sideways. Nichole sat in her car as oversight, watching the gunfight play out.

She had the original meeting place fully wired, but it did them no good when Emily and Lukas were surprised by the Shifting Shadows. The meet changed and all their prep work was for nothing, except the retired police car they had borrowed. It had a dash camera, which showed her the grim details only when Collin pulled into position.

She was two miles out, watching her friends get shot down.

It was part of the plan, but the Formula team at headquarters did too good of a job. Each member of the team was armed with real weapons but with rubber bullets. Everyone except Lukas and Emily wore custom armor, over which were pouches of red cornstarch covered by a thin black fabric, giving the appearance they had actually been shot.

But when three armed Shadows showed up to the meet instead of the one, plans were bound to change. She watched in shock as the bullets flew into the first Shadow, penetrating through his armor. He collapsed out of the camera angle.

Another bullet struck the next Shadow, and she saw his head rock back before he dropped.

Emily appeared then, or at least she assumed it was Emily. She shot Collin and Brooke who both went down then made her escape with the surviving Shadow, shooting Ryan on her way out.

Half a minute later, her phone chirped with a text from Emily: *Plan C. 3 min.*

Plan C was in action, and Nichole hated plan C.

She started the car and sat with it idling. Emily said she would be there in three minutes, and at two minutes forty-seven seconds, Nichole heard the squeal of an engine pushed to its limit.

Her timing had to be perfect. Too soon and someone might die. Too late and she would miss them entirely.

A glimpse of black was all she saw as she tromped the accelerator.

The sound of crashing metal on metal assaulted her ears. The airbag flew toward her face. All she saw was white.

Once she got her bearings again, Nichole reached for the door and stumbled out. Surveying the extent of the damage, she saw she had clipped the rear quarter passenger door, spinning the car into the shoulder of the road.

A moan came from the passenger side, and Nichole ran over to check on Emily. She tried to open the door, but it was crushed with no way to pry the metal doors apart. The side air bag completely covered the shattered window, so Nichole could only hear Emily's soft moans.

Circling around front, she could see through the windshield. The interior was filled with busted airbags. The driver was laying at an awkward angle, having flown forward not wearing his seatbelt. His left arm was caught between the steering wheel and the door, and he remained motionless.

Emily leaned forward, the seatbelt the only thing keeping her sitting up. Her jaw was covered in blood from a busted nose. What concerned Nichole was the broken window and what the glass would have done before the air bags went off.

Nichole tried opening the driver's door, but it was locked.

The sound of an approaching engine caused Nichole to look up. Thankfully it was one of her team.

Lukas stared down the scope of his rifle and took out two of the Shadows, leaving one for Emily to extract. He watched them leave in the SUV and slipped around to get the car the Shadows arrived in.

Knowing Emily, she would implement plan C. He raced down the road following Emily's trail.

The scene of the crash sent chills up his spine. Nichole was trying to get the door open to no avail.

"She is alive, but that is all I know. I cannot get in."

Lukas pulled out a lock pick set and worked the driver door. In less than a minute it was open. Nichole helped him pull the driver out and lay him on the side of the road before Lukas crawled in to get Emily.

"Emily, can you hear me?" His words were gentle as he took her hand. He flipped it and took her pulse. Steady and strong. "*Mein Shatz*, you have to wake up. We need to leave."

Her words were slurred as her lips barely moved. "Can't move."

He tried unfastening the buckle, but it was locked in place. He pulled up the leg of his trousers and unfastened the knife attached on his calf, using it to cut through the thick weave of the belt.

Free of that, Lukas angled her to assess her injuries. Her shirt was covered in blood, but it was just from her nose, which looked to be broken. Across her neck, her skin was rubbed raw from the seatbelt that probably saved her life. Glass stuck out from her armor, but none of the pieces went through the metal plates protecting her torso. Her arm had several cuts, but nothing looked major. Her legs had room to move, so he wouldn't have to cut her out. Not to mention, he didn't have the tools to do that.

"Emily." He grabbed her shoulders which caused her to wince and turn away. "Emily, I'll need your help."

Her eyes remained closed. "No. Let me sleep in just once."

"Emily." His tone was sharp and commanding.

The sound of sirens reached Lukas's ears as he pulled her from the vehicle. He glanced at the Shadow who was still unconscious. They needed him for answers. This plan depended on getting him out with them, but nothing today had gone according to plan.

"Lukas, get her out now." Nichole tore off her vest and threw it in the backseat of Lukas's car. Then she raced around to her car, putting the computer and communication array in his. By the time she made it around again, Lukas had pulled Emily out and was helping her to the car, half dragging half carrying her.

"Get out of here!" Nichole said as Lukas hesitated waiting for her to join them.

"What about you?"

"I'll find my own way out. À bientôt."

With a curt nod, Lukas drove away while Nichole knelt beside the Shadow waiting for the police.

CHAPTER 9
COUNTING THE COST

Flock Headquarters

Three days later, Collin stood in front of the directors, his peers and his bosses, and waited for their decision.

The executive director of the Flock, Felix St. James, stood from the conference table to address him. He was tall with a chiseled jaw showing through a shortly trimmed black beard with streaks of gray through it. "To say this mission was a total disaster would be giving too much credit to a disaster."

Collin moved to defend his team, but Felix kept talking. "I have never seen so much destruction, and what do you have that proves this was worth it?"

The answer was nothing, and everyone knew that, so Collin stayed quiet, staring blankly at the wall behind them.

Felix gave a sigh of resignation. "What was the purpose of this mission?"

"To prevent the Shadows from getting the weapons and gain information on their next strike." Collin practiced phrasing it in a way that it wasn't a technical failure. Before Felix could interrupt him, Collin continued. "The Shadows did not get the weapons."

"And that is due to Brady's team."

Collin snuck a look at Brady, whose lips were tucked in concern. "And Emily told us the location of their next attack."

"Houston, yes you told us. But it is one of the top ten biggest cities in the United States. We need more specific information. When is the attack? Where? Who is the intended target? We can't answer those questions because the one survivor you left is in custody of the law." Tapping his pen against the desk, Felix paused. "Let's table this for now and talk about the execution."

A chill ran down Collin's back, causing him to shiver involuntarily. He had been prepared for probation or even forced to leave, but execution?

"Starting with equipment."

Collin let out a quick breath, realizing they were talking about how he executed the mission, not about executing him.

"Seven custom design armor vests from Formula."

"Come on, cornstarch and red dye don't cost that much."

Stephon, the burley director of the Formula division, who had worked with Collin and Max on the designs, answered. "It was the design of the pouches and labor of sewing the top coverings." He then turned to Felix. "But really Felix, the cost was minimal and the design worth repeating for future missions." Turning back to Collin he winked. "How did it work, by the way?"

"They had no idea they were watching theatre."

"Four vehicles," Felix continued. "Three of which were totaled. Two in the crash and one by the bullet holes sewn through it."

"We weren't the one who shot it."

"Yes, but you were the one who authorized 'Plan C', were you not?"

Collin hesitated for a moment. Every member of his team hated plan C, but him most of all.

"While the cost of your assignment may be negotiated and explained away, the risk to your team is not."

Anger surged through Collin's veins. Anger with Felix for assuming he was the one who put his team in danger. Anger with Emily for implementing plan C. But mostly anger toward himself. Anger that he could not think of a better plan. And anger that he had put his team in danger. "It was one of the plans we came up with. I never intended it to be used."

"And yet, one of your team just got released from the hospital today."

Emily had protested going to the Flock's hospital, but after Lukas' description of her injuries, Collin hadn't taken no for an answer. She suffered a fractured rib and a concussion, along with her broken nose, which had to be reset.

Nichole was lucky to not suffer similar injuries, walking away with a sprained ancle and a black eye.

Although Emily had been the one to instigate plan C, it was Collin's job as team leader to take responsibility for their actions. "Plan A went out the window the moment the Shifting Shadows showed up with additional armed guards. And Emily made the decision that plan B would either be ineffective or more dangerous than plan C. We trusted her insight."

"But you still discussed something so dangerous."

Knowing arguing would be futile and may not be the best representation of the leader he wanted to be, Collin conceded. "I take full responsibility for what happened."

"But you were not the one who made the call."

"We work as a team."

"Yes, but Emily is dangerous."

Collin stepped closer, his hands closing in fists. "You can debate my decisions. You can correct my mistakes. But you cannot attack my people. If you have a problem, come to me alone, because they-" he gestured to the other directors- "don't need to know."

"We all need to know when someone is dangerous."

He was about to refute that but thought better of it. Emily was dangerous, especially to their enemies. He looked to Michael. "Are you not dangerous?"

A small smile pulled at the corner of his mouth. "I would like to think the Shadows say I am."

"Emily and Lukas are in a difficult position that the Shadows must think of them as dangerous and maybe reckless. They have a reputation to maintain, and if they don't it could mean their lives."

"Yes, I can accept that," Felix conceded. "But she is also a danger to her team and herself. Last year, you brought your team home safe. Her gunshot wound was the only injury."

"But-"

"Then, she decided to implement your most dangerous plan which could have killed her and Nichole."

"What are you saying?"

Felix paused before answering. "Bench her until she has finished her training and a full psych eval. Actually, that wouldn't be a bad idea for your team in general. You and your team are confined to base until otherwise notified. Understand?"

Collin nodded numbly and turned to exit before Felix finished.

"And one more thing. If this happens again there will no longer be the Rising Flock. Based on the individual's strengths and *weaknesses*, they will be reassigned or sent back depending on their usefulness to us."

Collin wanted to turn and punch the guy, but this was his boss, so he settled on slamming the door shut behind him.

Emily lifted her shirt and stared at the patchwork of black and purple in the bathroom mirror. She tried to take a deep breath, but every time it was a fight between her lungs and her ribs which left her gasping in pain.

Letting her shirt back down, Emily splashed her face with the cool water and looked up at her reflection. She tried to figure out who was staring back at her Emily Moore or Emily Keller. Maybe Victor was right. Maybe she was a killer. Or maybe not. Lukas had killed the two Shadows, while she had carried out the rescue.

Some rescue. She had been lucky. And if she kept making calls like she did, her luck would run out.

She pulled at the edge of her collar to reveal the bullet wound from the year before. She nearly died by the hands of Radenie's wife because of her success in infiltrating the Shifting Shadows.

The door swung open, and Emily hastily pulled her shirt back into position. Tonya walked in behind her. "Do you want to talk about it?"

"No." Emily walked out into the lobby area of the training center. Tonya was kind and one of the closest friends Emily had, but her professional job as a counselor made their friendship strained at times. The truth was, she probably needed to talk to someone, but she didn't want Tonya to look at her with pity or worse, horror, as she explained everything that went through her head in the seconds before the car crash.

The only person she trusted that much was Lukas. They had been dating for over a year now, and she knew she could trust him completely, but it was hard. He didn't have the dark secrets she did. He wouldn't understand her guilt. The guilt that made it easy to make dangerous decisions.

They were thrown into a dangerous world. And while a part of her wished for the simple pleasures of a stable job, marrying Lukas, and raising a family, another part of her whispered that she didn't deserve it.

She walked outside and let the massage of the sun relax her muscles. She watched as Sam and Max raced against each other on the obstacle course. That was what she needed to do, but her sore body pleaded against it.

The door opened again, and Emily knew Tonya had followed her out. They stood in silence watching the boys.

"I'll be fine, you know," Emily started.

"I'm sure."

"It was just a stupid call."

"That I doubt."

Emily looked over, but Tonya still had her eyes on the game in front of them. "What do you mean? That I deliberately did this?" Emily gestured to her side, but even that movement hurt.

"You're smart enough to see the right move."

"Are you saying what I did wasn't right?"

"I'm not saying that at all." Tonya finally turned toward her. "I am saying, I trust you to see the different outcomes and choose the best course. But…" She paused as Sam toppled over Max trying to pass him. "I've seen you take care of this team, but you also need to take care of yourself."

They stood in silence as Emily considered that. "I do."

"Would you have made the same call if I was in your spot?"

"No." The answer was too quick, proving Tonya's point.

Silence lingered as Emily drifted through her thoughts. There had been other options she had considered, but this one seemed the one she had the most control over. No, even that wasn't the reason. Was she trying to prove herself to her team? No, they trusted her and knew what she was capable. No-- she was thinking like Emily Keller, where danger wasn't a factor. She shot first and asked questions later. And that mentality had put her life and Nichole's in danger.

"What's done is done." Tonya's soft voice interrupted Emily's inner dialogue. "I'm not questioning your decision or even why you made it. I just… I don't want anything bad happening to you."

"Then we joined the wrong profession."

Both smiled knowing that running toward danger and risking their lives was an occupational hazard. "We put ourselves in enough tight situations. There's no need to take unnecessary risks."

Emily nodded. But what was unnecessary?

Brooke hid in the confines of the library. She always found comfort being surrounded by books. No matter what the characters faced in their adventures, their authors already knew the ending. Everything would work out in the end, and the challenges they faced only made them stronger.

She trusted her own Author in the same way. God had already written the final chapter. And whether she lived to face another day with her team or woke up in the arms of God, she knew everything would be okay.

But today she was hidden in the library for research. Something Emily had said caused her to dig through the piles of books beside her. The guards were sent by Radenie who controlled the Shifting Shadows, and the Commander of DARKNESS. Something Max had found in the research last year about her ring mentioned DARKNESS.

She plugged Max's flash-drive into her laptop and found any document including darkness in it, which only came up with two relevant results. One was the journal entry Max had read which described the star-gem that Brooke still had. That star-gem itself was a mystery they were still trying to figure out.

It belonged to the Radenie, the leader of the Shifting Shadows, or his heir. She had a personal history with the heir, Hunter Drake, or was he now the Radenie? That was another question she had to answer. He had gotten into a fight with Collin, and during that fight he lost the ring. Then Tonya found it as she tried to help Collin. And at the dance the next semester, she had given it to Brooke because it matched her dress. And that was how the Shifting Shadow's star-gem ended up in her possession. Hunter had tried to kill her twice, the first time for witnessing a murder he committed, the second when he sent men to take the ring back from her.

She pulled herself out of her memories and looked back at the computer screen. Having looked through Max's files along with any other electronic records, Brooke turned to the only thing left: books.

Hours passed as she skimmed through them. Anything that might have the slightest link to the Shifting Shadows or this DARKNESS. She read so long, her eyes hurt and focusing on the words harder just made them more out of focus.

"Come on, come on." She mumbled in frustration. There must be some hint, some clue of what they were up against.

"There you are," a man's voice said from behind. She recognized it but was so focused, she couldn't place it.

"If you're not gonna help, go away."

"Help with what?" Brooke looked up and saw it was Ryan. "We called you three times. All of the team has been looking for you."

"If you're missing a librarian," Brooke said, grabbing another book, "you look in a library."

"You were supposed to be at the evening run an hour ago."

She ignored him as she read the section on fictional organizations. It was, by all means, a stretch, but she had to try everything.

Ryan sat down in front of her. "Unless this is a matter of life and death-"

"It might be."

The book she had begun thumbing through noted an organization called Drknis (spelled D-R-K-N-I-S). It was a group of six organizations with a common goal that divided the world by its continents minus Antarctica. Each organization had a realm of influence with mutual resources as well as mutually assured destruction if any of them tried to double cross the other.

It originated in the book *La Dimensione Grigia* by Salvador Moretti published in 1952. Turning to her laptop--that was running dangerously low on battery, she looked it up in the Flock's database along with an English translation. With their language program, they could have a rough translation ten seconds after the page was loaded.

"Brooke, I'm trying to talk with you," Ryan said, possibly again.

"And I'm trying to ignore you."

"You said earlier you wanted my help."

"Oh." That got her attention. She looked up from the laptop, pointing back at the book. "I've found something that might give us some clues. Look up Salvador Moretti."

She turned back to her laptop and waited as the library searched their database for a result. Yes, they had it. She opened it and looked through the table of contents for DRKNIS. Pages 46-47.

While she waited for the pages to load and the translation to appear, she turned to Ryan.

"It says here," he started as he read off the information from his phone, "that he published *La Dimensione Grigia* April 3rd 1952 and was killed in a car accident April 10th, just a week later."

"That's not a coincidence."

"And although this book was published as fiction, there have been several investigative journalists that say everything he wrote was based on real people and real groups. Does it have anything on the Shifting Shadows?"

"Not that I can tell."

"There you are," another voice said. This time Brooke looked up to see Nichole. "We're meeting in ten. Are you coming or not?"

"Meeting? What for?"

"Apparently Collin's debriefing did not go as well as he thought. He has called a meeting."

"But-"

"Brooke," Ryan interrupted. "Whatever you've found can be explored tomorrow, yes?"

Reluctantly, she bookmarked her page and closed her computer, rubbing her eyes against the headache forming there.

"How long have you been at this?" Nichole asked looking at the three stacks of books as high as the table on either side of her.

"What time is it?"

"Almost eight," Ryan answer.

"Wow, I missed lunch. I guess I've been here..." She counted on her fingers. Messed up and had to count again. "Ten hours."

"Ten?" he let out a short whistle. "I bet you're hungry."

"Starving. But there's a meeting?"

"Yeah. At least Collin called it at the club so you can get some grub while we talk."

Brooke packed up her computer and stared at the stack of books. "I have to shelve these."

"Leave it to the librarians." Nichole grabbed her arm and pulled her toward the doors.

"But I am a librarian."

"Not here. Now get a move on, or we'll all be late."

Tonya sat beside Brooke at the club, sharing a few fries as Collin gave his spiel.

"First of all, I want to say, I'm proud of all of you. For a first mission, we did well, considering everything about our plan went out the window from the beginning, we did well." He paused for a moment before continuing, rubbing his temple.

"Is there a but?" Tonya asked, feeling his conflicting emotions.

Collin nodded and continued. "But the directors don't like how we handled it."

Sam stood up. "Then they should have been there."

Tonya's phone rang. She went to turn it off but it was her mom. She answered the phone and stepped out. "Hi, mom. What's wrong?"

"Why would you assume anything is wrong? What if I just wanted to talk with my girl?"

"Sorry, things have been rough recently, so I guess I was expecting bad news. Any good news?"

Hesitation hung on the other end of the call. "No. I'm sitting in the ER."

"What?!"

"It's- it's okay. Everything is fine now."

"Sitting in the ER doesn't sound fine!" Tonya brought her voice down, forcing herself to ask the next question. "Is it Tadi?"

"Yes."

Tonya was pacing now, her free hand on her head. She couldn't do anything except listen and pray. "What are the doctors saying?"

"They want to try a new medicine."

Tonya refrained from interrupting that this would be the fourth medicine change that year.

"But if that doesn't work, they want to move forward with surgery."

Fear punched Tonya's stomach, forcing her to look for a place to sit down. But all the seats were inside the club. She slid down the wall and sat with her back to it, clinging to the phone. There were too many variables for this surgery, not to mention the expense, something her family had no way of paying.

"Tadi will be fine." But her words were hollow.

"The doctors aren't hopeful."

"But we will be." Tears steaked down her cheeks, and hiccups contracted her diaphragm as she tried not to sob.

"I know you weren't sure about coming home, but..."

"You let me know what is happening. If you give me a few days, I'm sure I can make it down there."

Silence again separated their conversation. "He's been asking for you."

Tonya covered the phone as her cries came through her defenses. She needed to be brave for Mom. But all she could hear was Tadi's voice begging her to stay home the day after she made it back from her encounter with the Shifting Shadows the year before. "How is he now?"

"Sleeping."

"Good. I'll try to make it home this weekend."

"I thought you were helping your friend."

"I'll try to do both. There may be a way."

"But all that flying. If you can't afford–"

"Don't worry about me, Mom. Take care of Tadi. I'll be there when I can."

Hanging up, she stared at the phone in her hand, blurry with tears. Collin had already told her she could go to Houston to help Jasmine on Friday. She would just ask for a few more days to fly home and be back before anything else major happened. At least that was her plan.

She walked back into the club and took her seat by Brooke, hoping it was dark enough that they couldn't tell she'd been crying. It seemed like the meeting was over. Everyone sat back casually, and the topic jumped around wildly.

"And where were you all day?" Emily asked Brooke.

"DARKNESS," she managed between bites of her hamburger, which she ate as if this was the only meal she'd had all day. And that wasn't far from the truth.

Max snapped his fingers and pointed back at Brooke. "Of course, the warehouse of DARKNESS. Has your ring given you any clues as to its location?"

She shook her head. "I don't even know where to begin."

"Wait, what ring?" Emily asked.

"The star-gem," Brooke answered, reluctantly putting down what was left of her burger. "It belongs to Hunter Drake, who I guess is the new Radenie. According to Max's documents, which his father stole from the Shifting Shadows, the star-gem has the location of the warehouse of DARKNESS carved into it. Originally it was designed as a safehouse for the royal family of some small country in Europe. But then the Shifting Shadows stole the star-gems and the safehouses."

"So, these star-gems lead to the safehouses?"

"Yes. But I don't know how to read them. When you shine a light through it, it shows the stars at a certain place and a certain time of the year."

"And how is that supposed to lead us to that location?"

"It's like how sailors read the stars to know where they were going."

"But the stars change," Collin said. "Depending on what time of year it is."

"Right, which makes this especially tricky. I'm hoping to have an answer to when it was made before we try to find an astronomist who can read it."

"So, that was what you were doing?"

"No." Brooke went on to explain her attempt at research into who or what DARKNESS might be.

Collin nodded as he listened but got up and moved around the table to stand beside Tonya. "I need to speak with you," he whispered by her ear.

"Likewise."

After the conversation had died down, she followed him outside. "I'm requesting a week," Tonya began. "After my weekend in Houston, I have to visit my family."

The look on his face caused her to pause. Turmoil was etched between his eyes, and his lips were tight.

"Tadi needs me. You said to do what I thought was right. The rest of the team can handle whatever happens next. Anyway, I'm not a major asset to your team."

"What do you mean, you're not an asset?"

"During the last mission, when the bullets started firing, I stayed down. I froze. I couldn't find it in me to look up and return fire."

"Tonya," he stepped closer. He brought his hand up to touch her cheek, causing her heart to lurch. She wanted his comfort and assurance, but it was too much to hope. He drew back, and her cheek felt the cold of his absence. "You might not be front line, but that's not what our team is about. We take care of people, and you are the most caring person I've ever seen. A time will come soon when you will be the most important part of our team." She smiled, but Collin continued. "But you can't leave."

She took a step back, hoping she had misheard. "But you said–"

"I said you would be on call." He softened his tone. "But this is not my decision. Because of Chicago, the directors want our team to finish training before we go out again."

"But I'm leaving for personal reasons. I'm not planning on getting shot at."

"I know." He took a deep breath, looking away from her. "I'll see what I can do. But I can't promise anything."

Tonya nodded numbly.

Collin took her hand and looked down into her eyes. "Please understand, I'm trying to do the best for you."

"I should tell Jasmine I can't come. And Tadi?" She whispered the statement as a question, hoping Collin would tell her no, but he simply pursed his lips and nodded.

"So much for family first." She turned and walked away as quick as she could without running and hoped he didn't see the tears slipping again down her cheeks.

CHAPTER 10
PROMISES

Days later, Sam stood at the shooting range with his Sig Sauer in his hands. Even with over six hours a day for the last week, Sam was only starting to feel comfortable with his pistol.

There was no standard issue gun for the Flock so each member could choose what was most comfortable. Brooke chose a Smith & Wesson M&P Shield because it was a small gun that fit her well and was easily concealable. Emily's gun of choice was the Walther PPK. It was the gun the Flock gave her during Nepal, and during that week it had become her second skin. Sam chose his Sig Sauer M17 because it was sturdy and the weapon of choice by the United States military. It was a small comfort that his brothers, wherever they were, carried the same weapon to keep them safe.

Tatiana was behind them, watching them shoot. "Again!" she called, her Russian accent now familiar to his ears. "I want speed and accuracy. My grandmother could shoot better than this."

Brooke leaned over beside him. "And my granny could shoot a squirrel at fifty paces."

"Brooke Castleberry!" She straightened as Tatiana stepped closer. "You are this close to failing this class. You better spend your time thinking about your shooting instead of your retort."

On the other side of him, Emily winked and pointed her gun

toward Brooke's target and shot a perfect smiley face on the face of Brooke's silhouette.

"And Emily Moore!" Tatiana switched focus. "It is a weapon not a toy. Stunts like those will not get you anywhere."

"Really?" Emily continued firing at her own target, yelling over the sound of the gunfire. "They got me into the Shifting Shadows!"

Sam had heard stories of the stunts Emily pulled off in Nepal. Even if half of them were made up, which he somehow doubted, he was sure it was her spunk and sharpshooting that got her in.

He finished his mag and caught something out of the corner of his eye as he reloaded.

Michael stood against the door of the indoor range. Tatiana walked over to him. His relaxed posture never shifted, but she waved her hands in agitation, often gesturing back at them. Whatever was going on, Tatiana didn't want any part of it.

"Ceasefire!" At the sound of Michael's words, everyone set down their guns and turned around. "It has come to my attention that some of you think you are ready to go back out there. So, I'm here to propose a wager."

He let the words hang there dramatically. Sam felt his heart race with the sub-message that they would not be able to pass whatever test he threw at them.

"Usually, this final is given at the six-week mark of your training and again at the end. No one has succeeded at six weeks. You will not succeed at two."

"What is it?" Sam dared to ask.

"It's called the House of Death."

Lukas lifted the visor of his welding helmet and inspected his work. His experience with mechanics and electrical systems made him the logical choice to help the Formula division with their newest project, a new ROV (Remotely Operated Vehicle). But what it would be used for was still a mystery to him.

He had spent hours staring at a computer screen to help the Light division try to narrow down when and where the next attack would take place. But without a timetable, and with the size of the city of Houston, it was a daunting task. When the maps and schedules proved too much, he headed down to the place where he thought best and put his hands to use.

The frame had only a few more welds needed when he noticed Michael standing at the edge of the Formula workshop. "How long have you been here?"

Michael looked at his watch casually before shrugging. "Only long enough to see that last joint. I'm impressed."

Lukas stood to greet him. "What can I do for you?"

"House of Death."

Taking off his gloves, Lukas shook his head. "I didn't think we had to requalify."

"This has nothing to do with you."

"Then why are you coming to me?"

"Because it's your turn to defend."

Lukas grinned. Ever since he first faced the House of Death, he looked forward to the time he would be the torment of the new recruits. "Against who?"

"Your team. It will be you, Collin, Nichole, and Ryan against Emily, Tonya, Sam, Max, and Brooke."

"Okay." But there had to be more to this for Michael to suddenly appear while he was working.

"And whoever wins gets three days off."

Lukas nodded, considering what he would do with his days off. But everything he wanted to do, he wanted to do with Emily, who was on the other team. Oh well, maybe he'd take Collin up for a fishing weekend on the great lakes.

"Okay, how long do we have?"

"Seven hours."

Tonya looked through the crowded cafeteria, one face standing out, his red hair summoning her like a beacon. "Collin, I assume this was you?" she asked, implying the chance to go home.

He nodded, a sadness still in his eyes. "It was all I could do. But please don't thank me."

"What do you mean?"

"They have put constraints on your freedom. If by some miracle you do win, you can go home, but you cannot go to Houston."

"Why not?"

"You know that well enough. It's the next target for the Shifting Shadows."

"That's why we're proving ourselves, right? To prove we can handle an attack out there."

Collin reached out to touch her, but she stiffened. "Please, promise you won't go to Houston."

Tonya let out a tired sigh, why were all the areas of her life coming unraveled at the same time? "Fine, my priority is Tadi anyway." She turned and walked away before her patience snapped and she said something she'd regret.

She spotted Brooke, Nichole, and Max seated toward the back and joined them.

"So, do you think we can win?" Brooke asked.

It took Tonya a couple of seconds to realize Brooke was talking to her. "Of course, we can."

"But does anyone know what this House of Death is?"

Max leaned forward, using his breadstick as a pointer. "It's a course set with all kinds of booby traps and the like. We go against a defending team. Our objective is to take them all out and get the briefcase without being shot."

"Sounds simple enough."

"Except," Nichole interrupted. "You will be going against your own team who knows how you think."

Max motioned to her with mock outrage. "Who let the enemy sit at our table?"

"She's made it through before," Brooke said with a tinge of hope. "Maybe she could give us some hints."

"*Non, cher,* I want those three days off, same as you."

"Then if you're not here to help us, why are you here?"

Nichole reached over and stabbed a mushroom Brooke had picked off her pizza. "I was here first. You sat with me."

"Fair point." Brooke reached across and stole a fry.

A cheer exploded from the other side of the cafeteria, causing Tonya to turn in her seat. She caught the blur of motion as Ryan backflipped off the table. "Nichole Thomas!" he called, and the crowd quieted. "Thou vex me with thy flaming hair. Wilst thou come hither to prove thy metal?"

"Oh," Nichole said with equal parts shock and admiration, standing and making her way over.

Someone touched Tonya's shoulder, causing her to jump, but it was only Collin. "Come with me."

"What's going on?" she asked as they made their way through the crowd for a better view.

Collin leaned over so his breath tickled her ear as he talked. "Over this last year, those two have challenged each other to anything from Shakspearian duels to breakdancing."

"Really?" Tonya couldn't see herself breakdancing in front of her friends, let alone all these strangers.

"Remember who they are. An actor and a journalist. They are showmen who love a crowd."

"Do you know what this one's about?"

"Not at all."

They pushed their way through to see Nichole tying her blonde hair with flaming red highlights into a loose bun. "What will it be this time, fiend?" Nichole asked to the amusement of the crowd.

"Nothing like before, fair lady." Ryan gave a low theatrical bow. Rising, he turned to the audience and waved. "Max, the instruments."

A few moments later, Max made his way through the crowd with two fencing foils.

The clack of the foils and the cheer of the crowd sounded. They circled around the tables. One of the bystanders pulled back just in time to save his sandwich from becoming a shish kebob.

Ryan leapt onto a chair from which he had the advantage of height but couldn't move.

After several attempts to strike him, Nichole hooked her foot on the leg of the chair and pulled, leaving Ryan seated on the floor.

She pressed the tip of her sword against Ryan's throat and announced, "At last I have bested thee. Now admit thy scheme or the whole world will hear thy scream."

Ryan dropped his foil and lifted his chin, exposing his neck. "By my life, dear maid, I have seen none as fair and strong as thee. Wilst thou take me with thee or to a life of exile force me flee?"

The expression on Nichole's face never changed, but Tonya thought she could see the smile shining from her eyes. "Tell me plainly, tell me true. What is thine intention?"

Ryan rose slowly with the tip of Nichole's sword still at his throat. "To take thy money, thy reputation, and thy life."

The crowd booed.

"Then thou be a thief, a scoundrel, and a murderer."

"And that is but the beginning." Ryan stepped back and leaned over to grab his sword, but Collin stepped in and took it before he could.

"You best be on your way before the lady decides to become less lady-like."

The crowd whooped at his comment.

Nichole lowered her foil. Ryan gave a half bow and turned to walk out the door with the crowd parting before him.

◆

In two minutes, everyone was back to their seats as if nothing had happened. Lukas took Emily's hand and led her away from the table. Though her stomach growled for food, her heart hungered for time with him, alone.

"Where are we going?"

He kept his face forward, gently pulling her along. He finally stopped at a bench where the trails began. "Emily, we need to talk."

Nothing good started with those words. Emily's gut twisted but she did her best to keep a calm appearance. "Okay."

She turned to look at him, but he was staring straight ahead.

Silence hung between them, and she wished she could have taken at least her apple with her.

"Where do you think this is going?" he finally asked.

"This?"

Lukas turned and took her hand. "Us. You and me."

"What do you mean?" She knew full well what he meant, but she didn't dare say anything that might endanger them.

"Where do you see us in five years? We have been dating for almost two, and I think we have reached a crossroads. Are we going to be serious? I mean, I like our friendship, our comradery, our partnership. But if you see only that, I need to know."

She loved working with him. And they did make an excellent team, knowing how the other thought. But in her heart, she wanted him not only as a sparring partner, not only as a teammate, but as a man.

She wanted him to take her in his arms and kiss her. She wanted to wake up and know he was hers. She wanted to dance every dance with him. She wanted to fight every fight with him. She wanted to spend the rest of her life with him.

But still she hesitated.

Was this even fair to him? She had been so willing to put herself in harm's way in Chicago, but when she saw what it did to Lukas... Her gut twisted at the choice she had to make. If they both stayed, the odds were very much against either of them living to retirement. Death already stalked them.

It haunted her dreams. The visions so striking they came back unbidden. Tonya kneeling in a smoldering building, holding a small child. The sound of Brooke crying a desperate prayer. Nichole slumped over in a metal chair; her fingers broken. Sam and Max falling side by side from a barrage of enemy fire. Collin's body laid on the steps of a courthouse like his father. And Lukas's burnt hand as he reached out to her from a burning car, a gold band on his ring finger.

"No," Emily whispered before realizing she said it aloud.

Hope pulled Lukas's brows up, but they fell again as he read her face full of fear.

"This life we lead," Emily continued. She wanted to stop, but the words kept coming. "I don't see a future for us of any kind."

Lukas leaned back and looked ahead again. She tried to grab his hand, but he pulled it away.

"As much as I desperately want to be with you, I can't stand to see you killed."

She had been thinking about this decision since Chicago, honestly since Nepal, but it was all too real for her now.

"Then what are you going to do?" Lukas asked.

"Go back home." Why couldn't she keep her mouth from talking? "The university said I would be able to join the force with the degree and training I've had."

"You've made your decision then." Lukas's voice was soft and distant.

"No, just-" her voice broke as the tears came. "Just considering my options."

"So, you want to quit the Flock and become a police officer. A much safer profession." Sarcasm coated his words causing her to flinch.

"I know. But it's not my safety I'm concerned about."

"I do know that."

"I don't want to lose you!" Silence hung as the truth of the words ripped her apart. "The truth is I love you. I love you so much even the thought of your death brings me to tears."

"And you think leaving would fix that?"

"Yes. No. I don't know. I have to do something."

Lukas grabbed her hand, and his warmth softened her anger. "Death is a part of life, dear one."

"But what is this world we have found ourselves in?"

"It will pass in time."

"I don't think so. Michael and his father are proof of that."

He tucked her hair behind her ear, letting his hand linger on her cheek. "If you want to run away, take me with you. There's always a job for a mechanic."

"But I couldn't leave our friends. And we're really good at what we do. Maybe we are here for a reason."

Lukas simply nodded, dropping his hand to her shoulder. "There will come a time when we need to make that decision. But now may not be that time. So, are you still with me? Do you want to pursue life together, good and bad?" He gently touched her forehead with his lips.

A shock of electricity flew from Emily's head to her heart, and she tilted her face up, looking him in the eyes. "Yes. Yes."

Her heart felt like a magnet, pulled toward him with the deep promise of a future. Whatever future may mean. His lips were soft at first, full of tenderness and compassion, then turned harder with passion. His hand slid from her shoulder to her back as he pressed her closer. Her hand wrapped around his head, playing in his hair and answering his passion.

A moment later, they broke apart. Her lips burned but craved more. But she was content to sit back and look into his eyes. His chocolate eyes that held the promise of a future.

CHAPTER 11
HOUSE OF DEATH

Most people called it dusk, but Max preferred the golden hour. In high school, he dabbled in photography and this was the one phrase he came away with that he still used on a regular basis.

He walked beside Sam, the two of them wearing matching vests and carrying their real guns with wax bullets. They weren't deadly but would sound like real guns, feel like real guns, and hurt like crazy if you were hit. The two of them were taking the back door while Emily led Brooke and Tonya through the front.

The House of Death loomed ahead. It looked like a run-down Dutch Colonial. This was the one advantage they had that no other team had ever had-- an architect.

They had all afternoon to plan and prepare, and Max went into research mode. Dutch Colonial was a common design in the area, but with the layout of the windows and the general shape of the building, it left six basic blue-prints that it could be. The common facts were: there were two doors and one staircase, which were likely chokepoints; the walls were sturdily built and unbreakable unless they came in with explosives; the gables of the roof were too steep for a swing down into the upper-story windows; and the lower windows were barred.

Admittedly, this information gave no useful way of getting in, but it would give the most likely places to get ambushed.

What the blueprints didn't mention was foundation, which was a storm shelter specially built for buildings in the tornado alley. When Sam came back from reconnaissance with the pictures, Max was 72% sure this would work.

He set small shaped devices around the building, enough to shake it but not enough to do any serious damage.

Staring at his watch, he counted down for seven o'clock. The entire house shook, and Sam kicked in the back door. They made their way through the kitchen with surprisingly no resistance.

But just as Max thought that, Sam slammed into his shoulder, throwing both of them to the ground.

Bullets tore into the wallpaper above their heads.

"What a fine job of remodeling," Max quipped, rolling into a crouch and moving toward the breakfast bar separating them from the shooter.

Sam had already risen to his feet, and moved forward in a low crouch with his gun raised. He left to flank the shooter.

Max popped his head up and fired twice. Another trio of rounds flew toward him, some hitting the bar he hid behind while others flew over his head.

A loud snap sounded, followed by Sam's yell.

Gunshots sounded again, but this time none of them struck near Max. Rising up, he shot twice, one of which got Nichole directly between the shoulders, eliciting a sharp cry and a string of French.

Max ran forward to Sam who was clutching his side. "Go! I'm out. The girls need help."

Sure enough, Max heard the gunshots above him followed by a yelp.

He swept the area and moved toward the stairs. When his foot hit the sixth stair, he heard the click. His momentum carried him forward even as he saw the eighth stair disappear.

With a fumbling leap, his toe caught the edge of the ninth stair, and he landed with a busted lip and two bruised knees.

Before he could make it up, a crack sounded from above, resulting in his ribs screaming in pain. He'd been shot.

Max looked up to see who it was, but no one was in sight.

Lukas lay across the exposed rafters, the ragged burlap he brought acting as camouflage. No one would look up, the traps he left and the ambushes of the rest of his team would ensure that.

From his position, he could see the stairs below him and a good portion of the foyer. His gun felt sturdy in his palm, and his fingers itched for something to shoot.

The entire building shook, nearly tossing Lukas from his perch. He whipped his legs around the rafter and waited for the house to stabilize.

With all the noise and confusion, he couldn't hear if the first trap had sprung at the door. Aimed at the entrance with a pressure trigger, the cayenne pepper would have become a cloud obscuring the intruders from Ryan, who lay in wait there. If it got in their eyes or nose, the pain would be excruciating but wouldn't cause any permanent damage. It was only supposed to stop them from fighting long enough for Ryan to take advantage of the distraction.

Within a minute the three girls were within view at the bottom of the stairs. None of them were covered with the red dust. They stopped to look around, suspecting traps or an ambush, both of which waited for them.

Brooke looked up, straight at him for a long second, but finally looked back at her friends and shook her head.

Emily pointed and whispered something causing Tonya to nod.

They began their assent.

Lukas closed his eyes and focused on his breathing, keeping it calm and even. He waited to hear the crash of the trap, but it never came.

Opening his eyes, Lukas saw they had completely stepped over the sixth stair. How could Emily have seen it? Although it wasn't his best work, it should have been invisible.

They were now almost to the top.

He reached around and pulled the trigger, using only his right hand to aim, his left keeping him balanced on the beam.

His aim was a little off, hitting Tonya in the shoulder, but in this game it would still count.

Before he could change targets, two bullets hit the rafter he was on, jolting him with the velocity.

"Told ya!" Brooke shouted.

"Run!" Emily answered and pelted the board a couple more times before following Brooke down the hallway.

He would now have to twist around to shoot them, but by the time he could do that, they would already be gone.

Looking back down, he waited for Sam or Max to come through. He figured Nichole would probably get one of them, but the odds were in their favor.

Sure enough, Max came running into view. He didn't even pause at the bottom of the stairs.

A click on the sixth and the crash of the eighth stairs meant the trap had worked exactly as he designed it.

Lukas leaned around and shot again, this time with better aim, getting a solid chest shot.

Max looked around with confusion, not even realizing where the shot had come from, and Lukas dropped down in front of him.

The look on Max's face made Lukas laugh as he walked backwards to follow the girls. "You will have to excuse me while I go secure my days off."

Brooke tried to check each of the rooms quickly and quietly. The problem was, the doors creaked like crazy, and each of them were closed. Behind each could lay a trap or the briefcase they were looking for.

It was behind the third door when Brooke found movement. She recognized Collin and she saw his raised gun.

She got out two shots before leaping out of the doorway.

Crack. Crack. Crash.

The sound of glass shattering.

She waited for two breaths for him to fire back, but nothing happened.

Peeking into the room, Brooke saw the large shape of a broken mirror with jagged pieces still attached on the side.

She spun around with her gun to where Collin would have been standing. Instead, there was a short door, not even reaching to her shoulders. She crouched to get through, but instead of leading to a room on the other side, it was a corridor the same height of the door.

Her mind screamed at her that this was a trap, but she didn't see any other way to go.

The door slammed shut behind her, and the corridor went black.

Brooke tried to let reason overcome her anxiety. It was an old house, sometimes the way it settles causes doors to randomly shut.

But the slam was followed by the click of the door locking.

Her heart struck her sternum as it tried to get out. She hated dark spaces, and she hated being trapped.

With her Smith & Wesson still gripped in her right hand, Brooke used her left to feel her way through the corridor. It had to let out soon.

Her back ached from crouching over so long, her eyes strained to see anything resembling a door, and her lungs begged for a deep breath.

The stone scraping against her left hand turned to wood, and she stopped.

Knowing she wouldn't have a clear shot at anyone, she tucked her pistol back into the holster and used both hands to feel along the wood for a door knob or latch or anything that would let her out.

The wood was clearly a door, but there was nothing she could feel. Not even the hinges.

Using her shoulder, she shoved against the door. A light *click* answered her, revealing a strip of light where the door opened inward.

She slipped her fingers into the crack and pulled it open, stepped into the next room, and stood to her full height.

The bedroom in front of her was empty except for a briefcase on the bed. Her mind screamed TRAP! She took her gun from its holster and grabbed the briefcase. Now she just had to get out.

The window opened down to the front, but the fall from two stories was a little high for her. That left the door or the way she came. But she had heard the door behind her lock while she was in the corridor. That left the bedroom door as the only way through.

She opened the door to Collin standing there with another briefcase waiting for her.

She lifted her gun, but he raised his hand to stop her, his empty hand. What was he doing?

"Brooke, you don't wanna do that."

"Why?"

"In one of these cases is the evidence you're lookin' for. The other is a bomb."

"A bomb?"

"It goes off in-" Collin checked his watch- "two minutes or whenever you open it."

Brooke stayed frozen in position. "How do I know which is which?" It was a futile question, but she asked anyway.

Collin clicked his tongue. "Where would be the fun in that?"

"Then why don't we take both?" Emily asked from behind.

He turned toward her voice, and she shot him square in the vest. She jerked the briefcase from his hand and motioned for Brooke to follow her.

"We still have to get past Lukas," Brooke said, counting off who of the team was left. "And possibly Nichole. We haven't seen her yet."

Emily led them into one of the bedrooms.

"What are we doing here? I'm not jumping out that window."

"Don't worry, we're not." Emily slung her pack from her back and rummaged through her modified survival kit.

Brooke picked up a small hatchet. "Why did you bring this?"

"Never know what you might need." She pulled the rope out and started tying it to the bed post. "Seems sturdy enough."

"What are you doing?" Brooke knew but was hoping for an answer other than the obvious.

"I need you to open the window. We have one minute until this bomb goes off."

Brooke did as she was told. "Why not just throw them both out?"

"Stop asking questions." Emily joined her and tested the rope out. "We should be good. I'll go first."

Brooke nodded and watched Emily descend. Once safely on the ground, Emily waved for Brooke to follow.

Sliding the briefcase up to her wrist, Brooke tried to find a good hold of the rope.

"Stop right there!" Lukas entered the room with his gun pointed at her.

With both hands on the rope and her gun in the holster, Brooke did the only thing she could think of. With a flick of the wrist and a heave, Brooke threw the briefcase at Lukas shouting, "Bomb!"

She then dove under the bed and covered her ears.

He followed her lead, tossing the suitcase into the hallway and crouching beside her, using the bed as cover.

Ten seconds later the floor shook, a concussive boom sounded, and all Brooke could see was purple.

But it was all worth it. Emily made it out of the house with the real briefcase. They had won.

CHAPTER 12

YOU NEED US

Sam alternated the ice pack from his bruised leg to his dislocated shoulder, as he sat at the back table of the club with the rest of the team. He hadn't seen the trap until it was too late and the rope slung him half-way to the ceiling. He had worked his knife out of his pocket and sliced the rope, causing his fall to the floor and the dislocated shoulder.

He wasn't the only one at the table who came back less than unscathed. Max held an ice pack to his busted lip. Ryan laid a washcloth over his swollen eyes from the cayenne pepper trap that didn't quite work. And Emily re-wrapped the rope burns on her hands from jumping out the window.

"How did you know it was the bomb?" Lukas asked Brooke.

She smiled and shrugged. "Collin has a tell."

"I do not," Collin protested.

"He does." Tonya laughed, pointing. "That little eyebrow twitch. Yeah, that one."

"Tonya, you weren't even there."

"She taught me well." Brooke patted Tonya on the arm, careful to avoid the shoulder Lukas shot.

"Come on, Collin," Ryan complained. "We trusted you."

"I almost had Brooke when Emily shot me." Collin brought his hand up to his chest. "Admit it, Brooke. It was just a bluff."

Brooke raised a shoulder and cocked a teasing smile. "It worked."

Sam moved the ice pack up to his shoulder and sighed. "I think a few days off was worth this. I think I'm going hiking. There's a national park not far from here. What do you think, Max?"

Combing his fingers through his spiky black hair, Max shook his head. "I was thinking about the new Call of Duty that came out last weekend."

"Ooh. Yeah, I'm down for that."

Tonya's phone beeped, causing her to get up and walk out. Not unusual for her over the last few days.

Sam turned his attention to Emily. "What about you?"

"Hit the town. Paint it red. Brooke?"

Brooke looked distractedly after Tonya. "Home, maybe. To see my sister and parents. I think Lilly would like… Sorry, I'll be right back." She stood and followed Tonya out.

"Well, for those of us still working," Ryan said. "I'll be hosting a movie marathon at my pad."

"Superhero or sci-fi?" Nichole asked.

"Whatever we're in the mood for. I have the Marvel movies, the Star Treks old and new, the Lord of the Rings and Hobbits, and all the Star Wars movies."

"I'll bring some of my famous dip," Lukas offered.

Emily elbowed him in the side. "Is this your attempt to make me stay?"

"Is it working?" He winked causing her to blush.

Sam shifted back in his seat and enjoyed the banter. This was where he knew he belonged.

◆

Tonya tossed her suitcase on her bed and began packing. The text she had received was from Jasmine asking again for her help.

Collin had been clear when he told her not to go to Houston. And her family needed her in Arizona. Still, she hesitated to text back no.

She had just pulled up flights on her phone when it rang.

"Hey, Mom!" she answered, putting it on speaker so she could continue packing. "I have good news. I got the weekend off, and I'm almost packed. I haven't booked my flight, but give me five minutes and that will be done too."

"Litty." Her response was slow and drawn out, causing Tonya to pause.

"What's wrong?"

"We won't be home." The pause before her next words were excruciating. Tonya sat down at the edge of the bed to brace for more bad news.

"Where will you be?"

"MD Anderson."

Those words struck through her ribs, stabbed at her heart, and stole her breath, leaving her mind void of thoughts except for one word. *Cancer.*

"What?" Surely, she'd misheard.

"It may not be what you're thinking. They found something in the scans yesterday and want to run more tests."

"Why didn't they find it sooner? I mean, it's been two years!"

Tonya knew her mother was asking those same questions. This could not be happening.

She drew in her breath to ask the question she didn't want an answer to, but knew needed to be asked. "How bad?"

Her mother had always done her best to be honest with them but tended toward protection with bad news. And nothing could be worse than this. "They said it could be what's causing the seizures."

"What are they going to do? What are you going to do? What can I do?"

Hesitation was not a usual occurrence in most of their conversations, but it stepped in now. "We're still moving, but it's been postponed. I really need someone at the house preparing things. But… I couldn't ask you to come, but Tadi wants to see you."

"Then I'm on my next flight to Houston. I'll let you know when I'll be landing."

She hung up and fumbled through her phone to book a flight. But as she entered her destination another thought bullied its way in. *Houston. Promise.*

Collin had made her promise not to go to Houston. But she also said she'd be where her family needed her. And while there she could help Jasmine with her walk to end human trafficking.

She flipped back to messages on her phone to text Collin but paused with the infernal question. Is it better to ask permission or forgiveness?

It was still dark when Tonya's alarm clock went off the next morning. Even as someone who enjoyed the time before anyone else was up, this was too early.

She groggily brushed her teeth and hair and washed her face before dragging her suitcase down the hall.

She went to turn on the light before realizing it was already on and three figures waited in the living room for her. Nichole stood with her hands on her hips. Emily stood beside her with her arms crossed in front of her. Brooke lounged on the couch with her feet stretched out.

"Where are you going?" Nichole asked.

"I have to leave," Tonya answered, avoiding the question.

"Yeah, but if you're going to do something stupid," Emily said, "then we've got to know."

"Why would you think I'm doing something stupid?"

Both Nichole and Emily cast a quick glance to Brooke who reluctantly stood up but still kept a posture of relaxed conversation. "How bad is it?"

"What?" Tonya felt the blood start to drain from her face. How could they have figured it out?

"I- I eavesdropped on your conversation. I didn't mean to," she quickly added. "But you were kind of shouting at one point and I was concerned."

Tonya didn't know whether to feel angry over the intrusion of her privacy or grateful for having friends that cared. "It could be worse."

Brooke simply nodded, not asking any other questions. "I'm going with you."

"But I have to leave now to catch my flight."

"Wait!" Brooke darted past her to her room, coming back seconds later with her own suitcase. "Okay, let's go."

"But you need–"

"Tickets?" Nichole finished for her, holding up her phone. "Already purchased and waiting for us."

"You're going to Houston too?"

"Your friend needs you," Nichole said.

"Your family needs you," Brooke said.

"And you need us." Emily gently pushed her shoulder leading her out the door.

Nichole climbed into the driver's seat of the car waiting for them and hit the gas as soon as all doors were shut.

Houston

Seven hours later, Tonya got out of Nichole's rental and waved them on to go and help Jasmine with what needed to be done for the walk.

After a long debate, her friends finally drove off, and Tonya found herself staring up at the word on the sign in big black letters. Cancer.

Her heart pressed against her spine, her legs felt bolted to the ground, and her breath stuck in her throat. She couldn't even utter a prayer. Not that she knew what to pray. She wanted to plead for healing, wanted to yell at God for how unfair this was, wanted to curl into a ball and cry.

But she couldn't.

Instead, she focused on moving one foot in front of the other and walking through the doors. Her phone dinged with a text from her mom saying Tadi was in the middle of testing on the pediatric floor.

Tonya was walking toward the elevator when a deep voice called her name. "Tonya?"

She turned and saw a Hispanic man with the shadows of a short beard and wearing a t-shirt that read Houston Firefighter. Her mind sparked with recognition, and her heart felt a mixture of happy and shy. But where did she know him from?

"Litonya Miller?" he asked again, as if he was trying to make sure it was her.

This time his voice registered a memory of high school-- her crush stood in front of her. "Benji?" She stopped herself before asking what he was doing there because she knew she didn't want to answer that question.

"You look good," he said before she could think of a suitable question.

She felt the warmth of a blush heat her ears. "You too. So, you're a firefighter?"

Benji looked down at his shirt and nodded. "I'll get my five-year pin in September."

"Wow." All those feelings from years ago rose up along with the memories. She had a crush on him since middle school. They dated briefly in high school before he moved to Texas. He was her first kiss. And even after all these years was still a good friend.

"What about you?" he asked. "What do you do?"

"I'm a counselor for-" but she couldn't finish that sentence. The Flock was a secret organization, and she was thus sworn to secrecy. "I just got a job as a trauma counselor."

"So, you work here?" Benji extended his arms, indicating the hospital they were in.

"No," Tonya hesitated before answering. "I'm here on personal business."

He dropped his hands and nodded solemnly. "Right. How is Tadi?"

"How do you know?"

"Your sister Kachina is close to Liz who is close to my sister Miranda who told my mom who told me."

"Oh. And why are you here?"

"To check on you."

"Me?" Tonya took half a step back, forcing herself not to run into his arms and let him hold her until her fears disappeared. "I just need to see Tadi."

Benji nodded and hit the call light on the elevator. "At least let me take you out for coffee."

"We'll see."

The elevator dinged and the doors opened. "If you need anything at all. I'm just a call away."

Tonya nodded as she stepped in and let the doors shut between them. She brought her hands up to her cheeks trying to rub out the blush. What was her heart trying to do? Her mind was scrambling to focus, and her heart threw another rush of emotion at her.

No. Everything she tried ended up failing. She gave everything to her team, but in Chicago she ended up hiding from the gunfight. She supported Collin and his leadership, but now she had broken the one promise she made to him to stay away from Houston. She had to support Tadi, but there was nothing she could really do. Jasmine needed her help, and she couldn't let her friend down. No, she had nothing left to give to her childhood sweetheart, and she didn't want his heart crushed because of her.

Nichole looked around at the shelter and shuddered. "Who would have a rally here?" she whispered to Emily.

"That would be me." A woman in her mid-thirties approached. Her black hair was tied back in cornrows and a little girl of eleven stayed in her shadow. "I'm Jasmine, and this is my daughter Sarai. Are you Tonya's friends?"

Nichole nodded and extended her hand, introducing herself, Emily, and Brooke.

"Thank you for coming. As you can see, we have a lot of work that needs to be done in the next-" she paused to pull out her phone to look at the time- "six hours."

"How can we help?" Brooke asked.

"We still need to set up tables. I have registration mostly organized and-"

"Jasmine!" someone called from across the room. "Phone call for you!"

"Excuse me. I have to take care of this."

Jasmine left, but her daughter stepped forward. "Did you happen to bring any strong men?"

Nichole laughed. "No, just us. What do we need men for?"

Sarai smiled and motioned for them to follow her. "All the tables are in the trailer. We have a lot of work to do."

As Nichole came back in toting a table with Brooke, she couldn't help but overhear part of Jasmine's conversation. "But I was counting on you… No, I understand the city comes first but isn't a city made up of people? Are you just going to stand there and let this happen?... A threat assessment, and you didn't tell us?"

Nichole nearly dropped the table. Threat. Houston. Easy target. Shifting Shadows.

Brooke sent her a confused look, obviously not listening in on the conversation.

"Do you at least have someone in mind?... I can't just pull someone out of my shoe! We're expecting over one hundred participants… You know what, just put me through to him personally."

Though she was curious to hear the rest of the conversation, Nichole lifted the table again and followed Brooke.

When the final table was unloaded, Nichole looked around, calculating seats. "Are you sure this is all?"

Brooke nodded, her hands on her knees as she took a minute to catch her breath. "The trailer is empty."

"This will seat maybe seventy."

Sarai raced ahead of them. "I think there may be some more in the storage room."

From across the room, Jasmine covered the phone and yelled, "I don't want you out there by yourself!"

"Don't worry. My new friends will be with me."

Emily returned from her trip down the street to the dollar store with decorations, pens, and umbrellas. "The forecast is calling for rain."

"Just what we need," Jasmine huffed. "Our speaker canceled, the guys didn't bring enough tables, and the sound system won't work."

Feedback screeched from the speakers followed by Brooke yelling, "Not that one! The other one!"

"Which other one?" Nichole yelled back over the noise.

"And the clock is ticking down," Jasmine continued.

"Not to worry," another voice cut in. "I brought the cavalry."

Emily turned to see Tonya walking in with a man she didn't recognize. "I'm Benji, the cavalry."

Jasmine and Tonya shared a hug. Jasmine stepped back and shook her head. "Who would even want to come to a 2K in the rain?"

Benji raised his hand and smiled. "You have at least one person."

Tonya and Emily also raised their hands. "I didn't travel halfway across the country to just sit this out," Tonya said. "I'm sure everything will work out."

"Check. Check. Check. Check." Brooke's voice boomed through the speaker. "Cash, credit, or debit. Check. Check. Check. We're good."

"If you don't have a speaker, why is Brooke fixing the sound system?" Emily asked.

Jasmine shrugged. "She said something about if you pray for rain bring an umbrella."

Emily hefted one of the umbrellas. "I didn't pray for this."

"I don't think that's what she meant."

"You need a speaker?" Benji asked.

"Our mayor was going to be here but was forced to cancel."

"Give me a minute." He got out his phone and stepped away.

Emily leaned over to Tonya. "Who is he?"

"An old friend."

"Not too old by the looks of him."

Tonya elbowed her in the side for that comment but gave her a good-natured wink.

"That's settled," Benji announced, coming back. "Gary will be here in about an hour."

"And who is Gary?"

"Gary Simmons works for UAHT."

Jasmine looked at him in awe. "How do you know the head of United Against Human Trafficking?"

"Friend of a friend of a person who likes me and owes me a favor."

"Well, now I owe you one."

"Convince Tonya to take me up on my offer for coffee and we'll be even."

CHAPTER 13
THE WALK

Flock Headquarters

Collin made it up the stairs to the Light division and took another sip of his coffee. It was a day where there was more coffee than blood in his veins.

He walked past the meeting room where Reid Whitmore was arguing with someone on the phone and stepped into Juan's cubicle. "Anything new in Chile?"

Juan looked up from his computer but shook his head. "No. Same answer as yesterday and the day before."

"But if you do find anything…"

"You will be the first to know. Or second depending on what it is."

"Thanks."

Walking away, Collin considered just dropping that matter. It was probably just a weird piece of advice to keep them looking in the wrong place. Still, something tugged at the edge of his mind that this might just be the key.

"Collin! Collin!" Ryan ran up from behind him. "Have you seen Nichole?"

"I haven't. Have you talked to your boss Cynthia?"

"She said Nichole called in sick."

"Okay."

"I dropped by her apartment but she didn't answer."

"Maybe she was taking a nap?" But Collin doubted his own suggestion.

"When I tried calling her, her phone went straight to voicemail. And don't try to come up with an excuse for her. She never turns off her phone."

"Well, good luck finding her."

Collin tried to walk past, but Ryan grabbed his arm. "Do you know where the girls are?"

"Emily is in town with some friends. Tonya is in Arizona with her family. And Brooke is in Texas."

"Texas?" Reid leaned around the corner of the meeting room. "What part of Texas?"

"I don't really know. She's told me like four times, but none of the words mean anything to me. Panhandle? Above Lubbock? West of Dallas? I have no idea."

"Are you sure they aren't in Houston?"

Collin's stomach dropped with a sense of dread. "I told them specifically not to go there. Why?"

"I just got intel that the Shifting Shadows are targeting an outdoor event tonight."

"Like the walk Tonya was talking about?" Ryan asked.

"That is a real possibility," Reid confirmed. "And it's scheduled for less than an hour from now."

"Is there any way we can get a team down there in position?"

"Kelli!" Reid shouted, walking toward her office. Collin and Ryan followed after them. "I need you to pull up the tracking program."

"Okay." Kelli opened a program and looked toward Reid. "Who are we looking for?"

"Any of our people that may be in a sixty-mile radius of Houston, Texas."

"You track us?" Ryan asked.

"It's for your safety," Reid replied as if he said it a hundred times a day.

"Do you also track our internet searches?"

"No." But his answer came a little too quickly.

"We do have a right to privacy." Ryan's tone was sharp as he leaned toward Reid.

Collin held him back and nodded at the computer. "It looks like we have four people in the area."

"We'll contact their team leader and work with Knight to organize a preventative strike." Reid turned back to Kelli. "Who are they?"

Kelli was silent as she typed and looked back at Collin. "They're yours."

"Are you sure you know where your people are?" Reid asked again.

Houston

Brooke stood behind Jasmine and watched the people flowing in. The turnout had been better than they expected, especially with the rain.

It seemed that everything had come together at the last moment. A couple of volunteers were able to round up the extra chairs and tables. Tonya's new friend was able to get a speaker. Nichole's finishing touches on the tables looked stunning. And Brooke had fixed the sound system.

Jasmine stepped up to the mic, and Brooke switched the input on the speakers from the music to the microphone. "Thank you all for coming. I am touched by your care for this mission. Tonight, we will begin with the 2K, returning here for dinner, then Gary Simmons will speak. All proceeds from this event will go to United Against Human Trafficking."

In her pocket, Brooke felt her phone vibrating. Grateful that she kept it on vibrate so she wasn't a distraction, she checked the caller ID. Collin. What was he doing calling her on vacation?

She ignored it and slipped it back in her pocket. She'd call him back later. She never thought that later would be too late.

Flock Headquarters

Lukas threw open the glass door to the Light division's conference room and saw the rest of his team standing around the table along with Reid Whitmore. "What are they up against?"

"Chicago PD says the man we captured still isn't talking." Reid shook his head, looking directly at Lukas. "All we have is the fact he told Emily it would be happening in Houston and the fact that they had previously targeted an outdoor event."

"Which would still make sense with the weapons they tried to get," Lukas agreed. "But how do we know the walk event is their target?"

"The chatter we're receiving indicates they are dealing with the local gangs."

"Which is what they did in Chicago."

"Right."

"So," Collin interjected. "Are they going for a specific target or mass terror?"

"With the Barrett they tried to get from us," Lukas said. "I would assume specific target."

Reid laid his palms against the table. "We already warned the mayor who was the main speaker, and he has agreed to back out."

Collin nodded his head. "Good, that will lower the likelihood of a threat."

Lukas knew the opposite. "No, they will just change targets."

"That will give us time to get a team in place," Reid said, turning to give instructions to Kelli.

"No." Lukas pulled out his phone and dialed Emily. "If they are already in position, all this will do is create more targets. For each of their plans there are primary and secondary targets. If the primary falls through, the secondary is always to kill as many as possible."

"Do you mean-?"

Lukas held up a finger as he left a message. "Emily, this is Lukas. Call me as soon as you get this. The walk is the target." Lukas lowered the phone and looked at Collin with a stunned expression. "Did you already try to call them?"

Collin nodded. "Not that it did any good."

Pressing the transmission on his watch, Lukas tried another way. "Nightingale, this is Falcon. Call me now."

Emily's voice came through, her words mixed with grunts. "Now... not the best time... for a check in... Call you... back..." The last thing Lukas heard was the sound of a gunshot.

Houston

The rain drenched Emily's hair, plastering it against the back of her neck. She had given her umbrella to a twelve-year-old who walked beside her. Brooke and Nichole walked in front of her, while Tonya stayed behind at the shelter with those who didn't want to walk in the rain.

As the sky flickered with the flash of a lightning bolt, doubt flickered in Emily's mind. Collin had said specifically not to go to Houston, and all four of them chose to ignore his warning.

Nichole dropped back to walk by Emily. "Wipe that worry off your face. Everything will be fine."

"What if Collin was right?"

"He may be team leader, but this is our day off. We get to do what we want."

"No, today is my day off, along with Tonya and Brooke, but you were supposed to stay there."

"Meh. I had some sick days."

Emily squinted against the rain. "But still, don't you think we should've told someone where we are, just in case something happens?"

"The only thing that will happen is us making a statement and having fun at this fundraiser."

The entire sky lit up, followed by an almost instantaneous crack of thunder. "How far out are we?"

"Two more blocks, I guess."

Emily started jogging, and everyone picked up their pace to make it to the safety of the shelter.

Lightning flew across the sky followed by two cracks of thunder. But the second was not thunder.

Screams sounded behind her and the crowd pressed her forward. Emily pushed herself sideways and out of the wave of people.

Standing off to the side, she could make out the forms of three people lying on the ground. Behind the crowd another group came forward. Tall men dressed in black. All of them armed.

She reached around for her gun but instead felt the curve of her hip. Having flown there commercially, she had arrived unarmed. As soon as they landed, she bought a knife which she had in her calf sheath, but that wouldn't be enough to take out these men.

One of the men turned toward her, and she threw her body to the ground. She hit the asphalt as the man let loose a short burst of bullets.

Her arms stung from where she caught herself, but she rolled and got back to her feet, grabbing the knife strapped to her leg in the process.

The knife flew through the air and the man who had shot at her dropped. She turned toward the next, running to close the distance between them. Guns were long-distance weapons. If she could get in close, she might have a chance.

He let out two shots before she took him to the ground. Both rolled to try and find an advantage.

The ground bit into her back. His left hand pressed against her windpipe while his right punched her face.

Emily brought her left arm across her chest and grabbed his forearm. Her right went up to grab his tricep. She then trapped his leg with her own.

Spots swam between them as her body cried out for oxygen. And pain washed over her in waves that made concentrating on this move barely possible.

She threw up her hips and rolled, instantly changing their positions.

Once on top, she punched the side of his neck, targeting one of his carotid arteries. The change in blood pressure the strike caused knocked him out.

The sounds of grunts and screams were interrupted by Lukas's voice over her watch. "Nightingale, this is Falcon. Call me now."

Looking around, Emily saw the street was mostly clear, except for the wounded. But the enemy was still advancing. Emily searched the ground for the gun the man dropped and answered Lukas. "Now's not the best time for a check in. I'll call you back."

Her hand wrapped around the metal of his gun and let out a few rounds, trying to end these murderers before they took another soul.

Tonya surveyed their work in transforming the shelter into a dining hall. The tables were decorated in red and black, the sound system was set up, and the speaker was ready. The first of the walkers would be back at any minute.

The sound of rain amplified as someone opened the door, but what followed was a stampede. With the sound of the thunder growing louder, maybe it had started hailing and that was why they were running.

But the faces she saw had true terror written on them, not the annoyance or anger that weather brings. These were the faces she had seen in India when the plane was hijacked. These were the faces of her friends ambushed in Brazil. These were the faces of those who knew their lives were no longer in their own hands.

Tonya tried to slip her way through the press of people, eventually sliding through the door and into the downpour. What met her eyes made her lungs trap her air.

A girl lay in the middle of the street with two people on either side of her. The water pelted her face, and her eyes stared blankly at the clouds.

Tonya's legs pushed her forward without thought, and her lungs forced air in and out in rough spasms. This could not be happening.

"Get her off the street, now!" Tonya grabbed her feet while the other two grabbed under her arms.

A scream sounded around the corner.

Turning toward the sound, Tonya could just make out Nichole and Brooke running toward her arguing animatedly, but the storm drowned out their words. As they made their way closer, Tonya could just begin to hear their conversation.

"We need to get in!"

"Then we'd be sitting ducks!"

Tonya helped lay the girl inside the building for the other two to look after and joined her friends.

Nichole shook her head. "We've got to get to safety! We can hold them off if we get inside."

"Hold them off with what? Our umbrellas?"

"Trust me. We can create a barricade. We can use fire extinguishers if needed. We can find a way to fend them off."

Brooke's face lit up and she tapped their arms. "I've got an idea. You two get everyone inside. I should be back soon."

All Tonya could do was watch as Brooke ran in the opposite direction.

Flock Headquarters

Ryan looked around the room at his team and all the directors gathered. He let his gaze linger on Sam and Max. The three of them had been in a similar situation before when the Shifting Shadows went after Brooke one year ago. But this situation could not be handled with acting and misdirection.

"Local authorities are en route," Cynthia Lombard said, covering the speaker of her phone. As head of Coordinate division, she was in charge of coordinating with local law enforcement. And she was Ryan's boss.

"What's their ETA?" Ryan asked.

"Five minutes."

Ryan shared a look with Collin who shook his head. Five minutes may not sound like much, but it would be four minutes too late.

The door hit against the wall, causing Ryan to turn. Lukas stepped in, his face pale, his chin set, his watch clutched tight in his hands. "No one is responding."

Ever since they heard the gunshot, Lukas had been trying to reach Emily or any of the girls, while the others kept their watches off as they made various calls.

"How many of those CN28 drones do you have?" Collin asked Stephon Taylor, director of the Formula division.

"Seven. Why?"

"Are any deployed?"

"Yes."

"You knew the Shifting Shadows were targeting Houston. Are any staged nearby?"

"Right!" Stephon leapt out of his chair, dialing his phone as he walked out the door.

Ryan hated to just sit there doing nothing, but all they could do was wait and hope the girls could handle things.

Houston

Find cover! Emily's training yelled at her. *Or you'll be dead!*

She had succeeded in drawing the gunfire away from the innocents. But now they were firing at her. She raced toward the cars parked on the side of the road, laying down suppression fire as she ran.

"Nightingale! Nightingale!" Lukas's voice came over her watch. His voice tinted with panic.

Part of her wanted to answer, but the logical part of her turned off the receiver so the bad guys couldn't hear her.

The gunfire started up again, this time steadily coming toward where she was crouched behind the cars. She was tempted to shoot blindly in their direction, but she couldn't risk hitting any bystander.

A spray of bullets exploded around her, flying through the windows and the doors. She had found concealment, but she needed cover.

She peered over the car, let out a burst of gunfire, and dashed for the storefront behind her. It gave her just enough time to burst through the door before the bullets began flying again.

The sharp cracks of the gun muted as the door slammed, but it was short-lived.

The windows crashed, sending metal and glass shards through the store.

Emily raced to where she hoped there was a back door and took half a breath as she ran out into the alley.

She waited for a full minute but no one followed her. They had gone back to easier targets.

Slipping along the side of the building, Emily peered around the corner. No one was in sight.

The sound of distant sirens reached her ears, and she pressed deeper into the shadows as a dark van sped past.

They had done their damage and now were gone.

Tonya looked at the chaos around her and raised her hands to try to get everyone's attention. "Everyone, please remain calm and stay away from the doors and windows. If anyone is hurt, please come forward or get our attention so we can triage you. The rest of you, just focus on remaining calm. Everything will be okay!" The speakers projected her voice around the room, stopping conversations.

"No!" someone shouted from the back. "Everything will not be okay. Look at what they did."

Tonya looked beside her as Jasmine and three others tried their best to help those who had been shot.

"Everything will be okay," Tonya repeated. "Maybe not today. Maybe not tomorrow. Maybe it will take longer than you want. But there will come a day when you can say 'everything is okay.'"

"You're one to talk," a woman from the front said. If Tonya remembered correctly, she was one of the women who lived in this shelter. "You come in promising a better future for people, but you've never been through more trouble than not being accepted into the job you most wanted. But let me tell you, kid. Life's about to come and smack you hard on the side of that pretty head of yours. This-" the woman gestured outside- "is the real world."

Tonya held her anger. What did this woman know about her? Certainly not the fact that she was kidnapped and flown half-way across the world, and when her friends did rescue her, they had to save a plane from being hijacked. Then came her personal life of having to be strong for her brother who might have cancer and helping her family move from the only home she had known.

But she also didn't know what this woman had gone through. So, who was she to judge?

Tonya hesitated before speaking her heart, knowing only two things could happen. "The real reason I know everything is going to be okay is that I know that God works all things for the good of those who love Him and are called according to His purpose. I don't know if you believe in God, but I believe that the reason we're all gathered here today is to accomplish His purpose to destroy human slavery. Yes, bad things happen. It's part of living in this twisted world. But God can use every situation to shine His light."

Looking out at all the faces of worry and fear, Tonya felt her own disappear. She was where she was meant to be, doing what she was trained to do. "There will come a time when we can freak out over what's happening. It is wrong that there are men out there with guns that are trying to hurt us. It is wrong that our children have to grow up in a world full of violence. It is wrong that evil attacks the innocent. But now, help is on the way and all we have to do is remain calm and help each other out. For I am convinced that after the rain comes a rainbow, after the night comes the sunrise, and after hurt comes healing."

She stepped away from the mic and walked over to where Jasmine, Benji, and a few others were rendering first aid. Everyone had gathered to stop human trafficking, and now they had a taste of the fear and of the hopelessness those people faced every day. Some of the people would go home today and try to forget the whole thing. Others would go home with a new determination for helping those living in this fear.

The sound of sirens reached Tonya's ears, and she let out a breath. Help had arrived.

Brooke tried to catch her breath as she stopped at the shelter. She carried three bags full of medical supplies, blankets, duct tape, rubbing alcohol, belts… anything she could find that would help barricade the door and tend to the wounded.

She pulled on the side door, but it was locked. Pounding on it, she called, "Tonya! It's Brooke. I brought supplies!"

Looking around her for any signs of the shooters, Brooke's heart pounded as she knew she had to go back and find Emily.

Sirens sounded. The cavalry was nearby.

The roar of an engine made her turn, and only too late did she see the barrel of a gun through one of the windows.

She turned to run, but the gunshot reached her ears the same time the bullet hit her side.

It wasn't like she'd imagined it. There wasn't a tearing pain. The velocity didn't throw her to the ground. Maybe by some miracle it had missed her.

Looking down there was too much blood for that to be the case.

Brooke dropped the bags and clutched her side. Warm, sticky, liquid covered her hands, but her side was just numb.

Shock. One thought clearly articulated before her knees buckled.

She sank to her knees and felt the rain against her wound which started to burn. She had never been so thankful for the cooling shower. Darkness closed in around her, and her awareness washed away with the rain.

Flock Headquarters

Lukas watched as Collin flew a drone above the streets of Houston.

"Right in two blocks!" Max called, indicating the coordinates Kelli gave him. "You should be right on top of them."

The ringtone for Lukas's phone went off. It was Emily. "Are you okay? What is going on?"

"I'm fine. But they made a clean escape."

"Maybe not as clean as you think. Did you get their license?"

Emily rattled off the numbers and letters, and Lukas repeated them to the team. Hopefully someone could use that to track them.

"Found them!" Collin called. "Switching targets. I'll follow them back home."

"Local police are informed!" Cynthia said. "We'll keep them updated on their location."

"Great work, Emily," Lukas said back into the phone. "What is the damage report on your end?"

"I don't know. They got at least four or five before I was able to distract them. I wouldn't think more than ten."

"Okay, we have an ambulance on its way and the-"

"No!" Emily's scream cut him off.

"What's wrong? Emily!"

All Lukas could hear over the phone was the pounding rain. "Emily?!"

"It's Brooke," she finally answered, her voice harsh and full of fear. "I need Tonya and Nichole out here now!"

Lukas pressed the transmitter on his watch and hoped for the hundredth time that day he would get an answer. "Hummingbird! Mockingbird! This is Falcon. The threat has passed. Sparrow needs you outside now!"

"This is Mockingbird," Nichole started. "We are currently under-"

"Now!" Lukas shouted. He didn't know what was happening, but the fear in Emily's voice told him she was desperate for their help. And Emily was never desperate.

Houston

Nichole cast a quick glance at Tonya before throwing aside the chairs and tables that barricaded the door. Jasmine had set up a triage to one side while Tonya was trying to keep everyone calm. The people needed her there, so Nichole decided not to involve her.

Tearing down the barricade took Nichole longer than she thought, but as she opened the door, Sarai walked up to her with an umbrella, trying to be helpful. Nichole accepted it with a small smile and walked out into the rain.

What she saw sent nausea rolling through her gut. Brooke lay on the sidewalk, bandages, belts, and blankets strewn around her. Emily was kneeling over her, but having little success getting any of the bandages to stay.

Nichole popped open the umbrella and held it over them. "How can I help?" This wasn't the first time she helped patch together someone who had been shot, but she definitely wasn't taking lead on this.

Gesturing to one of the sacks, Emily told her to try and find a dry bandage.

"Come on, Brooke, stay with us," she muttered as she rummaged through the sack. "What were you thinking?"

Emily took the bandage from her, placing it on Brooke's side.

"Had to help," Brooke murmured with her eyes still closed. "Did we get them?"

Nichole took her hand. "Yeah, we got them."

The street lit up with red and blue lights as the first responders arrived.

"Can we go home now?" Brooke asked, her voice weak and strained.

"Soon," Emily promised. "Soon."

CHAPTER 14
FALLING APART

Flock Headquarters

Collin flew the drone over the fleeing SUV while Cynthia passed their movements on to the authorities.

"Collin!" Lukas's voice called followed by the slam of the door. "We need eyes over the shelter, now!"

"ETA?" Collin asked Cynthia, who simply shrugged.

"Now!"

That was not like Lukas. He was patient and understood the priorities of missions more than anyone else. He rarely lost his temper and never shouted. What had him so worked up? "Give me a few minutes."

"It's Brooke." His words were quieter now but shook with barely contained emotion. "She's been shot."

Collin forced his hands to remain where they were. His instinct was to turn his plane around, but there was nothing they could do even if they saw her. The priorities had to be in stopping those who shot her.

"Aren't you going to do something?" This time the question was from Max.

"What can we do? The ambulance is already on its way, and we are hundreds of miles away."

His team was silent, and Collin tried to pull his attention back to the screen. The red and blue lights from the police cars soon lit up the streets. Protocol dictated he should stay on site and provide air cover until all the suspects were caught and in police custody. But his mind fought to go and find Brooke.

"How bad is she?" he asked Lukas, his hand aching to move.

"I haven't heard anything from Emily in the last few minutes."

Taking a deep breath, Collin jerked his wrist, pulling the drone into a tight turn. "Sorry," he muttered to no one in particular, "but the police will have to fend for themselves."

He pushed the throttle, but by the time he made it back to the shelter, the first responders were already there. Setting the autopilot to a slow circle so he could hover, he zoomed in with the camera. A steady stream of people entered and exited the shelter. EMTs were assisting the wounded, but what caught his eyes were the black bags. Body bags. People had died, and there was no one there that could have stopped it.

Houston

Emily stared after the ambulance as it left with Brooke. This shouldn't have happened. Emily was the one to take the risks. She ran after a gunman defenseless and drew their fire away from the walkers. Brooke had left to get supplies to help, the job with the least risk, and she was the one bleeding out.

Beside her, Nichole stood in silence, a rare state for her, and they both watched the hustle and chaos on the street.

Emily knew they should help the rest of the people, but with Brooke's blood on her hands, she didn't feel inclined to do anything.

"We should call in," Nichole finally said, breaking their silence.

Right, Emily had been on the phone with Lukas when she saw Brooke. But what had she done with her phone?

The initial fear hit again. Brooke was shot. Then the terrible feeling of helplessness as she tried desperately to slow the bleeding. But blood soaked through one bandage and the next and the next.

Shaking herself back to the present, she tried to remember what she was trying to do. Phone.

After a quick mental scan, she felt her phone in her pocket. But as she went to get it, she froze, staring at her hands.

Blood.

Brooke's blood.

"Hey, it's Nichole." The voice was distant, barely decipherable through the static of the blood pounding in her ears. "Emily is fine. I have not seen Tonya yet, but she should be fine. Brooke is en route to the hospital."

Heat tingled up Emily's arms despite the pouring rain. Her ears burned and her knees shook. She needed to get her head back in the game.

Pushing her wet hair out of her eyes, she tried to take in her surroundings, but all she saw were details. Nichole's umbrella shedding water. A dark stain on the side of the building. The yellow jackets of the EMTs. The crying faces of friends huddled together. A boy staring blankly through the rain. The flashing blue and red lights reflecting on the water at her feet. The hiking boots Lukas gave her.

Lukas.

Before she realized what she was doing, the phone was already ringing. "Emily! Are you okay? What is going on?"

Tears mixed with the rain on her face, and she breathed in the sound of his voice.

"Emily?"

"I'm fine. There's going to be a lot of clean up. May need to stay in town for a few days."

"Negative." His voice sounded carefully masked as Emily tried to pick up any indication of what would happen next. "The four of you are called back immediately."

"Three," she quietly corrected him. "Brooke."

"Yeah. Michael knows. He will make sure she's taken care of."

"Taken care of?" Emily's shock turned to anger, her thoughts flying to when Radenie told them to take care of Roux. But of course, that wasn't what Lukas had meant. "Taken care of? You make it sound like just another thing on his agenda. On your agenda. She is our friend."

"Emily." His voice was soft and said her name in the way that always made her melt. "She will get the best medical care possible. The Flock is completely covering this, since it was on the job."

"On the job? We were on holiday."

"We're going to leave that out of the written report. We knew there would be an attack in Houston, so we sent the four of you as scouts."

"But Collin told us specifically not to go. We can't just go around telling lies."

"This way Brooke is taken care of and the three of you will not be placed on suspension."

Emily didn't give a rat's tail about what the bosses thought would look best on paper. Only if it would help Brooke.

"Fact is," Lukas continued. "We still need the three of you back as soon as you can get a flight out."

"You aren't going to book us one?"

"No. You got yourselves into this mess. You can get yourselves out."

"So much for this being 'official' business."

"Emily," he added quickly before she could hang up. "I'm glad you're okay."

"Yeah." She breathed out, looking around at the contained chaos around her. "Me too."

Flock Headquarters

Lukas set the phone down and stared at the big screen where Collin's drone hovered in a slow circle. What a mess! But he had to take his mind off Brooke and focus on how to stop this from happening again.

A small voice in the darkest part of his mind said there was no stopping this. The world was infested with evil, and there was no stopping evil.

Although that may be true, he *could* stop the Shifting Shadows. There would always be evil to take out, but as long as he was doing his job it would be one less tomorrow.

"Did we have any intel this would happen?" he asked Whitmore.

"If we did, we would have sent a team in. A well-equipped team."

"I know. But we're acting as if this attack is the Shifting Shadows. Is there a possibility that-?"

"Collin!" Lukas spun to see Michael, the vein on his forehead clearly visible. "My office!"

"But I'm-"

"Now!" The door slammed behind him.

Uncomfortable silence settled over the room until Stephon told Collin he would take over. Conversation filtered back after Collin left.

Lukas turned back to Whitmore, continuing their conversation. "How do we know this attack was orchestrated by the Shifting Shadows?"

"One of our informants called half an hour before the attack with information that it would be that evening at an outdoor event."

"Any other information?"

"None of your concern. It's my job to analyze the information and give you actionable intelligence. You are just here to help."

"We know this is going to happen again." Silence suffocated the room, but Lukas knew he only said what was on everyone's minds. "We need to stop it before it does."

"What do you propose?"

"Does your informant have access to reliable information?"

"Meaning?"

"Half an hour warning is nothing. We need to know what will happen next. And we need to know now."

Whitmore slammed his hand against the table. "Do you think we haven't tried?! My informant is in a very precarious situation after Nepal. He said Hunter is keeping everything close to the vest-"

"So, Hunter is the new Radenie," Lukas interrupted.

"It appears that way." Whitmore turned to look back at the screen.

Lukas thought back on his time with Hunter Drake. "Then considering there was only a week between the two attacks, we can expect his next strike to be within the next seven days. He was never one to vary attacks. If it worked once, it will work again."

"Then we should focus on the similarities between Chicago and Houston."

"You do that, and I will try to find the next attack."

Whitmore scoffed, "Good luck. The only possible lead we may have is sitting in Chicago. But the local PD hasn't been able to crack him."

The shadow of an idea crept up in Lukas's mind, and he smiled. "I may be able to do something with that. Ryan, step out with me for a minute."

To Ryan's credit, he didn't laugh outright when Lukas explained his plan.

"Wait. You're serious?"

Lukas nodded. The more he thought of his plan, the more he knew this was a long shot. But that was only plan A.

"And you think this will work?"

"Would I be asking for your help if I thought it would fail?"

"True enough." Ryan rubbed the scruff of his beard and looked over at his boss, Cynthia, through the glass wall. "She's done things like this before, and with the amount of press Chicago got, I wouldn't see any major objections on their end. Honestly, though, the techniques I prefer and have had the most success with are two-man operations."

"The problem is, he has seen your face. In fact, he saw Emily kill you. Nichole is the only one that he didn't see in Chicago."

Ryan shook his head before throwing up his hands in surrender. "Fine. I'll ask. But why would you think we can get anything when the police have had him for a week and got nothing?"

"It's only plan A." Turning, Lukas walked out to find Collin. Now was the time to secure plan B.

Opting to take the stairs over the elevator, Lukas went up the next floor to Michael's office. He raised his hand to knock but stopped as he heard the loud voices.

"You realize what will happen to you if you say that?" Michael's voice was tight and tired, as if he had been arguing his point for some time.

"Aye." Collin's answer was short.

"If you sent them to Houston to do recon, you disobeyed a direct order and will be suspended."

"And if I did everything I could to warn them not to go and they still went, they will be."

"Yes."

Silence lingered, and Lukas waited outside the door for what Collin would say next.

"It makes no difference that we were there when the attack happened?"

"Need I remind you, one of your people was shot? Which was exactly why they were told not to go." Michael let out a heavy sigh. "So, what is your answer?"

"Exactly what I said. They were on official Flock business, approved by me."

Lukas knocked on the door and opened it before Michael could respond. "What if we could stop the next attack?"

Michael pointed at the door. "Eavesdropping is not something I condone. Unless this is time sensitive information, I want you out."

Across the desk from Michael, Collin looked up with confusion. Lukas knew today he was breaking his carefully crafted rules of conduct. Don't raise your voice unless absolutely necessary. If you eavesdrop make sure you are never caught. And never strike anyone unless it will stop further violence. But today he had broken two but hopefully not the third.

"I have a plan to find the next target, but I will need Collin to coordinate it."

Michael turned his attention back to Collin. "You must have a lot of trust in your team."

Collin waved Lukas forward. "Tell us your plan."

CHAPTER 15
SETBACKS

Houston

It was past visiting hours at both hospitals, so Tonya sat at the edge of the hotel bed. Brooke's suitcase lay on the other bed, its contents strewn around like she had been looking for something.

It was typical of the messes that Brooke left. She would always come home and profusely apologize for it, and it would be clean by the next morning, or two or three. But the mess at least made their house look lived in.

Tonya tried to tear her eyes from the suitcase but couldn't. Brooke was lying in a hospital with a bullet wound, and it was all Tonya's fault. Why had they insisted on following her there? Why had she not taken Collin's advice?

She repeated the words she so often told her clients. "Don't focus on the past. There's nothing you can do to change it. The only thing you can change is the future."

Saying those words out loud did little to quell the uneasiness in her stomach. "Tonight was not my fault. I did not pull that trigger. I did everything I could to help."

But what difference did that make? The Shifting Shadows were to blame, or at least that was who she would blame until she figured it out.

Her phone rang with Collin's number. But she couldn't answer it. Not now. She had defied him, and now Brooke was injured. In Collin's eyes this would all be her fault. She couldn't face his disappointment. Not yet.

A small voice whispered she should pray, but she had no words for God. She had been through so much. Wasn't it enough that she had been kidnapped last year? Wasn't it enough that Tadi was sick? Wasn't it enough that her family had to move from the only home she knew? But now Brooke was shot. And the weight of it was all on Tonya's shoulders. When would it be enough?

Collin called again. And again, Tonya ignored it.

"Okay, God," she whispered. "I've got to admit I'm mad at you right now. You're supposed to be good. You're supposed to be in charge. What the heck happened?!" She forced her voice to stay low. No need for her neighbors to complain about her too. "God, You created the universe. You know everything that happens in our lives. If You are for us, what can be against us? I didn't think that was a challenge.

"But we live in a world full of evil. I've chosen to work in a profession that puts me in the middle of it. Is it even worth it?" She sighed and considered her options. "I want to help people, I really do, but is this the best place for me? I mean, I could work with children. People don't usually shoot at children. I've always wanted to work as a family counselor. That's what my degree is in. Maybe I need to step away from trauma and help Tadi. I know my purpose is helping people, but that doesn't mean I need to put my friends in harm's way."

Her phone rang again, but this time she answered. "Collin, I know I messed up. I'll take the blame. Fire me, suspend me, do whatever you want with me, but make sure Brooke is taken care of."

A pause hung on the line until Collin finally answered. "Your sacrifice is noted and rejected. I've already taken care of everything."

Surprise and relief flooded through Tonya. She hadn't really wanted to leave, but it seemed like the right thing to say.

"How's Brooke?" he asked.

"She got out of surgery an hour ago, but we were pushed out because we weren't family."

"What about her family?"

"Still driving in. Should arrive at about two in the morning."

"That's four hours from now!"

"Yeah, and they've already been on the road for three."

Collin let out a heavy breath. "How serious is it?"

The room blurred from the tears in Tonya's eyes. "She's alive, but that's all I know."

Silence hung between them as they both processed what might happen. Finally, Collin continued. "I know Brooke will have her family, but would you like to stay? I'm officially calling all of you back. I need Nichole and Emily for our next step, but-"

"You don't need me. I get it. I'm the one who started this trouble and-"

"Tonya, listen to me. You are the moral support of our team. You ensure our, what do you call it, psycho-social wellbeing. Right now, our team's psycho-social need is to know how Brooke is doing. Do you think she would like you to stay?"

Tonya thought of what Brooke told her of her family. They were tight. She wouldn't need anyone outside her unit. But this would also give Tonya an opportunity to check in on Tadi. "I'll stay until Brooke is in recovery and can speak for herself."

"I'd expect nothing less. And I will see you back at headquarters within a couple of weeks."

"Okay. See you then."

Brooke opened her eyes to white walls and the sound of beeping. Where was she?

The last thing she remembered was fixing the sound system for Jasmine.

Maybe she was in the hotel? How had she gotten here?

She tried to roll over and that was when she noticed the wires. Tubes went up from one arm to IVs, oxygen ran under her nose, and wires were attached to her chest and other arm.

"She's up," a floating voice said off to her left. It sounded just like her mom's voice. But Mom was home, seven hours away from Houston. If she was still even in Houston.

The first face she saw was Lilly's. Her sister's dark brown waves fell across her eyes as she leaned into view. "How are you feeling?"

"I'm fine." But as Brooke said those words something pulled at her side. Was it pressure? Heat? Pain? She reached down to touch it and sparks flew from her side, up her spine to the base of her head. "What happened?"

"You were shot."

"Lillian Joy Castleberry," Mom admonished. "You don't just say that."

"Well, it's true."

"How? What happened?" Surely she'd remember getting shot.

"Well, it all started one dark September night."

"Isn't it June?" Brooke asked.

"Okay, then a dark June night. The full moon was shining."

"It was supposed to rain. I- I think I had an umbrella."

"Fine. It was a dark rainy night in June. We were in Uncle David's cornfield."

"Lilly, stop please. Don't mess with me." Images and emotions came flooding back.

Red and black decorations around the room. Meeting some guy in a business suit. Lightning. Victory over the feedback in the speakers. Rain. Emily coming in with umbrellas. Panic. Sprinting through the dollar store looking for bandages. Arguing with Nichole. Pounding on the side door. Fear. Lying on the sidewalk soaked. Confusion. Hearing a gunshot.

The memories were out of order, but the message was clear. The Shifting Shadows had gotten to them.

"Where are my friends? Are they okay?" Brooke moved to get up, but her whole body ached.

"Easy there." Dad pulled up a chair beside her. "Your friends are okay."

"Emily? Last I saw she was going after them."

"Tonya will be here after lunch. She'll explain what's happening at work, but for now you need to rest."

"But they're in danger." The machine behind her started beeping.

"No," Mom tried to assure her, but she didn't know all the answers.

"They're always in danger. We're always in danger."

A nurse walked in wearing blue scrubs. "Miss Castleberry, you're awake! But your heart rate has spiked. Is everything okay?"

Brooke focused on taking deep breaths. In and out. In and out. She forced herself to nod as her eyes filled with tears.

"The doctor will see you shortly. Can you rate your pain on a scale from one to ten?"

Looking down at her side, all Brooke could really feel was a steady ache. "Um. I guess I'm okay. Maybe a two."

The nurse nodded and left, and Brooke turned back to her family. "I thought it would hurt a lot more to be shot."

Dad pointed at the IV bag to the side. "They have you pretty drugged up. You'll feel it later."

"Yeah." Brooke laid her head back and closed her eyes, the tug of sleep pulling her away from their conversation.

CHAPTER 16
CONNECT THE DOTS

Flock Headquarters

The next day, Sam stretched and tried to stifle a yawn as he stared at the white board. He had claimed an empty cubicle at Light division and pulled over a white board to compare the two different attacks. There had to be some connection between Chicago and Houston, but nothing stood out.

Max came up and handed him the cold half of his unfinished sandwich from lunch. "You don't have to figure this out on your own."

Casting a sidelong look at the ham and cheese, Sam shook his head. "I'll eat when I'm done."

"Yeah, and I'll sleep when I'm dead," Max took a bite out of the sandwich.

Sam ignored him and turned back to the board.

"I've been in Formula division all morning. Tell me what you got. Maybe if you explain it, you'll find your missing link."

"Likely," Sam grumbled but obliged. "Both took place in the evening in a crowded area with guns."

"That sounds like a pattern."

"Except it's not. It just so happened that the baseball game and the walk were both in the evening. For the game, it was during the fifth inning; they had shifted into a lull and weren't heightening security awareness for departure for another two and a half innings.

For the walk, the protesters were within sight of the building. If they were expecting something, they would likely be looking for it at the beginning of the walk or once the dinner had begun."

"So, you're saying the only thing we can expect from them is to attack when least expected?" Max winked. "And then Lukas was talking about the Shifting Shadows going after certain things. I remember him saying something about guns and medicine, but I really wasn't paying that much attention."

Sam pointed to a list written in purple expo. "Guns, people, medicine, and propaganda."

"In that order?"

"Lukas didn't say."

"Chicago was about guns, right? They target a senator that is heavy on stopping illegal gun sales. Technically legal and illegal, but that's beside the point. But she was killed, cutting off some of the initiative she was trying to implement."

"And that allowed the Shifting Shadows to arrange a drop with the Outfit," Sam continued. "And Houston was about people."

"Right," Max took up from Sam. "The original target was the mayor, but he was warned in time. Instead, they shot up the protesters. But what would have happened if they got the mayor?"

Sam paused to think of Max's question. But his mind went on another trail. "What if the goal was to take the mayor and wreak as much destruction as possible."

"I'd say they accomplished the second half, but what would they want with the mayor?"

Jogging back to his computer, Sam logged on to the news outlet and glanced over at his phone. It read five missed calls from Brooke. Why would she call him? And why so urgently?

As he picked it up, the phone started ringing again. It was Brooke. "Hello?"

"Sam!"

"Brooke, are you okay?"

"Shhhh. I'm totally fine. Except that's a lie. Yep, my room is filled with purple stars."

"Purple stars, huh?" Sam put it on speaker so Max could hear Brooke's drugged talk.

"Yep, purple stars. Which reminds me. I need your help."

"Isn't Tonya there to help you?"

"Yeah. She told me to rest and not to call you."

"So, you called me?"

"No. Siri called you." She started giggling then groaned from the pain it caused.

"I'm glad to hear you. But why did you call me?"

"Stars."

"The purple ones?"

"No, the red ones."

Sam shared a grin with Max. "They're red now?"

"No. You don't understand. Can you get into my apartment?"

"Only you and Tonya have the key. Are you asking me to break in?"

"I need you to get the star-gem."

"The what?"

Max grabbed the phone from him. "Brooke, this is Max."

"Oh, Max! How I've missed you. Uh-oh."

Another voice cut her off. "Brooke, this isn't resting."

"I haven't lifted a finger. No. I only lifted one finger to press the button."

"They can take care of things at work." Sam recognized Tonya's voice as she came closer to the speaker. "Boys, we better let you go so Brooke can rest."

"But I didn't ask him about the thing?"

"The thing?" Sam and Tonya asked at the same time.

"To find the alchemist. Nope. Architect. Nope, that's Max. Astronomer? Astrologer? Someone who can read the star-map."

"We'll find one," Sam promised. "But we can't do anything until Tonya gets back and we can get the star-gem from your apartment."

The line was silent for a minute, and Sam feared Tonya had disconnected it. But Brooke's voice came back in a rough whisper. "I'll be out of here soon."

"Yeah," Tonya agreed. "But you'll be in no condition to work."

"Nonsense." Brooke's voice was now weak enough that Sam had to strain to hear. "They hit my stomach not my head."

"We'll find him," Sam assured. "Just focus on resting."

Silence again answered on the other end of the line. Tonya said goodbye for both of them and hung up.

"At least we know she's alright," Sam said as he put down his phone.

"I don't know. She called you."

"Ha-ha. Very funny. But how are we going to find an astronomer?"

"I don't know. But I do know where we can find an architect." Max pointed at himself.

"Fine, architect." Sam stood from his seat. "Let's switch places. You do all the hard work of connecting the dots while I stand here and make jokes."

"And get the coffee." Max sat in Sam's seat and started typing on the computer. "And find a star-gazer while you're at it."

CHAPTER 17
INTERROGATION

Flock Safehouse Somewhere in Michigan

Two days later, Nichole stood on the other side of the one-way mirror and watched as they brought the prisoner into the interrogation room. His arms rested on the table, which was attached to a polygraph running in the observation room. She had learned not to trust polygraphs for the truth, but they were useful to indicate the hidden response of a spiked heartbeat.

Beside her, Ryan flipped through the file Chicago PD had given them. "According to his driver's license his name is Zachary Forsythe and lives in Milwaukee. But his fingerprints came back as a Zane Tennison, last arrested in Orlando for running guns three years ago."

"Last arrested. He has more of a record?"

"Yeah. It goes back ten years."

"Must have started young." Nichole looked back at the man handcuffed to the table.

She could sense Ryan nodding beside her. "But the interesting part is, according to his sentence, he should still be in jail."

"The Shifting Shadows busted him out?"

"That's what we're assuming."

Nichole took the file from him and flipped through it herself. "Are there any transcriptions of the interrogation?"

"No, but they couldn't get any useful information out of him in his week there."

"They did get information?"

"He wouldn't shut up."

Nichole looked back at the man who stared at his reflection.

"But they only turned out to be false leads," Ryan continued.

"So, we have to sift through anything he says?"

Ryan held out his hand for the file in exchange for a small box. Nichole took it and pressed the earpiece in. "What's your strategy?" he asked.

"Out-talk him."

She turned to walk out the door, but he caught her arm. "Don't take this lightly. There is too much at risk. And he can't know who we are."

He was right. If they couldn't find out what the next target was, more people would die. And that was a price they could not pay.

Stepping out to the hallway, Nichole found Reaper waiting for her. He stood tall enough to have to duck under most doorways. Tattoos covered his bald Hispanic head, traced their way down his neck, and slipped down the collar of his shirt. His real name was José Garcia, and she knew he was an avid gardener and horse lover. But everyone called him Reaper since he could reap any information the Flock needed.

Reaper had been one of her instructors for interrogation techniques, and though she didn't follow his methods, she did respect him and his work.

He opened the door and followed Nichole in, choosing to stand in the corner and watch.

Zane looked over at her with curiosity, his stringy black hair obscuring half of his face.

The chair squealed as Nichole pulled it out and sat down. Before she was even seated, Zane began to talk, his voice a deep baritone, but his words strung together with barely a break.

"Don't tell me who you are. Let me guess. Blindfolded as I came in, so secret facility. Not cops. I haven't seen a badge or any big letters. Not FBI. Your haircut is not regulation. Nothing military. Still in the United States. Not CIA. So, I'm going with a nameless organization that wants to know my connection to what happened in Chicago."

"Zane," Nichole leaned forward. "Do you mind if I call you Zane, or do you prefer the alias you gave the Chicago PD, Zachary?"

With a shrug of the shoulder, Zane dismissed her knowledge. "A rose by any other name?"

"I would not call you a rose. You need a shower and a new wardrobe."

Zane laughed. "Oh, you're fun. I'm assuming you're the good cop, which would make him the bad cop."

Nichole looked over her shoulder to Reaper standing with his arms crossed and face grim. "Let's talk about you, Zane."

"Nah," he leaned forward in his seat, matching her intensity. "You seem much more interesting than me. French? Working on American soil? On an American crime? Who are you working for?"

"I'm the one asking the questions. But first let me get my facts straight."

"Oh, take all the time in the world. I have nowhere I'd rather be than looking at your pretty face." His eyes traced down, lingering considerably lower than her face before looking back up.

Nichole slammed her hands against the table before remembering the polygraph recording and lifted them again. "You will address me with respect if you address me at all. Or I will leave and let Reaper take his sweet time with you. And I assure you, you do not want that."

"That may be true, but this is America. There are laws against police brutality."

"But as you said before, we are not the police."

Within two seconds, Zane's head hit the table. Reaper stood behind him with a smug smile and winked at Nichole.

Zane cried out in pain and clutched his nose. "You can't do that! I'm an American citizen! I have rights!"

"What about the rights of the two children who were killed?

What about the rights of my friend who was shot? When you target the defenseless, you have no rights!"

"By whose authority-?"

"We're done." Nichole stood up and looked at Reaper. "I'll be back in an hour."

"No! Wait! I'll talk!"

She knew better than to assume he had cracked with simple threats. "Oh, yes. I know you want to talk. That is all you want to do. But I don't want your words. I want the truth. So, I'll be back in an hour when you are more cooperative."

Closing the door behind her, she could still hear his muffled pleas.

Nichole walked into the observation room and Ryan offered her a bowl of popcorn. She gladly accepted and sat up on the desk to watch the scene unfold.

Fishing a key from his pocket, Reaper opened a locked cabinet in the side of the room. He then rolled out the bundle he retrieved on the table. Nichole couldn't see what was in it, but Zane leaned back and visibly paled.

Reaper picked up something and walked around to Zane's side. What was laid out on the table looked like a knife kit/ tool box from all Nichole's worst nightmares combined. Tweezers, clamps, spreaders, and knives of all shapes and sizes.

"That one he's holding-" Ryan explained- "was fashioned after the Vikings' Seax."

With the length just larger than his hand and the lines at clean angles, it wasn't the most intimidating. Reaper drew his thumb across the edge, causing a thin trail of blood to slip down the side.

A shiver ran up Nichole's spine. The fear tactic was working, and she was in the next room.

Zane squirmed in his chair, desperate to get away, but Reaper didn't even look up. With a shake of his hand, he put the blade down and walked out.

Two minutes later, Reaper walked into the observation room with a bandage around his thumb. "Don't tell me you already ate all the popcorn."

Ryan extended him the bowl. "How long are we letting him squirm?"

"Until it gets boring." Nichole reached across Ryan for the bowl in Reaper's hands.

"No, really."

"Relax, I set a timer on my phone for an hour. I wasn't lying to him about that part."

Nichole walked into the interrogation room and set down a cheeseburger, moving aside Reaper's instruments. "Are you hungry? You strike me as a cheeseburger extra onions and mustard guy."

She opened it and let the scent waft around the room.

With a wary side-long glance at the instruments, Zane extended his hands as far as they could go still handcuffed to the table.

"Ah, but in exchange I need information."

"And I told you I wanted to talk."

"I told you I'd be back in an hour. And here I am. Now, answer me honestly or things will go much worse for you."

Zane's eyes drifted back to the instruments. "What happened to the other guy?"

"He's taking care of our other guest."

"Other guest? Who-?"

"No. I'm the one asking questions. Who do you work for?"

"The Outfit."

"Wrong answer." Nichole picked up the hamburger and took a bit out of it. "I know it's been over twelve hours since you've eaten. You must be hungry. But if you keep lying to me, it will be another twelve and I won't offer you something this *délicieux*." She closed her eyes, savoring the flavors.

Zane slammed his fist against the table. "But I am telling the truth!"

"Really?" Nichole set the burger down slowly. "Because why would you sell weapons to yourself?"

"What?"

"I have video from the police cruiser that you shot up that there were two distinct groups. We know the first was the Outfit, but you are not. So, let's try this again. Who do you work for?"

"You don't have proof of nothing. By the time we saw the lights, we were already in our positions."

Nichole smiled at his confirmation. "In your positions. Preparing to shoot at police officers. All three of whom were critically wounded."

The smile on his face boiled Nichole's blood. She wanted him off the streets. She wanted him off the face of the earth. She wanted him in a hole so deep that Satan himself couldn't find him.

"See, I know exactly who you work for. I am well acquainted with him and his organization. What I'm trying to do is save people like this little girl." She pushed forward a photo of a ten-year-old girl with a wide smile and thick black hair. "This is your daughter, Zalia. Am I right?"

"Leave her out of this!"

"Leaver her out?" Nichole pulled out three other pictures from her file. "These two were killed in Chicago during the attack from your organization. The other is in critical condition in Houston after the attack two days ago. What if the next attack is in Orlando where she is in school?"

"They told me they would never."

"Ah, but they lie. What makes you think your daughter is safe?"

"We had an agreement."

"Was that with the original Radenie or his nephew?"

Zane hesitated, confusion and fear etched in his brows. "How do you know that name?"

"As I said, I know about your organization. All you have to do is tell me their name. You've all but admitted to working with them. It will go a lot easier on you if you just tell me who you are working for."

Zane stared at the picture of his daughter.

Nichole swept the other photos back in her file and pulled out her phone. "You give us just that, and I will let you talk to her."

He slowly nodded his head, his eyes never moving. "We call ourselves the Shifting Shadows."

"And who is the Radenie?"

"Hunter Drake." His answer was little more than a whisper, as if even speaking his name was dangerous.

Nichole nodded and spun the phone around, put it on speaker, and let him dial her number.

After a short chat, Nichole disconnected the call. "Now, tell me what the Shadows are planning, so we can save innocent people like your daughter."

"A bomb. In the last place you would expect one."

A thousand thoughts flooded through Nichole's head. As attacks had gotten worse all over the world, even the unthinkable had to be thought of. Bombs in schools. But it was summer break for most of the United States. Would it be another major event? Something where people were gathered together in peace?

"Don't go there," Ryan's voice came in her ear. "He's trying to get in your head."

"Be specific," Nichole told Zane.

"You'll need a pen to write these down." The hint of a smile curled his lips.

Disgust flooded like boiling water down to her stomach. She scrolled through her phone to the voice recorder and started a recording. "The exact locations, down to the description of the bombs."

Ryan was already on the phone with Director Lombard when Nichole came back to the observation room. The director would work with local law enforcement to verify the bombs and take care of them. This was the reason the Coordinate division was so essential to the Flock. Instead of spending the time and resources to send out its own people, the threat could be verified by the time the plane was even half-way there.

"It's all a lie," Nichole said.

Ryan hung up and turned his attention to her. "We still have to verify."

"He's wasting our time."

"Do you have so little faith in your abilities?"

"No, but I do not trust him."

"Nor do I. But if he is telling the truth and we treat him like he's lying, it will destroy any rapport you build with him."

"But if he is lying?"

"If he's lying, we'll move to plan B."

"Give me a chance to break him."

Ryan reached back and scratched the back of his neck. "Lukas gave us twenty-four hours. It will take time to verify his claims. If he is lying, I want him to spend a night in room 22A. You'll have one more chance in the morning when he's at his weakest to crack him."

Lukas was still putting the finishing touches on room 22A. Electrical wiring hung from the junction box as he stood on the ladder, using only the light of their lantern. "Emily, hand me the dykes!"

Behind him, Emily worked the nail gun, covering up the speakers they installed earlier. "The what?!"

"Wire cutters!" he translated.

After a minute of searching, Emily handed the dykes up to him. The thump of the nail gun continued. They had only a few hours to complete this room, and all Lukas had left to do was electrical.

Careful to keep the wires separate, Lukas picked up the timer balanced on top of the ladder. When finished, the complete circuit would run for two minutes every half-hour. This meant unshielded fluorescents, strobing red lights, swirling blue ones, and a siren going off at one hundred twenty decibels.

It would guarantee the prisoner would be sleep-deprived and his senses would be overwhelmed when it was time to pick up with the interview the next morning.

Within the hour, the electrical system was connected, baseboards completed, walls painted, and room 22A looked like any other room on the hall. Lukas slapped the dry part of the sound-proof walls as he stepped off the ladder. He did not want to be in here when he turned the breaker back on..

CHAPTER 18
BALANCE OF LIFE

Houston

Tonya took the elevator down from Brooke's room. If all went well, Brooke would be released in the next day or two. Her family was with her, and she was weaning off the heavy medications. Once Brooke was released, Tonya would be called back to headquarters. Technically, with this development she could come back any time, but Collin had been intentionally vague about coming back so she could spend more time with Tadi.

Resting her head against the back of the elevator, Tonya closed her eyes and listened to the dings. Thankfully the Houston hospital district kept the hospitals close enough together that it was simply a short walk to see her brother.

Tadi had just finished the last of the tests. She had promised him a smoothie from a shop there. Then he and her mom would be on the plane flying back home.

Back home. Where was her home? Her mailing address was in South Dakota, but that wasn't her home yet. Her personal driver's license read Arizona, while her identification for work changed with her assignment. But if she said home, her first thought was immediately the pueblo house on the rez, running around with her cousins, and Grandma's homecooked dinners.

Stepping off the elevator, Tonya ducked through the crowd and to the fresh air outside. It wasn't hot, but the humidity made the loose strands of her hair stick to the back of her neck. Within a few minutes, she was back inside the air conditioning and waiting for her people at the smoothie shop.

She looked around at the other people in line and saw many of the same expressions she felt: sadness, worry, exhaustion, smiles that didn't quite reach the eyes, and all manners of nervous tics.

"Litty!"

Tonya turned just in time to catch Tadi flying into her arms. She lifted him up, knowing that this six-year-old little wiggler would soon be heavier than she could carry. His hair was cut shorter than she was used to and he was light for someone his height.

"Look at what Benji got me!" He slipped down so she could see his t-shirt. On the front was a picture of a puppy looking up at her under a fireman's helmet.

"Benji?"

Mom rolled her eyes. "He told you to keep it a secret." People said she looked the spitting image of her mother, but Tonya wished she had half the dignity her mother carried herself with.

"But I never keep secrets from Litty. Like how I want a choc-a-laka."

"That was never a secret."

They spent the next hour enjoying each other's company and pretending the circumstances that brought them there didn't exist.

The time passed too quickly, and Tonya felt the tears welling as she looked at the clock. "I'll drive you to the airport."

"No need."

"But I want to."

"Fine, you can drive," a voice behind her said. She turned to see Benji holding his keys out, "but then I'm taking you home." He gently took her a few steps away from her family. "I know this week has been more than emotional, and the streets of Houston are not friendly to those who aren't entirely focused."

"But aren't you supposed to be at work?" He was being so nice, and she desperately wanted to accept his offer so she could spend her time soaking up every last minute with her family instead of worrying about city drivers. But it was still her habit not to accept help.

"I'm a firefighter, remember? Twenty-four hours on, forty-eight hours off." He gave her a wink and motioned toward the parking lot. "I'll pull the car around."

Brooke held onto the handrail in the hospital hallway and wondered why the world was spinning. When she was little, she thought she could literally see the world turning on its axis, but that would be impossible.

She closed her eyes, but it only made it worse. Constellations flew around so fast she wasn't even able to find the big dipper, which would always lead to the north star.

Opening her eyes, she stared at her room. Ten more steps? Yeah, she could do it.

Lilly came around the corner with a slurpy and a grin. "Glad to see you're up."

Why did everyone say that? The answer was obvious. If the bullet had been a few inches over, she wouldn't even be alive. A week before Tatiana was yelling at her to get up and over the wall. Now, even thinking about trying the obstacle course caused Brooke to grimace.

"What's wrong? You look as pale as a ghost."

"Thanks a lot," Brooke ground out as she forced herself to take another step.

Lilly was there then, walking beside her step by step. "You need to take it easy."

"No, I need to get better."

"But you can't do that by brute force."

"Who says I can't?"

"You did."

"Right."

Brooke sat down slowly at the edge of the bed and tried to take a deep breath, but even that hurt. "What the heck! I'm going star crazy. I need to get my strength back. But I can't even walk down that freaking hall. And every time I try to do research, I fall asleep."

"First off-" Lilly sat heavily beside Brooke causing the bed to creak- "it's stir crazy. Secondly, you can't walk down that hall for the *third* time today. You did just fine the other two. Your body is telling you to rest. And that's why you can't focus."

"I said star crazy for a reason. I keep seeing stars."

"Purple stars?"

"Depends. A few minutes ago, they were white and I thought I saw the big dipper."

"See, your research is paying off. A month ago, you wouldn't've known what that was."

Brooke sent her a sideways stare.

"Okay, I may be exaggerating a little. But the point is, you're being way too hard on yourself. Everything takes time. You told me that."

"But that was when I was talking about you finding a boyfriend."

"Finding a boyfriend. Recovering from a bullet wound. What's the difference?"

They shared a laugh, causing Brooke to groan and lean back in the bed.

"But in all seriousness," Lilly continued. "You need to rest."

"Yeah, you may be right." But her eyes lingered on her phone. Had Sam been able to find that astronomer? She was doing well enough that Tonya could go back and they could start figuring out where this star-gem led.

Brooke would fly back there eventually.

If they let her.

The thought blindsided her. Michael had been adamant about the Rising Flock finishing their training before being integrated into the rest of the Flock. Even the thought of walking down the hall to the elevator made her nauseous. How was she supposed to scale a thirty-foot rock wall and rappel down?

Unbidden tears rolled down her cheeks, and she broke.

She was always the weak link in the group. Hunter had been right in saying the Flock only chose her because she was a witness. Nothing about her measured up to her friends. Collin's leadership. Lukas's ability to adapt. Emily's fighting skills. Nichole's charm. Ryan's boldness. Max's intelligence. Sam's persistence. Tonya's compassion. And her what? What did she have to offer?

Tears turned into sobs, her jerking diaphragm causing pain to ripple from her side. But there was nothing she could do about it.

A firm hand pressed against her shoulder. "Breathe with me. In and out. In and out." The words were those of Tonya, but the voice belonged to her sister. "I don't know what worry is rolling around in your head, but it doesn't belong there."

"I know," Brooke whispered between breaths. "But it's real."

"Tell me."

"No."

The bed shifted as Lilly lay down next to Brooke. "Tell me what lies the devil is whispering so we can fight it with God's truth."

Brooke opened her eyes to Lilly's dark curls and caring eyes. "When did my little sister become so wise?"

"By hanging out with you."

Tonya stared out the window of Benji's car, watching the planes take off. They rode in silence as Benji wove back into traffic.

"Where do you want to go?" he finally asked.

"Home," she answered, but gave a quick sigh, "but there are people who need me."

"You told me Brooke has her family."

"But Jasmine needs–"

"No. You have needs too. I'm taking this day to take care of you. Even if it means momentarily kidnapping you."

Her body jerked involuntarily at that word. Benji had no idea what she had been through the previous summer.

"I meant it as a joke."

"Do me a favor." Her voice came out quiet and weak. "Never use that word in front of me again."

"I'm sorry. I would never do anything to harm you." His face was still on the road, but it twisted in hurt and concern. "I trust someday you will tell me why. But I solemnly swear that that word will never reach your ears from my lips."

They drove in silence for a little longer before Tonya felt comfortable changing the topic. "So, where are we going?"

"If my memory serves me right, you loved the zoo."

He was right, but it had been ten years since she had been to one. "How could you remember that?"

Turning slightly, he gave her a smile and a wink.

They spent the rest of the day at the zoo, talking about their jobs and any light hearted subject. The wind played with the loose strands of her hair, and the air was filled with a myriad of noises. Gone were the honking cars and the echoes of sirens. Instead, what met her ears were the screeches of monkeys, the calls of birds, and the amazed gasps of tourists, including herself.

The heat of the day was countered by frozen lemonade, and the loneliness of homesickness was countered by Benji and his jokes, which had not improved much since middle school.

Six hours elapsed before the whispers of responsibility crept back into Tonya's mind.

"This has been fun."

"Has been?" Benji turned from watching the orangutans. "The day isn't over."

"But it will be soon." Tonya put her hands in her pockets and shook her head. "I need to go back."

"Like I told you, everything is covered."

"Yes, everything is covered here. But I need to go back to work."

"Didn't your boss give you some time off?"

"Yes, but-"

"No buts. Take your time and relax so you can go back with your mind fully prepared."

"But you don't know–"

"I don't know that you're needed?" He pulled on the end of one of her braids. "Tonya Miller is not the only counselor. The world will go on without her. No one is going to die because you took a week off."

"You don't know that." Tonya tried to turn away, but Benji stepped in front of her and grabbed her hands.

"You said you were a trauma counselor. After the event, you come in and help them put it in perspective and move on with their lives. You can't do anything to stop bad things from happening."

But what if she could? That was what the Flock was trying to do now, right? But, of course, she couldn't tell him about them. Secret organizations were secret for a reason.

"Yeah. You're right."

He grinned, his smile always one that made her heart skip. "Then I've saved the best for last."

He led her through the crowd, not bothering to let go of her hand, and to the birdhouse. Benji stopped her before entering and pointed. "Look at them. Majestic. They can do something that none of the other animals can. The cheetah is the best runner. The lion has the fiercest roar. The otter, so fun to watch. The python, terrifying. The Panamanian frogs are poisonous even to touch. But these birds can fly."

Tonya chuckled at his theatrics.

"I'm serious. Look at their wings. Look at their feathers. Such color. Such shape. Such majesty."

"Yes. Beautiful."

She reached out to open the door, but he stopped her. "Take this also as a warning. Stay with your own kind. Others that were made to fly. Don't let a cheetah tell you that you're too slow. Don't spend too much time with the fish or you'll drown. And don't spend too much time with the penguins who look like birds but have forgotten how to fly."

Considering his words, Tonya found it ironic that he chose to describe her as a bird and she was part of the Flock. But was she really a bird? She knew in her heart she was where she was supposed to be. And her team were definitely her people. But was the larger organization? Did she really want to work for people who told her NOT to go to the danger? It was for her good, and Brooke had gotten shot because she disobeyed a direct order. But the best way to stop trouble was to be where trouble was.

A calmer life also called to her. A life without bullets and explosions. A life where she didn't go months without calling her family, where her friends didn't get shot, and where her biggest worry was how to balance work and life, which would always be a hard thing.

Benji opened the door, and they walked in. A duck waddled his way past, not caring about the people two feet away from him. A scarlet ibis watched them for a moment before stretching his red wings and taking off.

Tonya closed her eyes and reveled in the sound. Such joy from simply being alive and doing exactly what they were made to do. Hopefully, someday, she would have that joy too.

CHAPTER 19

COLORING OUTSIDE THE LINES

Flock Headquarters

Collin paced outside of Felix St. James's office. His secretary, Sheila, gave Collin a soft smile. Sadness pulled at the corner of her eyes as if she knew how this meeting would end. By the end of the day, Collin assumed everyone in the Flock would know the outcome of this meeting.

He had submitted the official report, and now it was time to face the consequences. This would be it. They would send him back to Ireland. Or would they? Did he know too much? He'd heard of secret organizations terminating their assets permanently. But that wouldn't happen here. They were the good guys. Right?

He clasped his hands together to still his nervous energy. Michael stepped out of the office and walked past him without a spoken word. The message on his face mixed regret with respect.

Stepping into the office, the first thing Collin noticed was the large oak desk Felix sat behind. It was perfectly clean with a single file sitting beside the computer. "Have a seat."

Felix leaned back in the chair with his fingers steepled in front of his face.

Collin sat in the overstuffed chair across from him and waited, his nerves drilling into his stomach.

"You've put yourself in a hard position." The tone in Felix's voice left Collin with no doubt. He was leaving this office without a job. "You disobeyed a direct order and one of your team was hurt as a direct cause of this. One thing I haven't figured out is this." He opened the file filled with handwritten notes and copies of emails. "If you put your team purposefully in danger, like you have in your report, why did six out of eight members of your team personally write me letters about your qualifications and requesting, some even demanding, you stay on as team leader of the Rising Flock and suffer no consequences for your actions?"

Collin leaned forward to read the papers.

"And before you ask. 'Brooke didn't send one because she is in recovery. And Tonya didn't send one because she didn't know.' Exact words from Nichole." Felix shuffled through the papers. "This is the most interesting one:

"'Dear Executive Director of the Flock, Felix St. James. I appeal to you as a man with great responsibility, to give us another chance. I am aware that Collin has taken blame for what happened, but honestly, if we had been any other group, you would have sent us there to do recon, just as he said. I implore you to look at our recent activity as examples of how we work; not our failures.

"'In Chicago, you saw how we adapted to change. Everything went wrong from the moment Lukas and Emily stepped out for that meet. But because of Collin's plan and our ability to work together, we were able to salvage it and bring one guilty party into custody.

"'In Houston, you saw the heart of our team to help others, even at the risk of our own lives. If Emily hadn't been there to interfere, the fatalities of that evening would be considerably higher.

"'Again, I ask on behalf of our safety and our team's unity, to keep Collin in his current position. He knows how we operate as a team and pushes us to be the best that we can be. With all sincerity, Nichole Thomas.'"

Felix put down the letter and stared at Collin. "Nichole certainly knows how to put a spin on a bad situation."

Collin remained silent. He wouldn't defend himself now. The blame had to fall on his shoulders to ensure Brooke had the care she needed. "What is to become of my team?"

Sitting back, Felix shook his head. "That's what confuses me. If you had truly told your team to go, I would expect to see more guilt on your face. Instead, I see protection and sacrifice. And none of your team said outright that you sent them. They use phrases like 'Collin has taken blame,' 'Collin saw we needed to take action,' and 'as a team we addressed the needs of those who were helpless.'"

The chair creaked as Felix leaned forward and looked through the papers to find Collin's statement. "I'm giving you one more chance to tell me the truth."

Collin stood with his jaw clenched. He had never intentionally lied like this. But his first priority was to protect his team, his second was to the Flock. "You have my statement. I have nothing more to say."

Felix rose with him and extended his hand with a folded piece of paper. "Then you give me no choice."

Taking the paper, Collin walked out without replying, not trusting what his tongue might say.

Sam stared at the whiteboard that took up an entire wall of the office. More colors filled his white board than a rainbow, and a pile of dried-up expo markers and energy drinks lay in the trash.

On the left were all the facts of the two attacks. Facts on Chicago written in red, facts on Houston written in blue, and similarities in purple. On the far right were four words written in Lukas's handwriting: guns, people, meds, media. Between them were possible targets with booklets of sticky-notes under each.

Somewhere on the wall was the answer they were looking for. He just needed one more clue.

He turned his attention to the printed photo of Brooke's ring. Max had said the star-map would only lead to a certain latitude. The problem was, anywhere along that latitude would show the same stars.

Max had also told him these star-maps were made in the late 18th century. By that time, the entirety of the globe had been discovered, so this map was not limited to a section of the world. If they were used to designate safe-houses, they would need a longitude as well. But the stars themselves would not tell him that.

There must be a hint somewhere else on the ring.

The picture blew up the ring to fill most of the page. The red gem shone in the light of the camera's flash. Twelve small diamonds circled it. The band was gold with no designs.

Sam looked around at the mostly empty office spaces. The Light division was on orange alert, meaning even if it was after hours, a few people would be still be in the office working to find the next target before it was too late.

In the next cubicle over, typing sounded from Kelli's desk. "Kelli? Do you have a magnifying glass?"

"Who do you think you are? Sherlock?" Her voice came from around the corner. "We don't use magnifying glasses to examine evidence anymore."

Sam got up and stretched. "Know where I could find one?"

Kelli rolled her chair back to get a glimpse of Sam. "You know you live in the 21st century, right? Just take a picture with your phone and enlarge it."

Born in the late 90s, technology had grown to be a part of Sam's everyday existence, but he fancied himself a man from another era who would use technology as a tool but preferred the old-fashioned ways.

"Or-" Kelli continued- "I think Dan might have one on his desk."

"Thanks." Sam ambled over to Dan's desk and borrowed the large magnifying glass. Dan kept threatening retirement but couldn't see himself doing anything else. He also couldn't see that his eyes were well past retirement age.

Sam studied each small diamond surrounding the larger red gem. Two of the them had small blemishes.

He picked up the light blue expo marker and drew a sketch, switching to dark blue for the blemished stones.

It looked almost familiar but he couldn't place it.

The door behind him opened and shut with a light click. Sam didn't have to look to know who had entered. "Hey, Collin! Come over here and look at this!"

Sam exchanged his blue markers for a red one and colored in the ruby (or what he presumed was a ruby) in the ring.

Collin set down his papers with a heavy sigh, causing Sam to turn. He saw a mask of resolve, but what thoughts and emotions he hid behind that mask, Sam could never tell. This would be a perfect time for Tonya to come in and say something magical to make Collin smile and realize being team leader did not mean carrying all the responsibility alone, but she was in Houston looking after Brooke. "How did it go?"

"About as expected."

Sam nodded and turned back toward the board, waiting for Collin to ask the next question. "What are we looking for?"

"Something that will give us the longitudinal coordinates."

"So, we're looking for a set of numbers?"

"That would be my guess."

Collin took a step up to the board, the papers behind him dropping from the desk to the ground. Sam picked them up and set them back, but he couldn't help reading the first line of the letter. "Collin…?"

"Twelve diamonds. We also need a way of knowing positive or negative." He reached down to pick up the photograph. "Maybe it's on the inside. But we can't see it until Brooke or Tonya come back."

"I think she would've taken a picture of the inside if that was the case."

"Yeah, but there's something familiar about this."

"That's what I thought!"

Collin picked up a black marker and connected the two blemished stones. But it was simply a line in a circle.

Sam took the marker from him, erased the line, and connected the rest of the diamonds with a series of different lines. The resulting design looked more like a spider's web. While it looked cool, he couldn't see any connection to a series of numbers or anything that might lead to a location.

Handing the marker back to Collin, Sam took a step back and unfocused his eyes, trying to see a pattern instead of details. Collin had erased his webbing and instead drew a single dot in the middle, connecting the two marked stones to it.

"That's it!" Sam called.

"A V?"

"Not exactly." He grabbed the eraser and shortened the length of one of the lines. "See it now? Latitudinal and Longitudinal coordinates are made up of degrees, minutes, and seconds."

"A clock!"

"Bingo."

"How do we know which is which?"

Sam picked up the photo. "I don't see any marks or indications on this side."

"The ring has to hold another clue."

"Yeah, but we have time when Tonya gets back."

Collin shook his head and picked up the papers from the desk. "I won't be with you any longer."

"Did you even read the letter Felix gave you?"

Sam thought he could see a tremble in Collin's hands as he brought the letter up. His bottom lip quivered, causing him to bite down on it. The façade he had up began to crumble as tears streaked down his face. He looked up to Sam and his brows lowered in confusion. "It says… It says I… I'm… I'm not being suspended. But how can this be? He knew I was lying."

"Maybe Felix values something more than truth," Sam suggested.

Collin looked back at the letter. "It says this is a reprimand for falsifying official documents. But because I chose to protect my team, and each member of my team chose to protect me, we get to stay together."

Sam slapped him on the back. "Great news!"

"But–"

"Why does there always have to be a but?"

"But there is a condition."

"Of course there is."

"We cannot disregard director orders again."

"Obviously he has to say that." Sam shrugged a shoulder and took a sip of the energy drink sitting on his desk.

"What does that mean?"

"Our jobs aren't exactly black and white. We don't live in a black and white world. And the bad guys we face define the word gray. As long as we get the bad guys and save the world, it's going to be a win. Today, Felix showed his true colors. If he didn't throw the book at us as the newest recruits here, as long as we come home with the win, that's all that counts."

"Rules are here for a reason."

"Yeah, to be broken. Or at least bent."

"A line has to be drawn somewhere."

Sam pointed at the wall. "And I drew mine on that white board. Whatever it takes to make sure Chicago and Houston don't happen again."

He looked back at the board, certain that Collin would eventually say those exact words, but hoping that by the time he did, another city wasn't added to that list.

CHAPTER 20

ROOM 22B

Flock Safehouse

Nichole began the interrogation again at dawn the next morning with a computer tablet in one hand and a cup of hot tea in the other.

"No food this morning?" Zane asked. His eyes drooped, one side of his face would twitch, but his grin still sent chills up Nichole's spine.

"You lied to me." She tried to keep her voice calm.

"Now, why would I do that?"

"You don't deny it."

"I did not lie."

"Then why were the buildings empty?"

His eyebrows raised, but his surprise was a mask. He wasn't letting any of his other facial muscles move. "I guess when they found out I was captured they moved the bombs. So, you can see, I'm really no help to you. They already changed their plans."

"Wrong answer." Nichole opened the tablet and logged into the account. "You think if you can make us believe your information is fake, we will stop questioning you. But I know you know the next attacks of the Shifting Shadows. You can save lives."

"Save lives? No, we're doing something much more important than that."

Nichole leaned closer. "And what, pray tell, is that?"

"Do you realize how many people are in the world? At the rate of their expansion, our national resources could very well be depleted within the next two generations."

"And you plan to fix global warming?"

"Don't pretend to be naïve, the only way to save our planet is to thin out the parasites destroying it."

Disgust boiled in the pit of Nichole's stomach. He wasn't talking about termites but precious human life. "And how do you plan to do that?"

The curl of his lip was the only answer.

Nichole's entire angle with this interrogation was to find common ground and build upon that. But the ground she thought she had established of valuing life was slipping away. She had reminded him of his humanity by letting him talk to his daughter, but the disconnect between his daughter's life and the lives he was taking made it impossible to reason with him.

"Tell me about your plans."

"You seem like a girl with a vivid imagination. But even your nightmares won't compare to what Radenie has planned."

She leaned forward, careful to stay out of range unless he decided to strike. Before she could say anything, two raps sounded on the mirror behind her.

Ryan waited for her in the observation room with a legal pad. "He's not going to answer any more of your questions."

"You don't know that," Nichole said, although she suspected he was right.

"We're going to try a different approach." He handed her the legal pad and mumbled under his breath, "I wish Tonya was here."

Nichole looked over the words written on the yellow pages. It was a list of possible ways and places the Shadows could attack.

"Our recordings are all set up and running. We're going to try a micro expression interrogation."

"That's a myth."

"If we fail, we aren't losing any more ground because there is no more ground to lose."

As much as she wanted to, Nichole couldn't argue that. She tossed the pad on the table with a soft thud. "But if we do this now, he will know this is our last-ditch effort. It's time for Lukas's plan B isn't it?"

Ryan's grim look was answer enough. Neither of them was fond of plan B, but at least it was better than Emily's plan C.

Nichole took up the pad and walked back in.

Emily dropped the bundle of tattered clothes at Lukas's feet in the hallway of the basement. "I don't know about this.

"Come on, Emily. You of all people should know why this is the only way this works." He took off his shirt, but the lighting made his usually chiseled muscles hard to see.

"I know. But think of this from Zane's point of view. I was in the car with him when it was hit. Shortly after, he was in police custody, still unconscious. I was on the side that was hit. It only makes sense if the Flock did grab somebody, it was me. Because how could I have gotten out before the police got there?" She had spent the last three days refining her argument. "You know as well as I that the details have to be right. Any small deviation and we lose him."

Lukas put on the shirt and motioned for her to turn around.

"Plus," Emily continued once she faced the wall. "You were in a secure position on top of the building. You had a clean getaway. How would the Flock have caught you?"

The jingle of his belt was the only answer.

"I can handle myself. I proved that in Nepal. I proved it in Chicago. Now won't be an issue."

Two solid hands rested on her shoulders, and Lukas placed a kiss on the back of her head. "I know you could do this. But this is my plan, so I will be taking the risks."

Emily turned back. Lukas's clothes hung loosely off his body with stains of blood and other things. She felt grateful for his protection, but she didn't need protecting. "I don't mind the risks."

"But I do." His face darkened.

"If this is the life we choose, if we go into danger together, you can't be thinking about my safety. Then I become your weakness."

Lukas took a step closer. "Let me ask you a question. Am I your weakness?"

The breath stuck in her throat said he was. The pounding of her heart said he was. And against her will, her lips admitted, "Yes."

"Then we will learn to make our weakness our strength. And the first step is to let me go out there and gain his trust. That is also why it must be me. With men like that, I can gain rapport with him much quicker than you could. It is just the way this game is played."

"Okay." She stepped forward, took off his watch, and snapped the metal handcuffs around his wrists.

Lukas shivered as he walked down the hall to room 22B. As much as room 22A was clean and spartan, made for the mental torture of overwhelming the senses with sound and light, 22B was the epitome of a castle's forgotten dungeon.

The cold seeped in through the soles of Lukas's boots. The metal of his handcuffs bit into his hands. The light was dim enough Lukas could just make out the outlines of two cots and a metal pot. The smell reeked of sewage and mildew. And the floor moved with what looked like insects.

The hinges of the cell door squealed in protest as Emily opened it. "Play nice. Make new friends. Stay out of trouble. And I'll pick you up tonight."

Lukas stepped into the cell and felt around for anything that would make this escape easier, but nothing stood out.

Emily closed the door, locked it, and walked back up the stairs, leaving Lukas alone in the dark to contemplate his next move.

It took another half hour for Nichole to finish up her interrogation and for Reaper to bring Zane down to him.

Lukas sat with his back against the far wall of the cell, and barely lifted his head to see who was coming, as if every muscle in his body ached.

Reaper opened the door and shoved Zane in, causing him to trip over the rough threshold. He then locked the door and walked away to the sound of Zane's shouts of defiance.

Silence followed, and Lukas closed his eyes, waiting for Zane to approach.

"Hey!" A kick to the ankle sent pain shooting up through Lukas's knee. "Who are you? And what are you doing here?"

Lukas slowly opened his eyes. "You don't recognize me?"

The dimness of the room caused Zane to kneel down and scoot closer to see even the outline of Lukas's face. "You're the shooter, aren't you?"

He gave a slow nod.

"Where's your wife?"

Lukas scoffed, letting his voice break as he did. "You know better than I. Last I saw of her, she was with you in that van."

Zane sat down on the edge of one of the cots and shook his head. "I don't remember much about that crash except for waking up in police custody."

"Crash!" Lukas shot to his feet and let his body sway for a minute as if he might fall. "Tell me what happened exactly!"

The details were sketchy. He didn't remember being pulled from the vehicle, but he did remember that Emily was with him and her side was the one hit. "But," Zane wagered to say. "Chances are she's still out there, and the Flock doesn't know about her."

"Why would you say that?"

"They were thorough about finding my loved one and where she is. They knew her name, had her picture, even knew where she went to school."

"Yeah," Lukas gave half a smile. "But they don't even have my name. They could never link Emily to me."

"On your feet!" Reaper's voice boomed.

Lukas shook his head and stared at Reaper in defiance. "I've had enough of your demands."

"Then you're ready to talk?"

"Not on my life."

"How about the life of this Emily?"

"You don't know a thing about her, who she is, or where she is."

"But I do. I know exactly where to start looking for your wife."

Rising to his feet, Lukas crossed the rest of the cell in two strides. "She has a full week's lead on you. I know you do not even have a description. You will never even see her coming."

Reaper unlocked the door, throwing it open. The hinges squealed in protest.

Lukas ran at him low, ducking under the braced arm meant for his neck. His technique was perfect as he went for the tackle. Reaper should have been on the ground, but he barely moved.

Stepping back with one leg, Lukas brought his fist up to Reaper's exposed chin. But something solid hit the back of his head, dropping him to the floor.

He struggled to get to his feet, but Reaper placed his boot between his shoulder blades. The last thing Lukas felt was the blinding pain from the metal baton before the world melted into oblivion.

CHAPTER 21
CLUES

Flock Headquarters

Tonya turned the key to her apartment and opened the door. It smelled vaguely of blueberries from the scented night-light they kept in the hallway. Books and papers lay strewn across half of the couch. Brooke's handiwork.

A breeze swept through the door, lifting one of the papers and tossing it to the ground at Tonya's feet. Picking it up, Tonya saw it was covered with Brooke's handwriting. The word darkness was scrawled across the top and below it were quotes, page numbers, and book titles.

Tonya tossed it back on the couch and pulled her suitcase back to her room. She didn't have a clue what Brooke had been working on, but she needed to find the ring.

She set her suitcase beside her bed and walked past the bathroom to Brooke's room, but something stopped her. Words were written across the top of the bathroom mirror in Brooke's hand: *You are a daughter of the King; a princess worthy of a storybook. The weight of the world was never meant for you. So, look up, take a breath, and smile.*

Smiling, Tonya took a breath and walked into Brooke's room. The ring was hidden right where Brooke had said, in her underwear drawer under a stack of feminine products. Not exactly original, but it worked.

The ten-minute walk up to HQ finally worked out the kinks in her knees from the flight. Her first stop was Collin's office on the third floor.

He was in the middle of a phone call and raised a finger for her to wait but followed it with a wave. When he finished, he motioned for her to come in. His office looked spartan compared to the last time she had visited. "Are you remodeling?"

Collin glanced at a couple of boxes that had all his personal things. "Long story. It's good to have you back." He stepped forward a fraction as if to give her a hug but stepped back to the desk. "To get you-" Collin shook his head and started over. "How's Brooke?"

"She's tough. She'll be okay, but it's going to take time."

"And how are you?"

Tonya shook her head slightly. "I need to stay busy or everything comes crashing down."

"I understand. To get you up to speed: plan B is in motion."

"Okay," Tonya said slowly, fully stepping into his office. "I didn't even know there was a plan A."

"Right." Collin gave Tonya a brief description of the report Nichole had sent him and Lukas's plan for what came next. "We have the videos of Nichole's interview of our prisoner. I would like you to look at them. You have training in how to spot lies."

"So do Nichole and Ryan."

"Ryan told me you were the best."

The heat of a blush crawled up Tonya's neck, and she took the flash-drive he offered. "I'll see what I can do."

A shadow fell across the doorway as Sam and Max entered. "You started the party without us?"

"You and I have very different definitions of party," Tonya remarked, earning a chuckle from Sam.

"You have the ring?"

Tonya held out her hand, letting the office lights make the ring sparkle.

"Great. I finally got in contact with Professor Sinclair from the University of Colorado, who was highly recommended by several sources. He said we could skype tomorrow or come in sometime next week."

"I don't think skyping is a good idea," Max interjected. "One thing is security. Since skype is added to the OS of Microsoft, it has the potential to be hacked. Do you really want to trust something when the company has to send out patches to fix the patches? And honestly, since we're dealing with the Shifting Shadows, I'd assume they have hacking ability to exploit this weakness. Second thing is lighting. The only way we can see these stars is when we turn off all the lights. If we turn off the lights, there is no guarantee he will see anything. And there is the possibility that the tablet or phone or whatever we use for the skype will wash out the lights. Thirdly-" Max paused, his eyebrows scrunched, as if he had the point and lost it. "Oh, thirdly, we have a hemisphere of stars. How is the professor supposed to know by one look where it leads? I mean, maybe he could, but I really don't want to depend on luck to solve this."

"Okay," Sam turned to walk out. "I'll email the professor to arrange a meeting."

"No, don't do that!" Max caught his shoulder and spun him back around. "It's clear text. That means it is the easiest to intercept. Literally, in less than ten minutes I could read any of your texts or emails that aren't encrypted."

"And if they are encrypted?" Collin asked.

"Depends." Max shrugged a shoulder. "That's one thing I haven't tried yet."

"Right." Sam rolled his eyes.

"What? It's illegal. You know, reading someone else's mail. It's a federal offense."

"Okay, boys," Tonya interrupted. "Let's get this done. Sam, call the professor. Set up a time, the earlier the better."

Collin cleared his throat. Tonya took a step back. Right, he was team lead. She was supposed to defer to his authority. That's what got her in all this mess to begin with.

"Just be aware-" Collin's voice still had the easiness it held earlier. He wasn't upset at her, just wanted her to remember his position- "we may not be able to make any appointments next week. If the Shifting Shadows follow their current pattern, which we have no reason to suspect they won't, we'll have another crisis by the end of the week."

"But we'll get there first," Tonya spoke softly. It wasn't a promise, simply a hope. But hope was something precious and powerful during uncertain times. "Any clues on that front besides the interview?"

Sam shook his head. "I tried to find any commonalities, any trends-"

"But with only two points," Max picked up mid-sentence, "it's too early to see a true pattern versus just coincidences."

"Too early!" Tonya's outburst surprised her, but she had seen too much to let this happen again.

"It's simple stats. We don't have enough to make predictions."

Tonya rubbed the flash-drive in her hand. "Maybe I do."

CHAPTER 22
ESCAPE

Flock Safehouse

Lukas came to propped in a chair. Someone was rubbing his arms. Voices were speaking but everything sounded to be in a different language. No, his internal translator just hadn't kicked in.

The spoken language is strange. You take phonemes common to a certain language, mix them in different orders, and they come out words with meaning.

"Was that really necessary?" A girl's voice. One he trusted. One he loved.

"Ask him. He's the one who attacked first." Deeper voice. Familiar but not personal. Like he'd heard it once or twice. But it registered as a friendly.

Pain from the back of his head resounded through his skull. He reached up and was surprised to find the back of his head still intact. Remember to disarm someone before picking a fight next time.

"Did he buy it?" The sound of his own voice bounced around his brain, amplifying the pain.

He opened his eyes to Emily squatting in front of him, holding his hands. Pain and anger burned in her eyes. "I would say if your goal was to eliminate any suspicion of a double cross, yeah, I'd say you're on his side. But the only way to know for sure is when you go back in."

"Okay." Lukas brought his hand back and let out a breath, glad that his head wasn't bleeding. He stood up and tested his balance. It was still good. "For him to think it's real, I need you to hit me."

The first punch caught Lukas off guard, making him stumble back a step. The second caught his eye sending tears flooding down his cheek.

Emily stood opposite him with her hands raised prepared to strike. "Are you ready?"

Lukas struggled not to groan. "A little too late for that question."

"You told me to make it real."

"Ja." He put a hand against the cool wall. "He'd know a fake if he saw it. He's the type who has experience with the rough side of life."

She reached up to touch his cheek, causing Lukas to wince. "That'll give you a nice shiner."

"I taught you too well."

"Who said *you* taught me to punch?"

He took her hand in his and traced her knuckles with his thumb. "When I met you, these were the hands of an artist."

She drew back with a sad smile. "But when you insist on going into situations like this, it's my job to get you out in one piece."

"I'm afraid that's my job. And that's why I have to do this." Lukas let go of her hands and turned back to Reaper. "Is it time?"

Reaper looked up at the clock mounted on the wall and nodded. "Whenever you're ready."

"Let's go."

Zane lay sprawled on one of the cots, so sound asleep not even the squeal of the door woke him. He must've been awake close to thirty-six hours at this point. The time of torture was over. Now was the time of trust.

Lukas tried to catch a few winks as well. Emily's plan was to break them out about one in the morning. There was no knowing when they would have the opportunity to sleep again. And even when they did, it wouldn't be restful if Nepal was any indicator.

Something crawled across his feet. Images of spiders and roaches and centipedes filled his mind. He threw off the threadbare blanket and sat up. Something scampered away, as did any ability to sleep.

He must've dozed off because he woke to Zane's voice. "Hey, are you awake?"

"Ja," Lukas answered without opening his eyes.

"We need to plan our escape."

"Why now? I've been in here for a week. You think I didn't try?"

"No, I think it's a two-man job."

Lukas finally opened his eyes. "How do you figure that?"

"It occurred to me when you fought with the guard. If you call what you did a fight."

"Hey!"

"No offense. But I've heard stories of you. And I know you could have bested him."

"With these on?" Lukas raised his hands to show the cuffs. "Besides, I've been in here over a week. I'm not exactly in top physical condition."

Zane scooted closer on the edge of his cot. "Is that black eye new?"

Touching his eye, Lukas nodded. "They think they can break me, but I've been through worse."

"Yeah, I read your file."

That took him by surprise. "My file? Who exactly are you that you had access?"

"I was wary of working with an outsider for the Chicago job. Radenie gave me your file to show you could handle yourself. I think he trusts you."

Lukas let out a scoff. "Hunter never trusted me."

"It's nothing personal. I don't think he's ever trusted any of us either."

Lukas got up and stretched. "Was this your first job with them?"

"Are *you* interrogating me now?"

"The cops got there too fast. Someone must have tipped them off."

"How do I know it wasn't you? You were never in the line of fire. They never saw your face." Zane stood up to match Lukas. "You had clear shots at the officers. Why did I have to take them out?"

Lukas took a step closer, almost standing on Zane's toes. "You never saw the reinforcements. The two more cars following behind. I figured you could take care of one police cruiser while I pinned down the other two. I was able to send Emily down there to extract you, but I couldn't make it out in time. Turns out, the backup wasn't police, it was the Flock. And that is how I ended up here."

They stood toe to toe for a full minute until Zane took a step back. "Whatever. How about this escape?"

"There is no way to tell time in here, therefore no way to time when the guard comes in."

"Does he always come in to get us?"

"Most of the time, no. But when I provoked him, he did. How are you in a fight?"

"Bare handed?" Zane shrugged. "Not so good."

"Then you'll provoke him."

"What? I just told you I couldn't take him down."

"Right. Which means, while he's focused on you, I can take him out."

"Okay. So now the guard is out, we have his keys and get out. What next?"

Lukas shook his head. "They were careful when they brought me up. Up the stairs, to the interrogation room or the torture room."

"Right," Zane held his head. "Not going back there."

"But I spotted exit signs at either end of the hallway. Not too hard to follow them out. Did you see what it was like outside?"

"No, they had me blindfolded."

"Then we will find a car and get out. But with our botched mission and the Flock on our tail, I'm leaving the country."

"Do you really want to be hunted by the Shadows too?" Zane lowered his voice.

"We were up against too many."

"It's one thing to fail. It's another to get caught. You've been in here for a week. Do you really think Radenie would believe you didn't crack? No, our best solution is to meet the Shadows for their next move and earn their trust again."

Lukas looked up at the hidden camera and gave a subtle wink. Zane would tell them exactly what they needed to know. "But how do we even know where they will be?"

"Leave that to me. The guns I was supposed to procure were to go to Houston and another city. We'll start that way when we get out."

The fact that Zane didn't tell Lukas the name of the city told him that Zane was telling the truth. Hopefully.

Emily glanced at her watch. It was two minutes past one. Time to move.

Pulling the mask up over her mouth and the night vision goggles (NVGs) down over her eyes, she walked down the hall. Two of the Flock security guards stood on either side of the door leading to the basement.

They were ready for her and put up enough of a fight to make it look good. Then she was through the door.

Her footsteps down the stairs echoed, waking up the boys.

"Who's there?" Zane called.

Instead of answering, Emily opened the door and unlocked their bindings. Once free, Lukas headed for the stairway, but Emily touched his arm and shook her head, running farther down the hall.

"Where are we going?" Zane whispered, but Emily ignored him and kept moving.

The hall dead-ended at a brick wall. She knelt and reached into her bag again.

"What a great jail break." Sarcasm and contempt oozed from Zane's voice.

Shouts of guards and the sounds of footsteps came from behind.

"And now we lost our only chance."

Emily pulled out a cord of thermite, shaped a small door, lifted her NVGs from her eyes, and motioned for the boys to back up with her.

Even with her eyes closed, bright light penetrated her senses accompanied with a loud hissing sound.

She counted to ten before running back to the wall. With the three of them, it took seconds to clear the bricks and work their way into the tunnel.

Emily led the way again, bringing back down her NVGs. She knew the guys were running blind, but so were the guards who followed them.

The tunnel was straight with no curves and no obstacles. It came out into the open air under the moonlight. She tossed Lukas the keys and pointed at what looked like a heavily armored SUV. She was a decent driver but had only been driving for the last year. If they were getting into a chase, Lukas was the one she would trust.

The vehicle roared to life, and Lukas hit the gas. The safehouse disappeared in the night.

"Where to?" Lukas asked once it was obvious no one was following them.

"West."

CHAPTER 23
RUNNING INTEL

Flock Headquarters

Collin stood in Felix St. James's office for the morning update. Lukas and Emily were driving somewhere to the southwest. Ryan and Nichole were on their way back from the safehouse. And the rest of his team were working to find the next target. According to the possible time-table, considering both of the previous attacks were on Fridays, they had approximately twenty-four hours to find the next location, get a team there, and stop the threat.

Felix rubbed his temples and tried to cover an exhausted yawn. "Cynthia, do we have any tips from the authorities?"

"Nothing they are willing to tell me."

"Stephon, how are we on finding any leads through the forensics?"

The burly man shook his head. "Just what we expected. Nothing more than yesterday. Reid said he would run down the only lead we have."

Felix turned his attention to Reid. "And how is that going?"

Reid shook his head. "Bulk ammo ordered online to a fake address, and the payment was run through several shell companies which we're still running."

"Okay," Felix closed the spiral he was using to take notes. "That's a wrap, unless anyone has anything else to add."

The door to the office flew open, revealing Tonya's flushed face. "It's a bomb." She breathed hard, as if she had run all the way. "And it's worse than we thought."

A few hours earlier, Tonya had risen with the sun, which was not unusual for her. She fixed a cup of tea and opened the door to go out for her morning walk, but something kept pulling at her. A life or death pull that if she didn't act now, people's lives were in danger.

Foregoing her walk, she grabbed her tablet and the flash-drive Collin had given her the day before, and called Max.

She had reviewed the hours of interrogation the day before, but something hadn't settled. If Max could write a program to slow the video so she could watch for micro expression, maybe, just maybe, she could get it.

Max met her at the door to HQ with a thick bundle of paper. "These are the results from the polygraph."

"Wait. He was on a polygraph? I didn't see that in the recordings. And why are we just now getting the results?"

"Because they wanted to get all the results before bringing it back to headquarters. Courier came in after midnight last night."

Tonya thought back. "Okay, but again, I didn't see any wires."

"There weren't any, at least not on him, and that's the beauty of it."

"You better start talking. And use simple words that don't go over my head." Tonya hit the button on the elevator and sipped her tea while it came down.

"They ran a charge through the table. Low frequency so he wouldn't feel anything, but enough to pick up his heart beat."

"Pick up his heart beat?"

"Yes." Max shook his head. "Pay attention. The wires coming from the table went under the floating floor and to the next room where a machine would draw out the vibrations it felt."

"No digital way to overlap them?"

"Nah, they went old-school. But it does have the time stamp at the bottom, so it shouldn't be too hard to overlay."

"Right." The elevator dinged and they both stepped on. Max unrolled part of the transcription, but all Tonya could make out were scribbles. "Do you know how to decipher this?"

"Yeah. That's what I was doing up last night."

"Did you get any sleep?"

"What is sleep?" Max laughed and shrugged. "Whatever it takes to get the bad guys, right?"

"Right." They stepped out of the elevator and Max clapped his hands. The lights were motion sensitive, but he thought it made him look cooler if he clapped and they came on. Whatever, the mad scientist could think anything he wanted as long as he could read that paper.

Two hours later, Tonya found what had been bothering her. It was assumed he had lied about the bombs and placements of them. While he was writing the targets, his face was away from the camera, thus negating her ability to read him. She checked with Max and his polygraph and confirmed a reading outside of baseline. That was all expected. What was unexpected was the fact he showed no signs of manipulation or deceit when he told them it would be a bomb.

"Max, it's a bomb."

Max stepped closer, looking over Tonya's shoulder as she ran the tape again. "That doesn't follow the pattern of the other two."

"You told me yourself that we don't have enough to make a pattern."

Max growled and grabbed a black expo, starting a new column on Sam's whiteboard.

"In this context. Why would they choose a bomb instead of guns like the last two?"

"Distance." Sam walked in from the stairway and took the marker from Max. "Higher number of casualties. More than likely an indoor target opposed to an outdoor one like the last two. The last two had specific targets with a large number of civilians. To me, a bomb isn't designed to take out just one person."

"Or," Max countered. "It could be a place highly guarded. It might be easier to disguise a bomb than a gun."

"True, and a bomb cuts out half the planning. Yes, you have to get in, but you're already out before anything goes amiss. Exit strategy is how we caught the second group."

"Guys," Tonya tried to interrupt.

"Maybe they're learning from their mistakes. Adapting. That's what we'd do."

"So, you're proposing our interference in Houston caused them to change their tactics?"

Max paused but shook his head. "But that would be wrong because we captured him before Houston happened."

"And this was part of the original plan."

"Guys."

"We have to know more about the bomb to know its intended target."

Sam nodded. "Yeah, but we can probably assume it's political since the Chicago attack was after a senator and the Houston attack was originally aimed at a mayor."

"Guys!"

"Because if they're going after structural failure, our targets are going to be very different than if they're going after soft targets."

Sam shrugged. "Soft targets. Hard targets. It hardly makes a difference if we don't know where to start."

"Guys!!" Tonya slammed her fist against the desk and motioned to the computer. "I may have a clue, but I need to concentrate."

Sam and Max both shut up and watched her work.

Skipping to the end, Tonya watched as they listed potential targets. She wrote them down along with the time on the bottom of the screen, tagging the time so she could compare to the polygraph results. Then she slowed it down, focusing on his eyes. The subject showed interest in several of them, but she wasn't looking for interest.

There it was!

"Max! Check 10:23:40."

She prayed she was wrong as she listened to Max roll out the paper and say the two words she feared. "You're right."

Collin watched Tonya as she stood propping the door open, the tablet clutched tight against her as if she didn't want anyone to see what she saw. "They're going to bomb a hospital." Her words, usually soft and comforting, carried a harsh bite that made him cringe.

"How reliable is your intel?" Reid asked.

She held up the tablet and set it down hard against the table. "Straight from our prisoner."

Expletives filled the room and the team leaders left in record time. Collin took the stairs down to the Light division, which fluttered with activity, and made his way to Sam's desk. Max sat behind the computer, and Sam stood at the whiteboard writing out facts and theories.

"What do you have for me, boys?"

Max answered without turning. "We've taken into account the trajectory of Lukas and Emily and have looked into prominent city hospitals. The last two attacks have happened in major cities. Although we don't have enough of a pattern to extrapolate information, we are assuming it will be the same, especially if they're going for a body count."

"Assuming?"

Max nodded hesitantly. "Our current hypothesis has a lot of assumptions."

"Did we recheck the original list he gave Nichole?"

"But he was lying."

"He gave us five names at once. He could've been lying about four and the fifth one wasn't in place yet."

"None of those locations were hospitals," Sam cut in.

"Are any of them near hospitals?"

Sam and Max exchanged a glance.

"Look again."

"But they were all to the east," Sam added. "You told us to look west, where Lukas and Emily are going."

Collin pinched his nose. He didn't want to miss anything because of assumptions, the only things they really had, but they also didn't have time to waste on a wild goose chase. "It will take you, what, five minutes, to find those five locations and see if they're near a hospital. Indulge me."

Collin waited as Max typed on the computer and Sam scrolled through his phone. "Indianapolis," Max pointed at the computer screen. "The location the prisoner gave us is a shopping mall two blocks from their largest hospital."

"But going there," Sam picked up, "would be based on a lot of assumptions as well. The prisoner didn't give the hospital as the location. It's to the east of the safehouse, whereas Lukas and Emily are heading west. And the last two attacks happened in an open area with guns."

"What are you saying, Sam?" Collin knew they needed to act fast, but they also had to be right.

"I'm just playing devil's advocate here. I don't know if I believe Tonya's magic, but who am I to say she's wrong. If it's a hospital, there are hundreds and thousands of them, even just following the direct path to wherever Lukas and Emily are going. There's also the possibility they aren't going to the next attack. With one day left, they may be going back to base. Or they could be found out."

"Very encouraging, but what I wanted was an answer."

"I can't give you a definite answer unless we're there."

"Okay. What about you, Max?"

Max turned in his seat to study Collin for a second. "We aren't the only group in the Flock. We can check this out while other teams check out other leads. Or we could follow Lukas and Emily and give them support."

Collin considered them for a moment before nodding. "I'm heading up to talk with Michael. Pack your bags."

Tonya sat in the protection of the outdoors clutching her head. She should be inside helping them find the next clue, going over footage again, or something. But all she could do was sit there and cry. She was emotionally compromised but had no idea how to fix it.

Three months before, the Flock had called her out to help with trauma counseling. It was the first time, and she had been excited to get out in the field. But when she got there, the remains of an oil refinery were all that was left. She saw the bodies burned beyond recognition. And the cries of the survivors haunted her dreams for weeks.

Bombings were devastating enough, but targeting a hospital was beyond cruel. The patients in there were already suffering. And the doctors and nurses needed to help the survivors would be in need of help themselves. They would have to move every patient and member of the medical staff (doctors, CNAs, laundry, maintenance, etc.) to a different hospital, thus creating a logistical nightmare of finding beds for all of them, plus the medical staff to take care of them.

Though that was bad, it wasn't what her mind concentrated on. She had spent the better part of the week in hospitals visiting Brooke and Tadi. It was the image of them burned beyond recognition, screaming in agony, that stuck in her mind.

She had to talk to someone to help get hold of her emotions. She opened her contact list on her phone but froze. Usually she would talk to Brooke, but she was in the hospital, or just got home, with her own problems. When it had to do with the job, she would talk with Collin, but he was obviously in the middle of trying to save the world. And if he found her emotionally compromised, he might bench her. Normally, she would bench herself until she got her head in the game, but they needed all the help they could get.

Continuing to scroll, Tonya saw her mom's name, but continued on. Mom didn't need to know the dangers she faced every day at her job. Or at least every week. No, she had enough to worry about with Tadi and the move.

Under that was Benji's number. As a fireman, he understood the horror she would face. And as someone not part of her team, he wouldn't be overwhelmed by what they were facing.

Before she lost her nerve, she hit call and waited through the rings.

"Hello, this is Benji."

"Hey, do you have a minute?"

"Yeah, what's going on?"

Tonya took a deep breath and told as much of the truth as she could. "Well, I'm just having a really hard day, and it's just going to get worse by the end of the week."

"Okay." His tone was calm, and he actively listened, which gave Tonya some comfort.

"It's a bomb."

She could hear him take in a sharp breath. "Those are bad."

"Yeah, and that would be an understatement."

"Right. If I can ask, what is your role in this? How close are you going to be? Working with the victims or the witnesses or the families?"

"I don't know yet. We got the call today, and I'm on my way." As soon as they told her where she was going. "I usually do psych evaluations with the survivors or just work on keeping everyone as calm as possible."

"Yeah." The line was silent for a moment as both were lost in thought.

"What- What do you do when you get a call like this?"

"Suit up, get in the truck, and drive. If I'm not driving, I go through everything I know about the situation and come up with plans of action."

"Yeah." This time Tonya let out a sigh. "Dealing with people, there's never one way to approach things."

"But that doesn't sound like your problem. I was there when the shooting happened, and I watched you take care of a room full of frightened and hurt people. You knew what to say and instilled in them the hope they needed at that time. I don't think you're worried about how to interact with people. I think your problem is in your head."

He got that right. She took a moment before answering. "All I see are the bodies of Tadi and Brooke." Tears started sliding down her cheeks, and she tried not to give in to the sobs again. "I feel grief. But I know in my head they're safe."

Benji didn't reply, and Tonya let the line hang silent for a minute as she tried to still her heaving chest. Finally, Benji answered. "I'm going to say something that won't sound comforting now, but hear me out. We're all going to die. It's a part of being human. And we'll all face grief. It simply means we have loved deeply. But don't let that trip you now. Save those you can. And at the end of the day, come back to your friends and remember what it means to be alive and enjoy life."

Max finished packing their equipment in the plane as Collin did his pre-flight check and Sam fished around in his bag for his ringing phone. Just as Sam answered it, the sound of bagpipes filled the cockpit, stopped short by Collin's answer.

"Hey, it's Collin."

"Sam here."

Collin scrambled to find a pen and wrote on the back of the check-list. "Los Angeles."

"Nah, nah," Sam was saying. "We have a meeting set up for next week."

"Two days. Is there a possibility you could be heading to a different location?"

"Yeah," Sam said, "that's how Michael filed it."

"We have a possible lead in Indianapolis."

"Remember to keep to your cover."

Collin put down his pen. "Are you sure you don't need backup?"

"Oh, I see. A secretary and a field agent don't exactly have the same goals in therapy. Tell them you compete in obstacle challenges or run marathons or something."

"If you need anything, let us know."

Sam chuckled. "No, you're right. But I'm sure you'll be fine. Just focus on getting better. We'll see you soon. Bye."

"Okay. Good luck. We'll be on our way as soon as we can."

"How's the wonder team?" Max asked Collin, assuming the call was from Lukas and Emily.

"They're fine. Heading to California, but we're still going east on the off chance they are heading to a second location, or I guess in this case it would be a fourth location." Collin turned his attention to Sam. "And how is our Sparrow?"

"She's fine. Wants to come back and be in the middle of everything again."

"Of course."

Tonya came up the steps with a bag over her shoulders and dark sunglasses on. Max took her bag and motioned to one of the seats. "Ready to fly?"

She just nodded and took her seat, unusually quiet for her.

Colin looked back. "We're wheels up for Indianapolis in ten. Last call for anything we may have forgotten."

Max looked back at the luggage and shook his head. "Everything's good back here."

Sam shrugged and smiled. "I'm missing my mind, but it's been gone so long I don't know where to look for it." He turned to Max. "Do you know where I might find an extra?"

"Nope." Max moved up and strapped in next to Collin. "But if you see one on our flight, I'll be more than happy to toss you out so you can get it."

"Ha-ha. And I'll keep a look out for a sense of humor for you."

Max rolled his eyes and looked back at Tonya for support, but she simply stared out the window. The situation clearly had her rattled. "We'll find it, Tonya. Everyone will be okay."

She shook her head, not moving to look at him. It was obvious the weight of the world hung on her shoulders. It hung on all of theirs, but they all wore it differently.

CHAPTER 24
TICK, TICK

Indianapolis

Ryan pulled up to the address Director Lombard gave them, which turned out to be a hopping place for lunch.

"How are we supposed to know our contact?" Nichole asked, slipping off her seatbelt.

"She said he'd know us." Ryan tossed his Yankee's cap in the backseat and ran his fingers through his hair.

Nichole chuckled.

"What?"

"No, you just look like you are picking up a girl for the first date instead of meeting with a contact to get help with our… problem."

"What? First impressions are important. Regardless of whether I'm trying to romance a girl or gain the respect of some hotshot detective."

"Yeah." Nichole finished a new coat of lipstick.

"You're one to talk."

"I'm a girl. It's expected."

"Fine then, Cinderella. Let's go see if we can save the world through the red tape of bureaucracy."

"You talk like that's a bad thing."

"Yeah, we shouldn't need permission to take down bad guys."

"It's for the common good." Nichole flipped the visor up and looked at him. "We all have to agree they are the bad guys, or we could face some real trouble with the people."

"But the bad guys don't need permission to blow up a building."

Nichole threw up her hands and opened the door. "Come on."

The restaurant was mostly packed with only a few tables empty. Knowing they were meeting someone from law enforcement, Ryan looked toward the back. Their contact would probably prefer a seat where he could see everyone, especially the front door, and no one could sneak up on him from behind.

There he was. Ryan motioned to a short stubby man. "That is our man."

"How do you know?"

They had met the previous year when Ryan's friend was shot by the Shifting Shadows in Ryan's penthouse in New York. "We've met before."

Their contact rose as Ryan and Nichole wove their way through the crowd. "A little far from home, Agent Smith?" Ryan extended his hand.

Smith shook it. "You do seem to get around, Mr. Murphy." He then turned his attention to Nichole. "And you must be Miss Thomas. Please do sit down."

Ryan swept his eyes around the room one more time before taking his seat beside Nichole. "Why are we meeting here? Or do you just like clandestine meetings?"

"The station is a little swamped right now, and I'm on my lunch break. Besides, I thought people of your organization preferred their anonymity."

Nichole nodded. "Thank you, and that is how we usually work things. But in this case, we need help, as much of it as we can get."

"Tell me what's going on."

"There will be a bomb at a hospital by the end of the week."

"I need details. Time? Location?"

Ryan relayed Collin's information to him and the assumption that it would happen on Friday like the previous attacks.

Smith leaned forward, lowering his voice. "How reliable is your information?"

"Honestly," Ryan said. "We're just checking every lead. But I'd rather be wrong and check every possibility than to overlook a lead and pay for it with people's lives."

"I understand. But we need reliable intel to take action."

"At least allow our team to come in and do a sweep."

Smith stopped and considered them. "Does your team have much experience doing this?"

"You know the catastrophe in San Francisco last March that didn't happen. That was us."

Nichole elbowed Ryan lightly in the ribs. "Not helping."

"No," Smith said, "I meant, does your team have experience locating and disarming bombs?"

"Locating, yes. Disarming, not so much. That's why we came to you for help."

Smith took another bite out of his burger before answering. "Do you know anything about this bomb?"

Ryan shook his head. "Only that we know for sure it will be at a hospital and people will die. Their previous attacks were directed at a single person of influence but also the largest number of injuries and fatalities possible."

"Single target with additional targets of opportunity."

"Precisely. So, if we could get a list of all hospital employees and patients."

Smith set down his burger. "I can't just do that."

"I know, HIPAA. But I don't need to know why they're there, only if they could be a target."

"I'll look into that, and we'll do a sweep of this hospital and amp up security for all the city hospitals. But because this is a hospital you're talking about, we can't just evacuate it for the search. It has to be done with care to not cause a panic. It will take a delicate touch."

"Then go in plainclothes."

Smith leaned back for a second and smiled. "Right. Actor. That's why they chose you. To make people believe the story."

"It works most of the time."

"And what about the other times. Do you just put others in danger because you're a civilian trying to be a hero? You run on instinct and luck. And because you decide to take on problems the police should handle, someday it will cost you your life and the lives of others."

"We rely on training," Ryan said, "same as you. We just have the flexibility to see the different angles. With my background in acting, I'm exceptional at handling the crowds and making them see what we want them to see. Or go where we need them to. We would never put anyone's lives at risk just because."

Smith looked at Nichole. "And you. Journalist? News-anchor? Politician? By your stance and your words, I can tell you are used to being heard and respected for what you say."

"Journalist."

"Yeah, and how are you two going to find this bomb?"

"We aren't," she replied. "Our team is. Our job is to coordinate with other organizations and divisions, like you, and then take care of the people. We make sure civilians are out of harm's way, so if anything goes wrong with our colleagues, they aren't hurt. And if anyone does see anything, we give them a believable story. We mitigate panic, which is extremely crucial with this situation. Like you said earlier, we can't just evacuate a hospital; there are too many people there that need help."

"So, you create coverups?"

"A coverup implies something bad happened that we are trying to conceal." Nichole paused for a moment. "I guess that is exactly what we are doing. But I don't see anything wrong with that. You do the same. You don't tell people everything you do to protect them."

"Fair enough."

"Then let us help you."

Smith tapped his fingers against the table, considering. "Fine. You can help. But stay out of our way."

"No problem." Ryan stood to leave. "Thank you for taking us seriously."

"I always take the safety of American citizens seriously."

"I know. That's why we chose you."

When visiting hospitals during her clinicals, Tonya always wore her pink scrubs with leopard print to make the children smile. Even if she was breaking dress code, no one ever seemed to mind because she could bring the one thing those kids needed: laughter. But today she pulled on maroon scrubs with extra pockets. Her job today was not to make people smile but to get the bomb and get out without anyone noticing her.

She stepped out of the hotel bathroom to see all three boys in matching maroon scrubs staring at the blueprints.

"If we're going for structural damage-" Max was saying- "then I'd set them here."

"That's if there's only one," Sam countered.

"If there's more than one, I'd still set one here but then have my secondary devices here and here."

"That's assuming he's going for structural damage," Tonya said, joining the group.

"That's how I would get the most casualties."

Collin shook his head. "I'm not sure they're going for most casualties. If that was the case, there was a more efficient way to take out a baseball stadium, and in Houston, I would have waited until everyone was in a central location. They've picked their targets for a specific reason. The stadium for the senator, the walk for the mayor--even though that changed, and the hospital for..."

"Medicine," Sam finished. "Lukas said four things were needed to start a war: people, weapons, medicine, and propaganda."

"If that's the case," Tonya said. "There's easier ways to steal medicine."

"But not to make it untraceable," Max continued. "In addition to injuries, panic, and fatalities, if you blow up the rest of the supplies no one knows what you took, and it has a collateral cost of everyone in the hospital. Then we have supply shortage for not only this hospital but also the other area hospitals and it may domino to other communities, bump the prices, who knows. And that's not even considering the fact they would now have hospital grade medicine. Anything from ibuprofen to morphine. They could sell it, they could mix it, or they could use it, like Lukas thought, to profit on both sides of a war."

"If they're going after the medicine." Collin tapped the blueprints. "This is where they'll strike."

"Okay." Sam picked up a black bag with a red cross on it. "Then let's get going."

The team split up. Collin and Tonya would start with the pharmaceutical storage while Sam and Max went for the structural weakness. If a bomb wasn't found at either place, they would do a full sweep, Collin and Tonya starting at the top, while Sam and Max went up from the bottom.

"What do you think it will look like?" Sam asked, carrying the bag with the chemical detection device.

"Be quiet," Max hissed. "We don't want anyone to overhear."

"Yeah, but I would like to know what I'm looking for."

"You'll know when you see it. But that's my job. You just keep an eye on that package of yours."

"Fine, but if I step on a pressure plate and we all go boom, I'm blaming you."

"Shhh. One, with all this foot travel, they wouldn't leave a pressure trigger that would accidently set it off. Two, if we all die, you won't be around to blame me."

Sam pointed at Max and grinned. "You do have a point there."

"Don't I always? But let's get a move on."

"Yeah, yeah." Sam followed behind Max into the hospital.

A tall slender man wearing jeans and a blue t-shirt with the hospital's logo greeted them. "You are the gentlemen the department sent over to assess our security?"

Sam nodded and patted his bag.

"I'm Shane, head of security and maintenance. Where would you like us to start?"

"With your structural foundation-" Max began- "as well as electrical and gas lines and-"

"Anything that has to do with the building," Sam summed up.

"Right," Shane turned. "Then follow me."

With a swipe of his key card, he led them down into the inner workings of the hospital. The first five minutes of the search was a bust, with Sam scanning anything that might look remotely like it could explode.

"I don't see anything out of the ordinary here," Shane said, turning to leave.

"Yeah, just give me one more pass. Don't want to overlook anything." Sam ran his fingers along the wall but pulled back with tacky white paint. "Did you recently paint the walls down here?"

"Down here? It's been before my time, so over three years ago."

Sam motioned to Max and put down his bag, examining the rest of the wall. "Only this part has the fresh paint." He then fished a crowbar from his bag.

"Wait! What are you doing? You can't do that!"

"Shane," Max looked around for anyone who might overhear. "We're trying to find a bomb here. If I was to guess why here, they've tied it into the electrical system so it has the needed power when it receives signal." He looked up and nodded. "This is close enough to a main support column that it will cause serious damage. Would you rather that happen, or for us to take down part of a wall?"

Sam paused, waiting until Shane nodded his head to start beating at the wall.

It didn't take long with Max's help to pull away the wood panel to reveal... well, just more wires. "I was expecting something screaming bomb!"

"Shut up and hand me that pen light." Max slid to the ground with his back to the wall, trying to look up the hole.

"Do we need to call in backup?" Sam asked as he handed Max the light.

"Don't touch your phone. We don't know how this device will receive the connection."

"Fine." Sam raised his watch to his lips and hit the transmitter. "This is Osprey. It looks like we found a device. Requesting backup."

"A little busy with our own situation," Tonya's voice came over the air.

"What did I say about not calling in?" Max ground out as he worked the device out.

"To not use my phone. And hey, we're not dead, so we're fine."

As those words came out of his mouth, the ticking started. The hairs on his neck and arms stood on end. His legs froze in place, and his lungs forgot to breathe.

"Um..." Tonya's voice came through clenched and hesitant. "Ours just started beeping."

"Us too."

"Get away!" Max yelled at Sam. "You could be the one creating this whole mess."

"I don't think so." It was Collin's voice that answered that time. "Ours has a timer saying two minutes."

"I don't see a timer on ours," Sam said.

"Sam!" Max snapped. "Screwdriver!"

Sam pulled a Philip's and a flathead screwdriver out of the bag.

Max held the pen light between his teeth, and took the Philip's screwdriver from Sam.

"You're doing great!" Sam cheered on. "I mean worst case scenario we all die. But that will happen in less than two minutes anyway if you don't do anything."

"Ah oh oo uh uh!" Max grunted around the light in his mouth. Which Sam interpreted as *Why don't you shut up?!*

Max tossed Sam the screwdriver and opened the case. Sam took the light from Max's mouth and held it at a better angle to see the wires. Three red numbers blinked up at them, counting down from a minute and a half.

"Now that we can see the wires, can't we just cut them?"

Max shook his head. "Failsafe. In theory, this is getting its power from the electrical supply, but it could have a capacitor so that if I cut that wire it would blow. Then according to the text book, we trace the wire from the explosive."

"If we separate the wire connecting the explosive to the detonator, it can't get the signal."

"Right, but there might be another wire hiding under it."

"So, we trace all the wires?"

"Yeah."

"With only a minute and fifteen seconds left?"

"Yeah."

Sam pulled the wire cutters out of the bag and waited as Max meticulously traced each line back. They didn't have time to do this, but they also didn't have time to fail.

The timer counted down to sixty seconds, then fifty, then forty.

"That one! Cut that one!"

The cutters snipped, but the timer kept counting.

Thirty.

"Is that supposed to keep going?!"

"I didn't touch the timer."

Twenty.

"Here, take it."

"But I don't want to hold a bomb!"

Ten.

"You can't go boom without power. And this can't go boom without the explosive."

Five.

"It's been great knowing you."

"Sam, I'll still know you in five seconds."

Three.

Two.

One.

Zero.

CHAPTER 25
POWER

A spark flew from one of the loose wires then nothing. They had succeeded. They had saved the day. They had-

The lights flickered and came back in an eerie blue.

"What just happened?" Sam asked, still holding the plastique in his hands.

"The power went out." Shane looked around the room. "We're on emergency generators."

"Why don't you and Max go and see if you can get the main power connected. Which way to the emergency generator?"

"Are you expecting another bomb?" Max asked.

"Yes. No. I don't know. But that's the next thing I'd destroy. And if the generator goes down this whole hospital will be in a world of hurt."

Shane pointed and called one of his men over the walkie talkie to meet Sam there. Max threw the parts of the bomb into the bag and slung it over his shoulder before chasing after Shane.

Okay, now to find the generator. Easy enough.

Sam ran to the end of the hall and up the stairs, coming out to a hall full of people in scrubs, plainclothes, and police uniforms. How did they get here that fast?

A man in a blue t-shirt matching Shane's touched Sam's arm. "Are you Sam Rogers?"

"Yeah. Where's the generator?"

Sam and his guide raced to the four large humming generators.

"No one's messed with the lock." The man said as he unlocked it and let Sam in.

"Yeah, I hoped but…" The sound of approaching sirens distracted Sam. "The reinforcements are here."

The man's radio beeped. "Be advised, we now have police on site."

"Now?" Sam turned and ran back the way he came, yelling over his shoulder. "Stay here in case they try something!"

Collin stood holding the defused bomb in the storage room with. Unlike Max's bomb, this one was shelved in a brown cardboard box. He had disarmed it with one minute left on the timer.

"I told you we'd save the day, Tonya." Collin wrapped the bomb and put it in their bag. "Let's get out of here before-"

A loud crash sounded followed by the flickering light of the power going off.

"Third bomb?" Tonya asked.

"I'm not sure it was a bomb." Collin left the room to look out the floor to ceiling windows. Below them a truck lay crushed under a power line. Sparks danced from the loose ends as electricity poured forth like the blood of an injured animal. Another truck pulled around, letting out six men in police uniforms.

"How much you wanna bet they're here for the meds?"

"I don't know." Tonya backed away from the window, out of their line of sight. "We learned in Houston they're good at adapting their attack. They could be going for body count."

Collin took one last glance out the window before retreating back to her. "I doubt it. What was the deal about hitting the power?"

"Panic? Get the real police here so they can blend in?"

Collin spoke into his watch. "Hawk, how's backup comin'?"

"Two steps ahead of you," Ryan's voice came over the coms. "They were en route five minutes ago."

"ETA?"

"Pulling up. Do you have a lead on the bad guys?"

"Negative. All I know is they're inside the building."

"Heading up... the back... staircase." Sam's voice came through between labored breaths.

"I'll let them know," Ryan said before signing off.

Collin took off running toward the exit sign leading to the staircase while Tonya ran in the opposite direction.

The door slammed against the wall as Collin launched through it. Two more steps brought him straight into the midsection of one of the men. His head bounced against the step with a loud thunk.

In the seconds it took him to regain his position, two men slipped past, ignoring the fight all together.

Collin grabbed for the waist of the third man, who turned and brought his knee into Collin's face. His tuck wasn't quick enough to miss the blow, but it glanced off his cheek instead of breaking his nose.

The man stepped up for the next step, but Collin pulled his knee causing him to crash into the stairs behind him. In three punches the man was out.

Collin spun to the men below him. He grabbed the man's helmet and forced his face to the stair. A quick shove to the shoulders sent the man rolling down.

The next man was quicker, guarding his head as he ran up. He ducked under a punch and caught Collin below the ribs, lifting him and tossing him over his shoulder down the stairs.

Pain pounded his body again and again before he finally came to a stop.

"Heads up!" a voice called from below him, followed by Sam's form jumping over him and continuing up the stairs after the rest of the men.

Collin groaned and rolled over. His latest attacker had fled, but the three he had downed still lay on the stairs above him.

It was up to Sam now. Collin's part was done.

When Collin had run to the stairwell, Tonya took off for the elevator. Stairs were not her thing, but if she had to take them, she much preferred to run down. Besides, with Collin and Sam chasing from below, working from top down seemed to be the most helpful.

At least that's what she thought four floors before. The beating of her heart in her chest matched the beating of her feet on the stairs.

She looked down, trying to catch a glimpse of them. They were two more stories down. She slowed her descent, not sure whether to hope their desired floor was between them or past her so she could stop them. She didn't like to fight, and she wasn't exactly good at it yet, but either way she had to stop them.

Pulling her keys out of her pocket, she slid her pepper spray to open and waited at the crook in the stairs.

When she judged they were half-way up, she charged down spraying the orange steam into the eyes of the two attackers.

She hesitated for a second, everything in her telling her cops are the good guys, but she had already committed. Her knee caught one of them under his chin, making him stumble backward. One hand caught the railing while the other rubbed at his eyes.

Tonya turned her attention to the other and threw her body sideways against him. He stumbled but caught himself, throwing a glancing blow against her ribs. She threw an elbow against his temple, and he toppled.

Someone slammed into her from behind. She braced herself against the unconscious man and spun, but the man fled with Sam on his heels.

She turned to her first opponent and saw him race after Sam. More running.

Sam's legs burned. His lungs ached. His feet slammed against the floor.

He burst through a door into a hallway. CNAs came in and out of doorways. Medical carts sat every few feet along the wall. Florescent lights shone against the polished floors.

That was when the chase ended.

The man Sam was chasing turned on his heel and brought his fist straight into Sam's nose.

Blood and tears fell down his face as he tried to see past the pain and focus on the next hit. It came as a punch to the jaw coupled with a kick to the ribs making him stumble back a few steps.

A kick to the back of the knee from a second opponent sent him sprawling.

A howl of pain came from the man behind Sam.

Tonya came into Sam's line of sight with a pair of bloody scissors, the distraction gave Sam just enough time to get up again.

The fight lasted longer than Sam's body appreciated, but it ended with the man in handcuffs. "They were even kind enough to bring their own," Tonya called, kneeling over the other attacker.

Sam stood and wiped at his face. His nose was still bleeding. "Here," a CNA handed him a washcloth. "Lean forward, pinch it and press it to your face. Hold it like that for five minutes. I'm June, by the way."

"Nice to meet you, June." Sam didn't give his name. The less everyone knew the better.

"Why did you beat up the police?"

"Those aren't real cops." The door to the stairs slammed open, flooding the hall with more men in police uniforms. "But they are."

Within seconds, Sam and Tonya were surrounded and staring down a dozen different muzzles. "Hands behind your head! Get down on your knees!"

Sam dropped the bloody rag and got to his knees. "Before you charge us with assaulting police officers, check their badges. They're not real."

The lead officer nodded to another who retrieved one of the badges. "Officer Nelson, they're right. These are forgeries. Good enough to fool the local guard, but they're not ours."

"Who are you?" Officer Nelson turned his attention back to Sam.

"We're a part of Ryan Murphy's team. He's the one who gave you the tip."

"Never heard of him."

Sam brought his hands together and hit the transmission button on his watch. "Hawk, we need a little help with the locals!"

A few seconds later, Nelson's phone rang. "Hello… Yes, but… No… Yes, sir." He hung up the phone. "Let them go."

Sam retrieved the washcloth from the floor, considered it, shrugged, stood up, and pressed it against his nose.

"What were they after?"

"Not quite sure," Tonya answered. "But you'll find the bombs we deactivated on the third floor and…"

"Wherever Max is," Sam finished. "Which should be the power source."

Officer Nelson nodded, sending two of his men toward the elevators.

"Osprey," Ryan's voice came over Sam's watch. "Check room 814. We don't have any info on that patient here."

Sam and Tonya followed behind Officer Nelson to the nurses' station. "Excuse me, ma'am. What information can you give me on your patient in 814?"

While Officer Nelson talked with the nurse, Sam tapped Tonya on the shoulder and the two of them slipped back to go directly to the source.

Tonya knocked on the door of room 814. "Hello?"

The lights were off, the shutters drawn, and the news played quietly on the television. "Hello?" she asked again as they walked in.

The patient lay propped in the bed, his cheeks were drawn, and his hair was missing in chunks. He lifted his hand slowly to mute the tv, and Sam stepped back into the hallway. He hated hospitals. They reminded him of his mother. No, that wasn't right. They reminded him of the cancer. This man had the same side effects she had. He would die. Did he have a family? Did he have anyone who cared?

But why were the Shifting Shadows after him? He clearly wasn't a threat in his current condition. It must be for what he knew then. And that could be anything.

After handing off the bomb to the police, Max made his way up to Tonya. She said she needed his technical help.

Sam stood outside the room talking with a police officer.

"Radiation poisoning. He was here for a conference when he started showing symptoms. Upon arrival, he was accompanied with someone from the government who designated his name as 'classified-do not publicize'."

"So, we're talking government-funded nuclear experimentation?"

"That, I don't know, and you shouldn't speculate."

Max squeezed his way through them and into the room. Tonya stood at the side of the bed. The patient readjusted himself.

"Rick Peabody, this is Max Davis," Tonya introduced. "He's more likely to understand what you're talking about."

"Do you know anything about nuclear reactors, son?"

Max pulled up a chair and sat down. "Enough to talk about one but not to make one."

"Good enough." Rick coughed into his hand, wiping away the blood with a towel. "My team of scientists are working on alternative power sources, namely the power of fusion reactions. They generate three to four times the energy of a fission reaction, however, the environment needed for these reactions to take place is an extremely high temperature. Now when I say high temperature what I mean is normally unattainable heat. One hundred million Kelvin to be precise. Which is approximately six times hotter than the sun's core.

"In addition to the needed temperature, the energy required to overcome the electrostatic repulsion is also very high. Right now, the only energy we've found high enough to create the right condition for this is a fission reaction itself. But theoretically, once it begins it can produce energy as long as it remains stable."

"So, you deal with radioactive isotopes on a regular basis," Max cut in.

"Yes, son, now listen. The dangerous thing about power is that it can be weaponized."

"Like the breeder reactors used in France."

Rick glared at Max until he shut up. "Any power form can be weaponized given the proper modification, and working with nuclear power, that modification is minimal. Even a miniscule manipulation of the safety barriers we use or the sequencing required for the process could lead to either nothing happening or everything blowing up."

"Is that what happened to you?" This question was from Tonya who looked at him with curiosity and compassion.

"No, but I am getting to that point. Two months ago, my team made a breakthrough. We achieved what we thought was our first sustainable power source."

"Why haven't we heard about it? Surely, it would have reached the news."

"Boy, you are getting on my last nerve, and I really don't have any nerves to spare. I will only continue if you cease your interruptions."

Max moved his fingers across his lips, zipping them shut.

"We named our project Hebat after the Syrian sun god, since we were essentially making our own sun. The week after we completed it, we were approached by a group of men claiming to be from the government demanding our research. I suspected they were up to no good, and I did NOT want my research to be used as a weapon. Because no matter how competent our government is or how secure their sites, it will get out and people will die because of it.

"I knew they would go to our superiors and maybe the ones above them until they found someone they could bully or bribe into getting it. So, I safely sabotaged our project. I talked with my teammates, and they agreed it was the best thing to do. We had to convince them the project was a failure, because only then they would leave.

"But that wasn't what happened. The night I came in to rearrange the control rods there was a containment breach, and I was exposed." He waved his arm indicating his current condition. "It was a low enough level that I was unaware I had been exposed until I was showing symptoms, and by then it was too late."

"So, the Shifting Shadows want you to make them a bomb," Max summed up.

"The Shifting Shadows?"

"The group that tried to take your project from you was here today to kidnap you. We stopped them just a few minutes ago."

"No, they weren't here to kidnap me."

"What do you mean?"

"They already have my colleagues. They were here to kill me because I'm the only one who knows how to stop them."

"How long do the doctors say you have?"

"That's the thing. Yes, it's bad and could be fatal, but the doctors have treatments that may help. I'm moving to the Mayo clinic tomorrow where these treatments will begin. This was the last day I would be here."

Max turned to Tonya with confusion. They had thought the Shadows would attack on Friday, but this was Wednesday. Their timetable wasn't as stable as they thought. And if their goal had been to take out Rick, why place two explosives?

"Who besides you knew you would be leaving tomorrow?" Tonya asked.

"The staff here and the staff there. I'm not really sure."

"That leaves a lot of people to check if we're going to find our mole." Tonya shook her head.

"If it was even a mole," Max said. "It could have been an intercepted email or some other communication."

"Then how are we going to keep him safe?"

"That's what the police are for, right?"

"Yeah, I guess." Tonya turned back to Rick. "How long would it take for your team to reproduce the process?"

"If they had all the supplies needed, like we did at our lab, I'd say a week or two. If they had to start from scratch, I'd say at least two months. But knowing my team, they'll be doing everything they can to delay."

"When were they taken?"

"Two weeks ago, when I was exposed."

"Okay, assuming they were at your lab, how long do you think they can delay?"

"Maybe an additional two weeks. But they've already had time to finish, so their time is up. You have to find them. And you," Rick turned to Max. "I have much to teach you about defusing this reactor."

CHAPTER 26
HEARTS OF MEN

Los Angeles

Zane gave direction as Lukas drove through downtown Los Angeles. They had been driving for over twenty-four hours, and even though he and Emily had taken turns driving, Lukas was having to stifle more and more yawns.

He pulled into a parking garage and drove up to the roof. There he pulled up next to a large white van. Everything inside him screamed this was a bad idea.

When he pulled to a stop and turned off the ignition, four men jumped out of the van and surrounded the car. He figured he could get out of there with some fancy driving, but this was a meet, so he got out and lifted his hands.

One of the men searched him, relieved him of his Glock, and shoved him toward the van.

A yell brought Lukas's attention behind him just in time to see Emily throw a punch straight against the man's jaw. "And if you ever try that again, I swear I'll kick you so hard you won't be able to see straight for a week!"

"Who's that?" one of the strangers asked Lukas.

"That is Emily Keller, the Huntress, member of the Shifting Shadows, and my wife."

"But there are no female members of the Shifting Shadows." He tried to grab her arm, but she alluded him.

"You must be new."

The man didn't bother to reply.

"Where he goes, I go." Emily hooked her arm through Lukas's.

"Where we are taking him is no place for a lady."

"I should hope not. I didn't break him and this guy out of a prison for nothing. I want in. Thought that would be the simplest way. Now, you either take us to the man in charge, or you'll see what I'm really made of."

The man she punched rubbed his cheek and shook his head.

"Fine. Everyone in the van. You'll find blindfolds on your seats. Put them on, and we'll take you to Radenie."

Emily tried to draw a map in her head as they drove, but it was a skill she had yet to perfect. She knew how many lefts and rights they took, but the stop and go traffic made it difficult to discern how long or how far they had traveled.

The slide of the side door opening told Emily they had finally arrived at their location. This was it.

She grabbed the edge of the door and cautiously stepped out. Someone yanked the blindfold off, and she blinked against the blinding light of the mid-afternoon sun. The fact they were brought in during daylight meant the Shadows weren't warry of prying eyes.

But that was unlikely considering the high-end neighborhood. The surrounding houses had small signs in their yards saying which security company looked after their valuables. That and the precise cut of the grass. The height of this particular lawn was slightly higher than its neighbors, which meant if they weren't careful, they would soon stand out.

The house itself was two-story, not including the loft or basement. Curtains covered every window. The windows themselves were floor to ceiling on the ground floor while the first floor (what the

Americans call the second), had windows that looked simple enough to open. The ground under the windows looked soft enough, no rose bushes to worry about sticking her on the landing. Not bad for a secondary escape route.

One of the Shadows unlocked the front door and let them in. The interior was polished marble with a double door leading into the living room. Plush carpet covered the floor, but that wasn't what caught Emily's attention.

A man with curly brown hair stood with his back to them, talking to someone. The set of his shoulder, the stance of his feet, and the familiar resonance of his voice all delivered one message: DANGER, GET OUT NOW!

"Radenie," Lukas began, "I assume that is your title now."

The man turned, revealing the enemy they had faced the summer before: Hunter Drake. "The Kellers," he replied, "just as I expected."

Zane stepped forward, pushing his way through them to get to Hunter.

"And Zane." Hunter nodded to him, but his glare made Zane stop.

"I swear, I didn't talk. The police know nothing of you and our organization."

"You withstood nine days of interrogation by the police, but it took the Flock less than forty-eight hours to crack you."

"What are you talking about?! I didn't tell them any of our plans."

"Then how did they know about Indianapolis? We had to move up our plans by two hours because they showed up."

"There's no way-"

"They even managed to locate and disarm both of the bombs we set. And they took out our team. Tell me, how did they know all of that if you didn't tell them?"

"It must've been them." Zane jerked a thumb over his shoulder at Emily and Lukas.

"Oh." Hunter glanced in their direction for a second then back at Zane. "As much as I wish it was, they didn't know anything about our next plans. I simply called them in as your backup."

"Which they failed."

Hunter looked up at them for an explanation.

"Everything about the meeting went wrong," Lukas said, "which would not have happened if you gave me the real details of the meet. I had four contingencies created for the location you gave us, but you went and changed the meet before we could scout."

"I couldn't trust you."

"Yeah, and your hesitation to trust us cost you the lives of two of your men and the capture of this one." Lukas gestured to Zane. "If you would have given us proper time with the real position, that day would have gone quite differently."

Hunter bit his lip, considering him for a long moment before giving a quick nod. "We'll see. Come in and have a seat. Everyone should be here shortly."

Half an hour later, eight of them gathered in the living room to discuss the plan.

"What are we stealing this time, boss?" a large man with a goatee asked.

"The hearts of men."

One of the other men laughed, but Hunter was serious.

"And how exactly do we steal the hearts of men?"

"Create a crisis that brings people together against a common enemy, who in this case is the United States military."

"You're turning the people against their own country?"

Hunter rolled his eyes and spread his hands. "You say that as if it isn't done every day. Even in this very spot fifty years ago this was accomplished. Thirty thousand people gathered in a peaceful march until the police intervened, killed four and arrested one hundred and fifty people. Do you think that reaction did anything to endear them to the people? We're trying a similar approach.

"First step, create the problem. Pedro, you are now Matias Gonzales, a refugee from Argentina who escaped after the US military burned your town to the ground looking for an escaped political prisoner. You were one of three survivors. You are here to protest the presence of the U.S. in Argentina." Emily looked over to

Pedro who stood a full foot taller than her with a goatee and a sleeve tattoo along one arm.

"Step two, make our problem everyone's problem. Emily, you look young enough to blend in on a college campus. I want you to go with Pedro, organize a protest, pass out flyers, and get people to come."

Emily looked at Lukas and gave a small smile. They were in. She turned back to Hunter. "I'm game, but it's currently summer break, and I'm not much for public speaking."

"Oh, don't worry. Summer classes are in session, several of the major frats are still on-site hosting parties, and the summer camps hosted are a major in for us. As for public speaking, you can leave that up to Pedro. You just make sure people are there. Meanwhile, Lukas and I will be working on step three, capturing a known military officer and getting him to admit or imply that they do have people in Argentina."

"Does the U.S. really have a presence there?" Zane asked.

"Whether they do or don't, it doesn't matter. The only thing that matters is what the people believe. And we can make them believe anything."

"How is rumor going to help us?"

"Patience." Hunter closed his eyes and took a breath before continuing. "After a couple of days of the protest meetings, I will arrange for the media to cover, if they haven't already. They do have a nose for trouble. Then, when we have the promise of media presence we will strike and the devastation will be aired live."

"We attack our own protest?"

"Yes, Zane, do try to keep up. It adds validity, it adds anger, and it adds a following."

"The only reason someone would attack a gathering of civilians," Emily continued for him, "is because they are a threat or to make a point."

Hunter nodded. "In this case, we add validity to our cause. The world will be in arms against America and all eyes will be on Argentina."

"Instead of…?" Emily asked, hoping Hunter would tell her the real crux of the plan.

He studied her for a moment before relenting. "Instead of Chile."

Stepping onto the UCLA campus the next day, Emily thought back to her first day at the University of BLITS. She had been so determined to prove herself and make a name for herself. Now, walking onto this strange campus, her purpose was to blend in and influence the people around her without them knowing.

It took the better part of the morning to hang the flyers, get the information on the electronic billboards in each building, and talk with a couple of professors to offer extra credit for students who came.

Slipping into the restroom, she pulled out a red dress that rode well above the knees and slipped it on. She pulled on yoga pants under it and tugged the dress up to her waist, tucking it in the waistband, and then threw on a baseball cap of a local sports team. She didn't even know who they were or what sport they played, it was only to help her blend in. The flats she chose were practical, and she threw her messenger bag back over her shoulder.

Her first target was a group studying in the library. She'd need an accomplice for this one though, for her next target she could use a phone conversation, but it was discouraged in a library.

She chose a table close enough to the largest group to be overheard but not too close to disrupt the social distancing of studiers. She set up her laptop and texted Pedro to meet her.

Five minutes later, he sat across from her with his back to the group of students. "I'm not sure I can do this," he started. "There's a reason I fled Argentina. I can't do this, or they'll find me."

"Like they're really looking. They think you're dead. This is the best way to get the backing you need and let the world know what happened."

The typing from the other table had slowed. Chances were, they were listening in.

"But a college campus? These kids don't care. They're entitled, selfish, and won't do anything even if they do come." The students turned in their seats to catch a look at the one insulting them. He was good. "I'll wager you're the only one that shows at six tonight."

"I wouldn't be so quick to bet against this generation."

Pedro got up and left. Emily looked over at the students and gave a small smile of apology.

"What was all that about?" one of them asked.

"He's speaking tonight about equal rights around the world. I've convinced him people do care about more than just their home. But we've been struggling to get supporters who will listen. Maybe he's right. No one cares about Argentina."

"Hey, we'll be there."

"Really?"

"Yeah, and if it's something worth supporting, you'll have that too."

"Thanks." She pulled a flyer from her bag and set it on the table. "See you tonight."

Ducking out, she pulled her dress down into place and tugged the yoga pants off and into her bag along with her hat. She straightened the dress and applied an extra layer of red lip gloss and deep blush before walking over to the SUB where she had spotted the fraternities hanging out earlier. She pulled out her phone, opened the door, and walked toward the coffee stand where most of the students congregated.

"No, you're not standing me up again! I know I'm changing plans, but you always do."

One of the boys let out a low whistle. She had their attention.

"Yes, it's just that I need the extra credit and it doesn't sound like a boring pitch like the rest of them."

She got in line, held her phone against her ear, and grabbed her wallet out of her bag.

"I was hoping you'd go with me to, you know, not make it so boring. But I'm sure I can find someone to go with me."

Covering the mic of her phone, she ordered a triple mocha Frappuccino with extra whipped cream.

"You have no right to talk to me like that. We're done." She disconnected and threw her phone in her bag, stalking to where the others were waiting for their orders.

"Excuse me," a good-looking boy with jet black hair approached her. "I couldn't help but overhear what was going on. Whoever was on the other end is a fool."

"Well, now I'm not, and I have a free evening except for this talk for an hour."

"Extra credit?"

"You overheard that?"

"I'm observant." He flashed her a smile, showing off his dashing white teeth.

"I caught that much."

"How about I go with you to that talk and buy you dinner after?"

"Only if you bring some friends."

"And why would I want to share you?" His smile went from charming to lustful, and Emily forced herself not to step back.

"I have friends, and we can turn the evening into quite the party."

"Yeah, I can arrange that. You bring the girls. I bring the kegs."

Emily smiled, hoping it didn't look half as fake as it felt. Thankfully the barista called the name she gave, and she walked away with her frappe.

Lukas drove the van following Hunter's directions, having only a vague idea of where he was going. When the exit Hunter pointed out read Los Angeles Air Force Base, Lukas finally put all the pieces together.

"We cannot just go onto a military base and take one of their leaders."

"Of course not." Hunter rolled his eyes. "I have a plan."

"This one I need to hear all the way through before I'm getting any closer."

"Relax. Today we're just doing recon."

"Recon looking for what exactly? Who is our target? Does he ever leave the base? Because we are going to need security to even get close." This time Lukas was not going in blind.

"Trust me. I have everything covered."

"The last time you said that, I was captured by the Flock and Emily was in a car accident. Forgive me if I do not trust you or your plans right now."

"They why'd you come back?"

Lukas shrugged as he took a right at the light. "I knew you would need me. And the Shadows pay well."

"That we do. So, just trust that I have everything in hand."

They came to a stop at an unmarked building with no windows.

"You know where we are?" Hunter asked.

"I can assume."

Hunter handed him a stack of ones and a stack of fifties. "Go in and get all the information you can on a Colonel Brice Fulton. And take as much time as you want. We have all day."

Disgusted at what Hunter implied, Lukas tossed the singles back at him. "Come on with me, then."

"I have a certain reputation to uphold."

"I doubt that. If anything, one of the girls in there would recognize you."

Hunter didn't say anything, but his lips drew in a tight line.

"That's it. Fine, I'll get the information." Lukas opened the door and got out.

Hunter hit the side of Lukas's head with the stack of ones. "Remember to keep cover. Just because you're a married man doesn't mean everyone needs to know that."

CHAPTER 27
INTO THE FIRE

El Paso

Max leaned against the side of the jeep at the airport in El Paso and waited as Collin finished his post-flight check and Sam and Tonya loaded the equipment. How many thousands of miles had their team flown in just the last two weeks? And that wasn't even counting the two thousand miles Lukas and Emily drove to get to Los Angeles. It was interesting to think just how small the world was becoming when a little over a hundred years before it would have taken all day to get to the next town just thirty miles away.

He himself had flown the short jaunt over from the mayo clinic in Arizona, where Rick had given him a crash course on the nuclear power plant they would be facing, to El Paso, the closest city with an airport to the secret base where Rick and his team were stationed.

Emily had called in and asked for Ryan and Nichole to serve as backup in Los Angeles. They said the Shifting Shadows were trying to steal the hearts of men, and those two would be the best defense.

As Collin came down out of the cockpit, Max waved him forward. "We're fueled up and ready to go! I have the coordinates Rick sent!"

Collin tossed his gear on top of the hard cases containing everything needed for reconnaissance to a full-blown invasion. Although if that was the case, Michael had a team on standby to join them, and they were explicitly ordered NOT to go in alone. But it never hurt to be overly prepared, unlike Houston.

The road to the badlands of New Mexico started in the mountains but quickly leveled out to desert.

"How much longer?" Sam asked from the back.

"We'll get there when we get there." Max looked in the rearview mirror to see Sam's smirk at his comment. "Rick gave me the coordinates, but I think pretty soon we'll be going off road."

"I'll bet there's not even a sign saying, 'Exit here for super-secret nuclear testing site.'"

"It's not an actual testing site. It's experimental for power only. We're not going to find alarms blaring with an automated voice telling everyone to get to the minimum safe distance."

Three hours later, Max would wish he never said those words.

Rolling up to the front gate, the sound of sirens reached Sam's ears.

"What's going on?" Max asked the guard, handing over their credentials.

"I'm sorry. No one is permitted entry right now."

"Are they testing something?"

"I really can't answer that." The guard handed back their IDs.

Max backed out and turned the jeep around. "Sam, can you-?"

"Already on it." The blueprints of the site were already up on his computer, and he scanned the perimeter. "It looks like the easiest access point would be cutting through the fence two miles west of here."

"And did you pack the suits?"

"Nah, I forgot to pack the radiation suits when going to a potentially radioactive situation."

"Sam."

"I left them on the plane."

"Sam!"

"Of course, I brought them!"

He reached behind Tonya and pulled a duffle from the back seat, tossing each one a suit.

"So, now what's the plan?" Tonya asked.

Collin started to say something, but Sam spoke first. "We improvise. Cut our way in. Use the map to find the central power. Then play it by ear."

"And if everything explodes?" Collin asked, folding his suit up in his lap.

"That's what I meant playing it by ear. Surely there will be a countdown, or if we see people still working it means it won't actually explode."

"This isn't the movies," Max interjected, "and it's not like a bomb. If there is something wrong with the power, it has safeguards that will shut it down before something big goes boom."

"Then why are the alarms going off?"

"I don't know. But if everything is going south, there won't be any warning. It will just go boom!"

"Stop here."

Max pulled to a stop on the side of the road, and everyone pulled their suits over their clothes.

Sam was the first dressed and ran to the fence with the wire cutters, leaving the rest of the team to grab the equipment. "The good thing about the alarms going off, is that no one will notice the additional alarms we're causing."

"You're sure breaking in is such a good idea?" Collin asked.

"It's Rick's team." Max slipped through the hole Sam made. "If any of us were being held in there, would you think twice?"

Collin shook his head and followed Max through.

Sam wasn't sure what he expected, but a hike through the desert in a full-body suit was not what he had in mind.

With sweat pouring down his back, Sam finally caught sight of the facility. Twin columns of smoke coiled from one end of the largest building. Good news, people were still on site trying to put out the fire.

"If that thing goes boom-" Collin pointed to the building- "we don't have time to run back the way we came."

"Meh," Sam shrugged. "Looks like we have our choice of vehicles to borrow for our escape."

"Then let's get in and out before everyone evacuates."

Running toward fire felt like such a bad idea, but Tonya was not known for her good ideas. Especially after Houston. At least this one wasn't hers.

She followed behind Max, trying to keep the orange suit in sight as the smoke grew thicker.

The respirators in their suits made the air breathable, but only for so long. They didn't have oxygen tanks. And their suits were made for radioactive chemicals, not smoke inhalation and the heat of fire.

Max turned around another corner, causing Tonya to jog to keep up. She wasn't sure where their point of no return was, and it was usually Max who kept a sharp eye on the logistics, like getting back out alive. Her job usually was to take care of their emotional states rather than their physical ones.

"This should be it!" Max's muted voice yelled through his suit. He reached for the handle but pulled back in pain. "It's too hot!"

Sam moved Tonya out of the way and readied himself. With his left foot firmly planted, he kicked near the lock and drove his weight and momentum into it. The wood around the door cracked and splintered away, and the door swung open.

The smoke swirled a deep black, making the interior of the room impossible to see. Collin stepped up between them with the thermal binoculars up to his mask. "I see two heat signatures. There and there. Go!"

Tonya followed Collin while Max and Sam went for the second person. Tonya lifted the person's knees and led Collin backwards out the door and through the halls, following the glowing red exit signs.

Using her back to open the door, Tonya breathed in the cooler air mix and scanned the area for a good escape vehicle. The blaring of the facility's alarms mixed with the wail of a fire truck.

"Pickup at your three o'clock!" Tonya jerked her chin in the direction of the old work truck.

After setting both of the rescued men in the pickup's bed with them, Tonya stayed in the bed with Max to assess their injuries while Collin and Sam got in the cab and drove off, trying to reach safe distance.

The first man's body lay completely still. A hole in his forehead said this was an execution. The second man's breaths were shallow and unsteady. His clothes were burned and his body was covered with red welts. His lips moved, trying to form words.

Max unfastened his breather and threw back the hood.

The man's body shuddered as he struggled to take another breath.

Collin brought the pickup to a stop by an ambulance at the gate, but it was too late. Their rescue mission had been for naught.

From the moment Max saw the smoke, he knew their chances of finding and rescuing all three members of the team alive would be a miracle. And that was a miracle God didn't give this day.

Sitting in the back of the truck watching the EMTs performing CPR, Max's mind replayed everything Rick told him. His team consisted of Big John, although his name was Simeon. They called him Big John after the western song about a coal miner who was big and quiet and ended up saving his fellow miners before the mine collapsed. He was like that, always taking the risks to keep his teammates safe.

By the looks of it, the man with the gunshot wound was Big John.

The second member of the team was H.D. A city slicker who took the job as a chance to help provide sustainable energy. He was the designer of this model of reactor and dreamed that this could one day power a city the size of New York.

He was the man who managed to whisper two dying words in Max's ear. "Find Susan."

Susan Ammons, the third member of the team, was previously working with the Navy as an engineer on the designs of nuclear submarines. She was the one responsible for all the safeties to ensure the power plant wouldn't just explode. She was the one who had saved this entire site from being melted when the fires hit. And the Shifting Shadows had taken her to design the core again at their base.

But where was their base?

"Max!" Collin called, stepping out and slamming the door shut. "Come on!"

Max shook his head, trying to clear his mind of those thoughts, but they kept coming back. This could have been his team. Shot. Burned. Taken.

"Max!"

A black van pulled up beside them. Michael got out and pointed at Collin with a glare that could penetrate. Max jumped out of the back, joining the rest of the team on the far side of the truck.

"Tell me you got them out." Max heard Michael's voice before he saw him.

"We did," Sam replied, "but we were too late."

Michael nodded, looking back at the ambulance. "It happens. Did they say anything?"

Max opened his mouth, but it felt too dry to talk. He swallowed and tried again. "He told me to find Susan, the last member of their team."

"Do we have any leads?"

Everyone shook their heads. Max looked back at the flames rising from the building.

"Then let's find leads. Split up and talk to witnesses. You know what to ask, what to look for."

An hour passed, the fire still burned, and they were no closer to finding any answers. The only lead they had was a farm truck with Texas plates, which this close to the Texas border could mean anyone.

With the firefighters still trying to contain the blaze, there wasn't anything more they could do there, so Michael ordered them back to headquarters to try and put the pieces together.

CHAPTER 28
THE STAR-GEM

University of Colorado

After a frustrating weekend of dead-ends, Tonya left the detective work to Collin and the Light division, and left with Sam and Max to meet with Professor Sinclair about Brooke's star-gem.

The mountains set the perfect backdrop for the university as students ambled around in the foreground. Tonya felt comfortable at universities, spending the last eighteen years in school. Now that she had graduated with her master's she was finished, with no intention of going back for a doctorate.

The opening notes of her ringtone pulled Tonya out of her thoughts. Her heart dropped with dread as she saw the call from her mom. She couldn't handle any more bad news. "Hey, Mom."

"I know you're at work, but I wanted to thank you for sending the help."

"The help?"

"Yeah, Benji showed up this morning at our doorstep with a horse trailer and his friends to help us move."

"Oh." Tonya shook her head, trying to figure out how Benji had arranged all that. It was a full day's drive from Houston to Phoenix. And the fact that he arrived that morning implied he had convinced some of his friends to drive with him through the night to get there.

"It seems we'll be able to move in one day. He even offered to help us unpack."

"I... that's..." Her thoughts couldn't form into words. Unbidden tears pooled in her eyes. The fact that someone she once knew had organized such a blessing overwhelmed her. "Give him my thanks."

"I will. I'll let you go. I just thought you might need some good news."

"Yeah, Mom. Thanks."

Tonya tucked her phone back in her pocket and turned to follow Sam and Max to the professor. Sam threw her a wink before continuing on his way.

Professor Sinclair gave good directions, and they found his office without a problem. The man who greeted them was a tall, thin man with a balding head of red hair. "Good morning. Are you the amateur star-gazers I talked with on the phone last week?"

"Yes, sir," Sam said, stepping in the office. "We had an appointment for ten."

"Of course, please do come in and have a seat. I must say, your story has me intrigued. You said this star-map would lead you to a location."

"Yes," Tonya confirmed, "but before we begin, let us call in a friend. It's her map, but she was recently injured and was unable to make it."

"By all means."

After two rings, Brooke answered. Tonya set the phone on speaker and laid it on the armrest of the chair.

"Before we see the map," the professor began, "do we know anything about it? Northern or southern hemisphere? When it was made?"

Max pulled out his phone and scrolled through his notes. "According to folklore, they were made on the 28th of March in 1795."

The professor turned in his seat, moving his fingers along the spines of his books. "The skies are changing. It's not like the sun, where it is the same every year, though technically not true, which is why we have leap year. You see, the major constellations may be in a similar location, but we have the movement of the planets, the passing of certain comets, et cetera. Ah, yes." He pulled out a thick volume and set it on his desk with a heavy thud.

"How could you possibly know what the stars looked like that night?" Tonya asked.

"People have been studying the heavens since time began. We can look back hundreds of years and see what Copernicus, Kepler, Galileo saw. So, after many years of research regarding this, I, along with some colleagues of mine, created these sky charts. Our main purpose for creating these was to establish a history so we could predict future patterns and movements. I never thought it would be useful to actually know the past."

"You mapped every day for the last two hundred years?" Max shook his head skeptically.

"No, just the major occurrences of the years. This book holds the late 18th century."

Tonya leaned over to Max. "What are the chances our date has a significant occurrence?"

"About the same as all this actually leading us to the Shadows."

"You don't think it will?"

Max glanced back at Professor Sinclair before leaning over to Tonya. "They know we have it. They've known for over a year. I think if we do find anything, it will be an empty warehouse."

"Or a trap," Sam cut in.

"Or a trap," Max agreed.

"I hate traps."

"Ah, here it is." The professor pressed the pages flat and turned the book around. "March 28th, 1795."

"Woah." Tonya leaned forward to get a closer look, but nothing looked familiar.

"Why was this day important?" Max asked.

"You see this alignment here? It happens every twenty-five years."

"I guess the odds were in our favor."

Tonya took off the ring and nodded to Sam, who got up and turned off the lights. Max turned on the flashlight on his phone and set it on the table.

Twisting the ring slightly so the light would come up through the base, Tonya waited for the stars to appear.

It did not disappoint.

The room sparkled with red stars quivering as Tonya struggled to stay absolutely still. It was like being enveloped in a kaleidoscope.

Sam tried to take a picture with his phone, but with the flash on, he caught only the white ceiling.

"It's more magnificent than you could even describe." The professor shook his head in awe. "See there," he pointed, "that is Canopus, the second brightest star. See its companion there, Sirius, so we know we're in the southern hemisphere, which I have lesser experience with, basing most of my studies here."

"Well, that rules out half the globe," Max whispered to Sam.

"Over half," Sam corrected. "Most of the landmass on earth is in the northern hemisphere, while the southern is mostly made up of water. This leaves us with Australia, most of South America, roughly half of Africa, and some of the islands of Southeast Asia."

"You forgot Antarctica."

"Of course not, but it wasn't settled until the early twentieth century and then only by scientists. Not ideal if someone from the eighteenth century was looking for a safehouse for a Duke and Duchess."

"And these constellations," the professor said, joining the conversation, "while gorgeous, can't give you which of those landmasses."

"But they can give us a latitude, right?" Brooke's voice startled Tonya, who had forgotten she was there.

"Yes, but it will take much studying. May I borrow it for a few days?"

"No," they all said in unison.

"I'm sorry," Tonya explained, "but finding the location is very time sensitive."

"Well, even if I can give you an exact latitude, I can't give you the longitude. You would still have the entire globe."

"Don't worry about that," Brooke said. "Leave it up to us."

Texas

Brooke lay propped in her bed with piles of paper surrounding her. While Tonya, Max, and Sam were finding the latitude from the professor, she was running possible calculations of the longitude.

Max had discovered that the smudges in the diamonds surrounding the gem might corollate to the minutes and seconds following the degree.

Brooke couldn't find any differences in them under normal light. Until they could find another way to examine the ring, that left four possibilities (two more if the ring was upside down). As for the degree, Tonya had sent her a snapshot of the inside of the ring. It was crisscrossed with a dozen different lines, but there was only one place where the lines intersected.

She reached over to get a protractor out of her desk, but even that simple move pulled at her wound too much. Pain ripped up her side, and black spots danced before her eyes.

When would this stop? When would she be herself again? Would she ever get better?

Taking a deep breath, she reminded herself it had only been a little over a week since the accident. No, not accident. Attack. And it would take time to recoup.

Lilly opened the door and walked in. Her sister was a mind-reader.

Brooke muted her end of the phone and pointed at her desk. "I need the protractor."

"And your meds."

"Yeah, I'll take them later."

"Later you're going to wish you took them now."

"That may be, but I'm not getting addicted to those things."

Lilly tossed the protractor into Brooke's lap along with a bottle of ibuprofen. "This is what you've been taking."

"How long?" Brooke popped two in her mouth and washed it down with a swish of water.

"Since this morning. You told me you wanted a clear head to solve this puzzle. Is it working?"

"Yeah. That's why I need this." Brooke set the center of the clear semi-circle on the intersection and lined up the angle. "It is exactly seventy degrees."

"So, what does that mean?"

"I should have a map around here somewhere."

Lilly grabbed it from the pile of papers and sat down beside her sister. "Latitude or longitude."

"Longitude. The lines going up and down. The rest of the team is working on the latitude."

"Is it positive or negative?"

"I don't know. Right now, the degree is negative, but if we flip it, it becomes positive."

Lilly shrugged and looked back at the map. "So, how many possible locations does that leave you with?"

"Hopefully two. When they find the latitude, it should narrow down our search and tell us which way the ring is oriented, giving us only the minutes and seconds to figure out."

University of Colorado

After spending the whole afternoon with the professor (who talked more than Max, if that could be believed) Sam was relieved both that they were out of there and that they left with the answer they were looking for.

A few feet away, Max was on his laptop, working with Brooke on finding the coordinates of the stronghold of DARKNESS, and hopefully the location of the nuclear scientist. Max hadn't talked about his time with Rick, but it had clearly shaken him up. A man who always insisting on having every detail in a plan laid out with multiple contingencies, had run into a burning building without a blueprint or a plan.

The expression on his face was classic Max. Double furrows dug between his eyebrows, and an expression of concentration, indistinguishable from a scowl, focused on his laptop.

"It's either Chile or the middle of the Indian Ocean."

Something about Chile sounded familiar, but Sam couldn't quite place it. "So, we're going to Chile?"

"Yeah," Max's eyes looked distant as he talked. "But I need to drop off some things at HQ and pick up some equipment before we try to take on whatever we'll face."

A chill ran through Sam's body having nothing to do with the evening breeze. He was missing something, and unless he figured that out, something bad was going to happen soon.

CHAPTER 29
RISKY MANEUVERS

Los Angeles

Emily looked around at the crowd packing the lawn. She should have been proud she had succeeded in gathering over one hundred people to this event. Instead, she just felt sick to her stomach.

Pedro was a gifted speaker and spun his tale with passion and emotion. Even knowing every word he spoke was a lie, Emily felt her anger rise as he spoke of his wife and sons who were killed in the fire. He even showed the scars on his hands from trying to get them out. She had no idea how he actually got those scars, but it pushed the crowd over the edge. These people were ready for war.

If she wasn't careful, the anger inside her would destroy everything she was working for. These students and young adults wanted a cause to stand behind, but were blind to the causes in their own backyard.

Emily slipped away and paced on the far side of the building, far enough away to not hear Pedro's words but close enough to hear his tone and know when he would be winding down. This crowd was not so different than the one in Houston. That one fought against the very real war against human trafficking. War had found them and at least two died.

This crowd wanted to do something good, but this was all based on the lies of the Shifting Shadows, and it would end in the same way.

How do people even know what truth is? For a split-second

Emily wondered if she was falling for some elaborate deception, but she had seen the bodies, had heard the screams of the innocent, had felt the blood of her friend. She had to stop that from happening again, but she was just following Hunter's plan, enabling his violence.

Emily stepped into the shadows at the sound of heels coming around the corner. The half-moon illuminated platinum blond hair with red highlights that was pulled up in a professional twist.

The stranger slowed to a stop in front of her and shuffled through her purse. "Emily, I know you're here. I got the contract. All I need is an introduction."

"How'd you get that?" Emily stepped into the light to talk with Nichole.

"I'm hurt that you would doubt my ability. I am the best at what I do. And the Flock might have pulled some strings. The producer never even blinked about a foreign reporter doing a fluff piece on American collegiate life."

"You and I know this is much more than a fluff piece."

"Yeah," Nichole continued walking toward the gathering. "But let's get this started."

Reluctantly trailing behind, Emily shook her head. "I don't think an introduction at this time of night would be a good idea. You know nothing good happens after dark."

"You must not have been to any of my parties."

Emily chuckled and patted Nichole's shoulder. "How do you think I got this wisdom?"

"But seriously," Nichole continued, "an introduction now would be perfect. It would show the Shifting Shadows I was already invested in this from the beginning. I would be their perfect choice."

"Fine." But the smile of having a friend with her again died on her lips as Emily rounded the corner. The voices of a hundred people chanting in unison sent chills down her spine. Memories came flooding back. Memories she had kept suppressed that threatened to destroy her every time they resurfaced.

She tried to look past the ghost of Thea's face and focus on her next step. She listened to the cadence of Nichole's heels and watched the swing of her stride. Anything to keep the memories from overwhelming her.

The peaceful protest. The feeling of doing something good. Laughing as she shared her sandwich with her sister out of a paper bag. Then daylight turned to night and more people showed up. She had foolishly assumed they came from work but later found out they were there to cause trouble… Which they did.

"Emily, you coming?" Nichole's voice broke through Emily's thoughts and pulled her back to reality.

"Yeah, right behind you." She just hoped that this was not a repeat of that tragic night.

Lukas walked out of the Shifting Shadows' safehouse and got in the passenger seat of the old van.

"Where's Emily?" Hunter asked, starting the vehicle.

"She is at the rally, where you told her to be."

"No, I told you Pedro could handle the crowd just fine on his own tonight." He backed down the driveway and onto the street. "But we can pick her up. You at least brought her outfit."

"No." Lukas's cheeks burned at what Hunter had asked him to do. "She has no part in this extraction."

"You misunderstood me. It was not a request. We're picking her up, and she will walk out of the club with our target."

"No, you misunderstand me. You gave me the assignment to capture the colonel. You gave me suggestions, but I made the plan. All you need to do is drive us to your location."

What Hunter didn't know was Lukas had an ace up his sleeve. Ryan Murphy. Classically trained actor and master improviser.

Lukas had given Ryan free reign as long as he got the colonel out alone. But that meant no plan.

Ryan had already been at the club for an hour and continuously texted Lukas with updates.

You're picking up the tab, right?

Not if you already used the money I gave you.

They have lame music here. Are you sure we're at the right spot?

He doesn't come for the music.

He's here.

Hunter pulled to a stop in the club's parking lot, and Lukas sent back a reply.

So are we.

Now it was the waiting game. Lukas just hoped it wouldn't be long.

Colonel Brice Fulton was not a punctual man, so Ryan arrived well ahead of schedule to establish his cover.

Peeling off a couple of fifties from the stack Lukas gave him, Ryan opened his tab with a bottle of bourbon and a wink to the bartender. "Now, which of these lovely ladies is Cinnamon?"

According to Lukas's research, this was the girl favored by their target.

The bartender pointed to a dancer at the far end with light brown hair swaying above her hips. "Be careful. That one bites."

Ryan took the bottle and forced out a laugh to cover his disgust. His mother had taught him to treat every woman he met with respect. But he was no longer Ryan Murphy. He slipped into the persona of Tony Wright, a mix of the adventurer/inventor Orville Wright and playboy/genius Tony Stark.

Flashing his most charming smile, Ryan flirted his way to the back, ending up with three girls and a bottle of chardonnay before reaching his desired seat. From there, he had the best view of the crowd, and in turn, the crowd had the best view of him.

When Colonel Brice Fulton came in, Ryan knew him by his short brown hair, broad shoulders, and slight limp, as well as the way his eyes settled on Cinnamon, who sent a wink in his direction.

The blonde sitting on the arm of Ryan's chair ran her hand down his chest, giving him a seductive smile. "Do you want a dance?"

Ryan caught her hand and turned it as he stood, placing her other hand on his shoulder.

She gave a short laugh that betrayed her nerves. "This is not what I meant."

"But it is what you want," Ryan whispered in her ear.

Her expression went from flirtatious to curious. "But the music."

"Don't worry about that." He leaned down and picked up a napkin, writing out a short list of songs.

He then made his way over to the DJ, stopping only to turn and blow kisses at the girls waiting for him. "Hey, man. Do you take requests?"

The DJ looked over with tired annoyance. Ryan grinned a little too brightly and waved the napkin like a white flag.

"Yeah." The DJ took the list and scoffed. "You do realize where you are?"

"Ah, yeah. But I know the best way to win a lady is to dance."

"Man, the best way to 'win a lady' here is to pay."

Ryan pulled out a couple of twenties and laid them on the table. "A wager then. If you play my list, I can get any girl to dance with me without touching my wallet."

Looking through the crowd, the DJ nodded to Cinnamon. "See the girl at the far end. Get her to dance with you."

Ryan smiled and stepped away before turned back and pointing to the lights. "And do you control those?"

"You ask too much."

Making his way back to his seat, Ryan spotted Brice at the bar and came up beside him to order another bottle for the ladies. "It's pretty crowded for a Monday night," Ryan observed, hoping to start some small talk.

"It's summer in California. This is the least crowded night. Once you get the college kids and tourists, that's when you have a crowd."

"What about you? I don't take you as the type to party on a work night."

Brice studied him for a second and took off his glasses. "Who said anything about work? I pulled the weekend duty, so Monday is the new Friday."

Interesting. That meant if all went according to plan, it would take days for anyone to notice he was missing. "Well, cheers to the weekend."

Ryan watched Brice down half a glass before walking back to his seat. And that was when the music changed. "Watch this."

He gave the bottle to one of the girls and pulled the blonde to her feet. They stood, touching hands for a moment before the beat dropped. The dubstep pulsed through Ryan's blood, joints, bones, and muscles.

They moved as one, hips jarring, shoulders shimmying, their feet the only things anchoring them to reality. Ryan brought up one of his hands and touched the back of her opposite shoulder, leading her in a spin. As she came back around, he stepped to the side in a lunge and moved his hands around her waist and neck, lowering her in a slow-motion dip. He held her there, waiting for the swell of the music to bring her back.

Spinning her out, Ryan let go and caught the arm of the next girl, bringing her in.

He let the music move him and continued to dance until the end of the second song. Time to win a bet.

With a wink to Brice, Ryan extended his hand to Cinnamon. She shook her head and rubbed her fingers together in the universal sign for money.

Ryan leaned closer and whispered in her ear, "That's a shame, because the DJ there bet me you wouldn't dance with me." He leaned back and took a step away before adding. "Tell you what, if you dance with me, I'll split the winnings."

Cinnamon considered him for a moment before joining him for a whirlwind of a final song. Ryan tried to keep an eye on his target, but just keeping up with the dancer in front of him took all his attention. The expression he did manage to catch gave Ryan an idea.

As the final note of the song cut off, he pulled her close and landed a firm kiss. He expected the following slap but not the stab in the foot from her stiletto.

His foot pulsed with pain, and he scrambled back. Brice stood with anger fuming but made no attempt to follow Ryan. He had lost any attempt to get him out peaceably, so that left a good old bar fight.

"You know you wanted some of that!" Ryan grabbed the empty bottle of bourbon and stepped toward him.

Brice's jaw strained, barely concealing his anger. "You should leave."

"Are you gonna make me?" Ryan took another step. He was close enough to throw a punch or be thrown by one.

"No, they are."

Ryan turned and caught sight of the bouncers coming toward him. Shoot. None of the plays or musicals he's been in had bouncers.

Knowing he had mere seconds, Ryan looked back for anything he could use and spotted the colonel's cell phone sitting behind him on the seat. He just had to be quick.

He grabbed the phone and raced through the club. It was a small place and didn't take long to get to the doors. Two bouncers and the colonel followed him out. He didn't have time to warn Lukas and had to hope he would be on the alert.

A van pulled up beside him, and Lukas jumped out. "Go! We have this covered!"

Ryan threw the empty bottle at a guard and hit him in the middle of his forehead. The man collapsed before Ryan could even turn and start running.

The sound of the fight grew more distant as Ryan made his way to his car. The van pulled away with the two guards laying at the entrance of the club. So much for making a clean getaway.

CHAPTER 30
LIGHTING THE FUSE

Lukas sat in the back with the prisoner while Hunter drove. The prisoner was impressive, already making two credible attempts to escape when the van slowed for a light and a turn.

Colonel Brice Fulton.

In addition to the file Hunter gave him, Lukas had done his own research on the man. Career military, he had joined up straight out of high school and had spent the last seventeen years in the Air Force with several tours in Iraq and Afghanistan. He didn't have a wife or children, and he was often away from home for months at a time while he was deployed.

He was known to frequent several clubs like the one they found him in. And he had acquired quite a gambling debt to a local bookie by the name Fredrick von Konikrike. Lukas guessed he misspelled Königreich meaning kingdom. Fredrick from the kingdom of what? Lies. He wasn't even of German heritage. He simply thought having a German name would make him more intimidating.

The day before, Lukas had visited Fredrick with a picture of Brice. He said the guy owed him sixty grand but promised to pay him back in one large payment by Friday. Something about that conversation hadn't settled well. What made him so certain? And was this all connected?

Lukas looked across at the man blindfolded and bound in front of him. What did he have planned?

The van pulled to a stop, and Lukas jumped out, pulling Brice with him. The waves beat against the shore lit by what was left of the moon. Hunter led them to a beat-down shack about a mile out from the marina where they stopped. The marina had half a dozen boats tied up, which would make for a good escape if that needed to happen.

Hunter pulled Brice along beside him as they walked across the hard sand. Closer up, the shack looked as if the smallest wave could knock it over. But that was the reason Hunter had chosen it. No one would press their luck investigating such a condemned building.

Once in, Hunter sat the colonel in a chair in the center of the room, removed his blindfold, and re-bound his hands to the arms of the chair. A camera was set up facing that seat. Two empty chairs sat beside the camera. A simple cot was set up on the side, and a blue and white blanket hung as a backdrop in the back. Something inside Lukas said something was wrong, but he couldn't name what it was.

Stepping to the back of the room, Hunter turned on a light, blinding their prisoner but leaving them in the shadows.

"Your name is Colonel Brice Fulton, is that correct?"

He hesitated a moment before nodding. "And who are you?"

"You will learn of us soon enough."

"What do you want from me?"

"We'll get to that in a minute. First, I want you to know how serious we are." Hunter opened an envelope and pulled out several pictures. "We want you to know what's at stake."

Brice said nothing, simply staring ahead, ignoring the pictures.

"It would be a pity if the wrong people got this. Either your bosses or… what about the media. I have a friend who would do anything for a scoop."

"I haven't done anything wrong or illegal."

"Oh, that doesn't matter. Especially after the police find her body floating in the ocean with the morning tide."

"You wouldn't dare!" He lunged for Hunter, but his bindings held tight.

Hunter leaned forward, letting the frame of his face come into the light. "We do not make idle threats. I do not make idle threats."

He leaned over to Lukas and tossed him the keys. "Get the bag out of my trunk. And don't forget the spare battery and jumper cables."

Ryan pulled up next to Nichole's blue rental at the motel and grabbed the target's phone. It hadn't been his intention to steal the man's phone, but now that he had it, he might as well see what he could get from it.

Opening the door, he heard the shower running and saw Nichole's shoes by the door. He settled on the couch and pulled out the phone. The lock screen had a picture of a cat and nine dots that opened the phone with a pattern.

He tilted it against the light, hoping on the off-chance the oils of his fingers had left the pattern, but to no avail. Smudges covered the phone in random patterns but nothing over the dots to get in.

The shower turned off, and Ryan could hear Nichole softly singing to herself a tune in French.

He opened his laptop and pulled out his phone charger. Luckily Brice's phone and his own had the same connection, but his computer didn't recognize it. In order for his computer to read it, it had to be unlocked.

"Did they get the guy?" Nichole asked, looked over his shoulder at the computer.

Ryan looked up at her wearing fuzzy purple pajamas with a towel around her head. "Yeah, they got him. But he left this behind." He handed her the phone. "Problem is, I don't have any clue how to crack it."

After several wrong attempts, she handed it back. "We'll just hope there's not a limit of times you can put in the wrong answer."

Lukas opened the back of the van and pulled out Hunter's black bag. He added in the jumper cables and tossed the bag over his shoulder. He then reached for the extra battery. His stomach dropped with a feeling of dread. Working as a mechanic for the last five years, he had never seen anyone carry a spare battery in their trunk, and this one looked brand new. It was bought purely for torture.

He picked it up, but it was lighter than he expected. Part of his mind tried to reason it away that he had been working out more, but he knew that wasn't it.

Walking across the open beach, only the cover of darkness protected him from the prying eyes of whoever might be up at this time of night.

Lukas opened the door without knocking and found Hunter and Brice deep in a heated discussion.

Hunter turned and had his gun half-way out of the holster before he saw Lukas. "Knock next time."

Lukas set the battery down and tossed Hunter the bag before leaning against the back wall, watching the scene unfold.

"Now, all you have to do is admit the United States military has forces in Argentina."

Brice straightened in his chair. "We do not, and even if we did, I wouldn't tell you."

"The American people have a right to know."

"All the American people need to know is the military is defending the cause of freedom and the interest of the United States around the world."

"And does that include murdering innocent civilians and burning villages to the ground?"

"No. Not unless the situation is dire and for the greater good."

"What about the greater good of the people? A wife who will never see her husband again."

"It is hard, but what about all the sacrifices our service families make?" Brice shook his head. "They sacrifice as much as our men and women in uniform."

"I'm not talking about sacrifice." Hunter reached into the bag and pulled out the jumper cables. "I'm talking about murder."

He attached two of the ends to the battery and held the other two inches from the colonel's face.

Brice did his best to pull away. "I had nothing to do with Argentina."

"Then you admit it, there is something happening there."

Lukas glanced back at the camera. A small red light glowed on the top, meaning it was recording.

Hunter probably planned on using the recording of the confession to sell or give to the media to create more of a rise. And Hunter was careful to keep his back to the camera, but his voice could still condemn him. If Lukas could only steal the camera and give the recording to the police it would be enough to bring Hunter down for kidnapping, and at this rate, torture.

"I admit to nothing. The US government does not condone what you are talking of, and I myself have never been to Argentina."

"Ah, but it's not just about Argentina. You see, the American military has a presence all over the globe. If what happened in Argentina is true, what are your forces doing in the middle east, in the eastern European block, or anywhere else in the world?" Hunter leaned down and attached the neutral end of the cable to the metal leg of the chair. "If we make the world see that even one unit is evil, then they will begin to doubt it as a whole. And when doubt is planted, well… rebellion isn't far behind. The people will rise against you, and you can't fight the people."

Hunter brought the other end of the cable against Brice's chest. He screamed, a muffled groan at first but after a few seconds he couldn't hold it back.

Lukas walked outside. The shack was far from sound proof, and someone needed to keep an eye out for a random Samaritan coming to help. Or that was the excuse he would give Hunter if he asked. Another scream followed the first followed by minutes of silence. Was he letting this go too far? He had proof enough to send to the authorities.

Chances were, he could get the SD card out of the camera while Hunter was caught up with the interrogation and make it back to the car without Hunter being the wiser. But if he did that, he and Emily would lose any inside connection. Would taking him out now stop the coming attack? Or did he already have things in motion that would ensure the dominoes start falling?

The main question stopping him from action was how elaborate was this con they were pulling? If he could get Hunter arrested, great. But if Hunter had the locals in his pocket, all would be for naught and the Flock would lose the only advantage they had against the Shifting Shadows.

Another scream came from the shack causing Lukas's muscles to coil in anticipation. He could not let this keep happening.

Doing a final sweep of the perimeter, Lukas walked back in.

Brice's head hung limp against his chest, sweat covering his bare chest and arms.

Hunter looked up toward Lukas, his eyes sparkling in a maniacal brilliance. "Where did you go?"

"Securing the perimeter. This building was not designed to keep in the noise."

"But it is far enough away from anything, there would be no attention to gain. I chose this location for a reason. Don't doubt me."

Lukas worked his way closer to the camera. "It wasn't that I doubted you, but a couple of years ago I was on an extraction detail. Our target fought us every step of the way. I hit him with a sedative that knocked him out for the distance we could travel by car. But when we had to travel by foot, we couldn't carry his dead weight around. His yells caught the attention of a local who then called the authorities. Since then, I've always been attentive to anyone who might overhear what happens."

Hunter hesitated before nodding. "Very well-"

A groan came from their prisoner who lifted his head slightly and opened his eyes. "Is that all you have?" His voice was raspy and weak.

"Yeah." Hunter turned back to Brice and undid his bindings. "We got the information we needed, and it's well past midnight. You can sleep. Lukas here will keep guard, and I'll be back in the morning."

Hunter patted Lukas on the shoulder and walked out.

Lukas's initial reaction was annoyance over having to stay awake and alert through the night without even being asked. But then he would have plenty of time to get the tape to the police and call in the cavalry by morning.

Ryan was just starting to nod off when a phone rang. It took him a second to realize it was his phone on the table and not the one in his hand.

"You do realize what time it is?"

"I need your help."

"I figured. Otherwise, you would wait until the morning to give me a ring."

"Can you make a duplicate of an SD card?"

"Yeah, the Wal-Marts around here are twenty-four hour, right?"

Lukas hesitated.

"Where are you?" Ryan sat up and put on his shoes, realizing he never changed into his pajamas.

"I just texted you my location."

It took a moment for Ryan to open the map on his phone and plan a route. "I should be able to get the equipment and be there within a couple of hours."

Lukas let out a tired sigh. "Fine, but if you can make it here any faster, it would be greatly appreciated."

An hour and a half later, Ryan pulled up to the old shack. The stars reflected off the ocean in a hauntingly beautiful way, and the crash of the waves called a warning. A chill ran up Ryan's back, but there was nothing there for him to fear.

He grabbed the bag with his laptop and supplies and went to grab the colonel's phone but it slipped. In an attempt to catch it, his thumb caught the pattern and the phone opened. Setting his bag back down, Ryan scrolled through the recent texts. Most had to do with work or family, but three days before, he got a message from an unsaved number.

Everything's in motion.
Be at the club Monday at 10.
Meet Cinnamon.

Acknowledged.
We agreed half up front and half in a week.

Check your account again.
The money should be there.

Affirmative.

Ryan switched to his phone and texted Lukas he was there and to meet him outside.

A few minutes later, Lukas walked out with the camera under his arm. "I feel like an idiot, but I can't seem to find the SD card or film anywhere."

Ryan took the camera from him and handed him the phone. "I'm afraid we've been had."

They stood there in silence for a few minutes as Lukas read the texts and Ryan searched for the camera's card.

"And you think these texts are from Hunter?" Lukas asked.

"Yeah, it would be the only thing that makes sense. Why else would he be there at that time on Monday making contact with the one person we had information on?" Ryan turned the camera over. "Are you sure he didn't take the SD card?"

"Something is off about this."

Lukas walked back in the shack with Ryan on his heels. Brice lay sleeping on the cot against the wall facing away from them. Lukas took the car battery and attached the cables. He stood for a moment before striking the other two ends together.

Not so much as a spark.

It was a fake. Everything in this room was a fake, including the capture of this colonel. If he was even a colonel.

Ryan took the phone from Lukas and opened the contacts. At the top read the name Elias Duncan with the phone's number under it.

He turned the phone to Lukas and shook his head.

In two steps, Lukas crossed the floor and grabbed Brice aka Elias by the scruff of his shirt. "Who are you, and what are you really doing here?!"

Elias struggled to get his feet under him and clutched his stomach.

"You can stop this pretense. I know the battery was a fake. As was your name and why Radenie wanted you."

"Radenie?" Elias's face visibly paled. "That was Radenie?"

"So, you know about the Shifting Shadows."

He blinked several times before answering. "Who?"

Lukas let go of his shirt and landed a solid punch to his diaphragm. "You best answer me. All the torture and interrogation you went through was fake, simply an acting job for money."

"I didn't-"

"Don't try to deny it. We have evidence on your phone."

"Hey! That's private property!"

"Do you think we care? Now, you will answer our questions and answer them truthfully, or I will go get the real battery."

"You wouldn't."

Lukas shoved Elias back on the cot and leaned down inches from his face. "Innocent lives are at risk. Things have been set in motion. The fuse has been lit. And you could be the reason people live or die. Do you understand?"

Elias nodded quickly, fear contorting his face.

"Now, let's start at the beginning. Who are you?"

"My name is Elias Duncan. I'm an actor. About a month ago at the club I met that guy who was in here, except he said his name was Bill. We quickly hit it off and became good pals. One night, I told him about my gambling debt."

"With Fredrich von Königreich?"

Elias sat back in surprise. "Yeah, how do you know about him?"

"We had a little talk about you. Come to think of it, he never did tell me your name."

"Bill said he had a way of abolishing my debt. All I had to do was act the part of a corrupt military officer. So, a couple of days ago I went to his house and we recorded what I would say to be dubbed over the performance tonight."

"And what exactly did you say?"

Elias squirmed in his chair, trying to get away from Lukas. "I don't exactly remember."

"You don't remember." Lukas stood and pointed to Ryan. "Go get the battery."

Ryan turned and put his hand on the doorknob.

"Stop!" Elias cried. "Please don't. He said it was for a movie."

"I very much doubt that," Ryan interjected. "No one insists on half before and half after for a legitimate job. Just answer my friend's question."

"Fine, I told the people to stand up and fight for our brothers and sisters to our south, that the military abuses its power and should be forced back home, and-" Elias hesitated, looking to the ground- "that everyone should meet downtown at the courthouse on Wednesday night to make their voices heard."

Lukas paused for a moment, running his fingers through his hair. "If you had a recording session last week, then why the façade here? Why have us capture you and go through that interrogation?"

"This was filmed to be shown on Wednesday. The speech was recorded for the radio."

"When will it be airing?"

"I don't know. And I told you everything I do. Now, will you let me go back to sleep. I have to be ready for the morning."

"What happens in the morning?"

"My death scene."

Lukas walked out, letting the door slam behind him. He hoped the fresh ocean air would help him think, but the questions kept clamoring for his attention. First and foremost was how to change

Hunter's plans for the morning. This wasn't a death scene like Elias thought, he knew too much and was too much of a liability if the authorities found him. No, Hunter would ask Lukas to shoot him and take care of the body. No doubt--that's what his uncle would have done.

Lukas turned at the sound of Ryan joining him outside. "What's your plan?" Ryan asked.

"We have to steal or destroy the recording before morning. We have to stop him before Elias ends up dead."

Ryan stood staring at the marina for a minute. "What if we bring the cops in?"

"We have no proof."

"Not for Hunter. But what if we call in men loading firearms on a boat in the early hours of the morning. Do it shortly before Hunter is supposed to show, then you take Elias and get out. Say you heard the sirens and didn't want to be found out."

"Hunter didn't leave me a car. And what am I supposed to do with Elias?"

"Say he freaked when he heard the sirens and told you who he really was. When you saw he didn't have any real information, you left him at the bus station to make his way back home. As for transportation-" Ryan tossed Lukas his keys- "you could say you stole one."

Lukas nodded, looking around at the empty beach. "This just might work."

Emily rolled over and opened her eyes to light coming in the window. She had fallen asleep waiting for Lukas, a wasted effort considering he never came in. His shoes weren't tucked under the table, his keys weren't laying by the door, and the blankets were still folded over the top of the couch.

The clock read half past eight. She had slept past her alarm, that she hadn't remembered to set the night before.

Dressing quickly, she pulled on a red sundress and set a matching pair of red sunglasses on her head. Nichole was meeting her and Pedro at a local café in thirty minutes. The living room and dining room were empty except for Pedro.

"Where's everyone else?" Emily asked, grabbing the orange juice from the refrigerator.

"Spread out over the city looking for some guy your husband let go," Pedro said as he finished his breakfast.

"Lukas? I thought they were interrogating someone last night."

"That was the plan, but I heard the police showed up."

"Cops?" Emily set down the bottle and tried to keep a straight face. "Did they get anyone?"

Pedro motioned to the police scanner sitting on the table. "Nothing yet, but your boy is in some serious trouble."

"As are you if you miss the meeting with that reporter we met last night."

Nichole sat at the café with her laptop open and a breakfast croissant beside her. She had the ability to spin any story if she had the right information. Five minutes after their arranged time, Emily and the man who called himself Matias walked in.

She focused on Matias and gave a friendly little wave, motioning for them to join her. "Thank you for meeting me," she began.

"No, I must thank *you*." Matias gave a small bow. His polite demeaner would make any girl smile, as long as she didn't know he was a liar, using her to stir up the crowd. "Without your help and support, no one would know about our cause."

"Yes, well I got quite an introduction to your story last evening. When is your rally planned?"

"Tomorrow night at the courthouse. I already have a radio announcement being broadcast this morning that will bring people to attendance."

"Okay." Nichole typed a few things on her computer before

continuing. "And do you have any pictures to show? I can have my people show our viewers the pictures while we do a voice-over. This will give people more of a connection to you and what happened."

Matias nodded.

"Great. Here's my business card. Please email me those pictures. And, for the record, how do you spell your name?"

After going over the logistics she would need, along with the important details from his story, she was ready to go.

"Thank you for meeting with me, but I really must get back to work. I will see you tomorrow night. I'll be there a little early to set up and do interviews with some of your supporters."

"Very well," her guests rose as one. "We will see you there."

CHAPTER 31
TRAVEL PLANS

Flock Headquarters

Max needed a new plan. He couldn't just jump on any plane and fly down to Chile. He needed his equipment, which would not pass airport security. The Flock has their own airplanes, but it required paperwork for any flight and approval from Felix himself for a flight out of country.

He stepped off the elevator and made his way to Collin's office. The door was closed but the sound of Michael's voice carried. Max couldn't make out his words but caught the intensity of the conversation.

Rapping twice on the door, he waited. Michael opened the door and motioned for him to come in and closed the door behind him. "As I was telling Collin, I appreciate your help along with the rest of your team, but for a full-blown invasion of a suspected trap, I need to send in a more experienced team."

"I don't think so. Rick trained me to dismantle their reactor."

"We have men who have spent years defusing bombs. Do you think your three days with a scientist gives you more qualification than them?"

"Yes." Max knew he was walking on thin ice, but he had to be on the team going to Chile. "No one has ever dealt with this type of reactor."

Max turned to Collin who looked done with the day at a quarter after ten. "Let him join the team. There will be plenty of well-experienced men to watch his back. He has my permission if that's what you want."

"No," Michael turned to face Collin. "What I want is your team to stop acting like they're heroes. That only gets our people killed. In the last two years, how many of your people have been shot, kidnapped, or otherwise injured on the job?" Michael continued before Collin could answer. "Your people need more experience."

"And how else are they supposed to get it? We took care of the situation in Indianapolis."

"Only after a truck ran into the hospital's power source and the police came to back you up. I'll be leading the team in Chile myself."

"You need me," Max tried again. "If weaponized, this is three times more powerful than a regular nuclear bomb."

"And you need a pilot," Collin added.

"We have several available pilots. And you're not just a pilot. Your team is still running an op in Los Angeles. They need you here." Michael took a breath before continuing. "The hardest part of leadership is trusting your people to do their jobs and overseeing from headquarters. While I'm gone, you report straight to Felix. If you need anything, he will help."

Michael opened the door to walk out. "Max, I'll see you at the tarmac in one hour. Don't be late, or I'll leave you behind."

As Michael walked out, Collin motioned for Max to close the door behind him. "I know why I want to go." Max sat in the chair across from Collin. "But why do you?"

"Something about Chile." Collin leaned back in his chair and rolled out a kink in his neck. "Two weeks ago, someone gave Ryan a tip to stop investments in Chile. Juan has yet to find anything, which in itself is strange. Then I hear from Emily a couple of days ago saying Radenie is planning something in Chile and trying to divert all attention to Argentina. Yesterday, you told me the star-gem leads to Chile. Then an hour ago Sam hands me this."

Max took the paper from Collin and spent a moment deciphering Sam's handwriting.

> *Chicago – weapons*
> *Houston – people*
> *Indianapolis – medicine*
> *Los Angeles – media*
> *El Paso – nuclear power*

"These are out of order."

Collin nodded. "Yeah, but what if El Paso happened earlier than expected because of our break in Indianapolis? Look at what it spells, and don't tell me it's a coincidence."

"Chile? What does this mean?"

"We received multiple warnings and clues. It's almost as if the Shifting Shadows want us to find them."

Max put down the list. "Well, we suspected a trap with the ring. They've known we have it and would eventually figure out where it leads. That's why Michael wants to send in the big guns."

"I know, but..." Collin paused. "You said the ring could lead to two locations in Chile, right?"

"Yeah, Brooke and I couldn't figure out the minutes from the seconds on the ring. I gave Michael the most likely location, but honestly either of them could be targets if hidden well enough. The satellite images we received showed nothing."

Collin drummed his fingers against the desk for a moment. "How's your Spanish?"

"Three years rusty, and yours?"

"Non-existent. We'll need to bring Juan."

"And Sam. If Chile is anything like what Brazil was, I want Sam with us."

"Okay," Collin stood with an idea gleaming in his eyes. "Tonya can take over here for me. The team trusts her and her crisis decisions are sound. Get the word to Juan and Sam to meet us at the tarmac in an hour. I have a lot of planning to do."

"Do you want me to pack your things?"

Collin pulled out a bag from under his desk. "Already packed. Now, let's get a move on."

Collin checked his watch as precious seconds ticked by waiting for Sheila to let him into Felix's office. "The director is ready to see you now."

Before he could even get fully through the door, Felix spoke. "The answer to your question, Collin, is no."

The sting of his words cut but Collin stepped in. "No, you don't want to put surveillance on the second possible location? Or no, Juan is too valuable an asset here to be temporarily assigned to my team?"

His response caused Felix to look up from his computer. "They said the mountains were too dense to make out details of either location by satellite. The surveillance would need to be done in person. And Collin, you couldn't pull off being a native Chilean if your life depended on it. And I'm afraid it would."

"That's why I'm requesting Juan."

"Juan from the Light division. You need to talk with Reid to get his approval."

Collin handed him a piece of paper. "I already have his permission. All I need is your signature."

Felix picked up a pen but hesitated. "Michael said you wanted on the plane, but I'm the one who vetoed that because your team in Los Angeles needs you here."

"Tonya can handle that. The team respects her, and what could I do here that she couldn't?"

Felix released the pen with an answering thud. "I've about had it with you and your team going on missions you're not ready for. Last year was one thing, you were working alone. But the Flock is more than just the nine of you. Just because you got the information doesn't mean you have to be the one that followed that information to save the world. We work together to accomplish that goal.

"You and your team are civilians. It was a controversy when Peter created your team. The type of work we do gets civilians killed. Do you really want to be responsible for the death of your team?

"The only reason I approved Lukas and Emily for Knight division was they already had rapport with the Shifting Shadows. The rest of you are analysts, scientists, and public relations. Your team is not supposed to go running across the globe getting in trouble and needing our other teams or the local police to come in and rescue you."

Collin tried to hide his anger and disappointment. "I'm not asking to join the attacking force, just a secondary recon team. On the off chance that we guessed the wrong location. Something big is happening. And you need more eyes on the ground."

Felix considered him for a long moment. "Reconnaissance only. And if you do find anything, report it straight to Michael."

"And can Juan go with us? He's the regional expert of the area."

"He's also a valuable asset here."

Collin kept silent, waiting him out.

"Fine." Felix picked up his pen again and signed the paper. "And if I hear of you taking any part in this, you will be delegated to flying cargo for the rest of your service with us. And you will have no part with the rest of your team."

CHAPTER 32

FORTRESS OF DARKNESS

Chile

After a cold night of surveillance in the mountains of Chile, Sam stretched his stiff legs and gratefully accepted the cup of coffee from Max, who was taking over his shift. Though Sam considered himself exceptionally great at geography, when he thought of Chile, he thought of the beaches and not the mountains that made up most of the country.

"Anything useful?" Max asked.

"No movement. No lights. No vehicles. As far as I can tell the place is abandoned."

"But there is a place here," Collin said, leaning against the hood of the car. "Which means there's a real chance this was used at some point by the Shifting Shadows."

"What about Michael's group?" Juan asked. "Have we heard from them?"

Collin nodded and rolled his shoulders. "He said they found a structure where Max said it would be, but it also appears abandoned. Their plan is to go in at noon when the sun is on their side. We should expect a call shortly after with what they find."

"And what is our plan?" Sam asked, letting the hot mug warm his hands.

"To sit here and watch this secondary target. If anyone does come, we are not to do anything but call for backup."

"But backup is thirty miles away in the mountains with no road straight between us."

"Those are our orders, and we will do everything in our power to obey those orders."

Juan pulled Collin over to the side, and Sam continued to sip his coffee, listening in on their conversation.

"Why did you bring me out here? I'm grateful to be out of the office and considered useful, but what do you want me to do?"

Collin put his hand on Juan's shoulder. "You know the culture. You know the language. If we do meet anyone here, we would greatly rely on you and your abilities."

"Fine, but know if this comes to shooting, you do not want to count on me."

"We have you covered."

Looking back to the mountains, Sam wondered what they were in for. Once they had landed, Michael had decided Max would stay as lookout with Collin and would deliver specific instruction over the phone to qualified bomb disposal experts. Though Sam was relieved to have his friend watching his back, he did feel bad for Max not getting in on the action.

There was always the possibility that the sight they were watching was the real safehouse. Then Max would have the chance to disarm his reactor. But Sam hoped and prayed it wouldn't come down to that.

Collin watched the hands on his watch slip past noon. The attack on the other target had begun. He wasn't sure what he hoped they would find. It would be a shame if all the work decoding the ring was for nothing, but an ambush meant that people would probably die.

Time ticked on past 12:15, past 12:30, edging closer and closer to one. Michael should have called in with something.

"We have movement," Sam's voice said from Collin's right.

"No way," Max said with awe. "That mountain isn't a mountain. The camouflage is genius. The entire mountain has opened. The base wasn't out here but inside the mountain the entire time."

Collin pulled out his phone and dialed Michael. It went straight to voicemail. "Michael, they're here. We found them."

"What's the plan, boss?" Sam asked.

"We wait for reinforcements."

"I don't think we have time to wait." Max handed Collin his binoculars and pointed.

Collin groaned as he saw what Max was pointing at. A truck pulled an old transport plane out to a make-shift runway. If they took off, there would be no way to follow them.

"It looks like they're evacuating the site. Who knows what weapons could be in there or where they're taking them? Max, you're with me. Sam, Juan, I need you to stay here, keep lookout, and stay in contact with Michael and his team."

With that, Collin grabbed his tactical bag and began his run with Max on his heels. They stopped in the cover of the structure and watched for an opening.

Men in kakis and brown jackets loaded crates onto the plane. The crates all looked identical.

Only two men were loading the plane, making about a two-minute break to sneak in, find the bomb, and take care of it.

Collin held up two fingers, and Max flashed a thumbs up before running to the plane.

Max ran through the plane, trying to read the names on the crates, looking for weapons, but his Spanish skills were basically non-existent.

"Osprey, put Juan on. I need some help translating."

"Here."

Max shook his head at all the identical crates in front of him. It would take way more than two minutes to search the area.

Coming to the first crate, he read each word aloud. "Efectivo."

"Cash," Juan answered.

"Medicamento."

"Medicine."

"Uniformes. Never mind, I got that one. Uniforms. Armas?"

"Guns."

"Great."

Collin's voice interrupted the dialogue. "Company."

Looking out the back of the plane, Max could already see the men coming toward him. He couldn't sneak out without being seen, so he ran toward the front of the plane and leapt over several crates, hoping to hide there until they left.

As they got closer, Max overheard their conversation, which happened to be in English.

"I swear, that woman's more trouble than she's worth. She already built the device. Why won't Radenie just be done with her already."

"You know the answer. The boss has always had his eyes on larger prizes. One bomb may be useful, but the ability to make them, imagine what he could do with that."

"Yeah, but he's not the one dealing with her."

A lapse in conversation tempted Max to look up, but he had to trust Collin would give him the all clear.

"It looks like we're about finished here. All we have left is that bomb."

At least Max wouldn't have to waste any more time looking through these boxes.

"I don't know about this."

"She said it was safe for transport."

"But do you really trust any word that comes out of her mouth?"

"More than I trust you."

"Come on, man." The voices grew softer as the men left to get their last load.

Max held the transmission button on his watch and whispered to the team. "They're bringing the bomb out next, then taking off. And the girl's here."

"We can't let the plane take off," Collin answered. "Even if you do defuse the bomb, they'll still have the uranium."

"Then Collin, take care of the plane. Max, get the bomb. And I'll get the girl," Sam said.

Sam loaded the pockets of his kakis with any tool he could possibly consider essential: a swiss army knife, a night vision monoscope, a couple of syringes of sedatives, a lock-pick set, and a flashlight/taser. He then made sure a round was racked in his Sig and put it back in the holster. The idea was to get in and out without anyone noticing he was there, so the gun was his final option.

"Are you sure you don't want me to come with you?" Juan asked.

"No, we need you to be our eyes and ears up here. If you can hail Michael, that would be greatly appreciated. And..." Sam grabbed a rifle from the back and handed it to him. "If anything goes wrong, wreak havoc."

"But I cannot shoot."

"The bad guys won't know that. All you have to do is aim in their general direction and pull the trigger." Sam turned around before adding a final comment. "Oh, and don't point it at me."

With that taken care of, Sam made his way down to the opening in the mountain. He didn't have any schematics or blue prints or any general idea of where they might be holding her.

The cave was much larger than he expected. Albeit, they had been hiding an entire airplane in there so he shouldn't have been surprised. It seemed as if the entire mountain had been hallowed out. Someone could launch three hot air balloons and still have room to maneuver them about.

The smell of salt-water wafted across. They were miles from the sea, so Sam assumed one of the tunnels led to the ocean where he knew they had a boat.

A woman's scream pierced the air, echoing around the spacious cavern. Two men hauling a crate didn't even flinch at the sound.

Following the scream came laughter Sam only heard in horror movies.

His body wanted to turn tail and run, but he pushed forward, staying in the shadows of the wall, toward the sound of the laughter.

He followed the path to the right and came to an abrupt stop at the sight of two guards. One held his arm and cursed in Spanish. "La chica está loca."

"Sí, pero el Diablo todavia tiene uso para ella."

Sam fingered the syringes in his pocket, thinking through how to get close enough without them sounding an alarm.

The woman shouted again. The men turned as one to look at her, giving Sam the opportunity he needed.

Driving the needles into their shoulders, he pressed down the depressors and hoped they would drop as fast as was advertised. The first man fell forward, hitting his head against the metal door, while the second man succeeded in throwing a solid punch that connected with Sam's jaw and made him see stars.

He stepped back and crouched, regaining his center of balance, and tackled the man, hitting him in the stomach and pushing up in the best football tackle he had. The man hit the floor and didn't move.

With a quick search of the sleeping bodies, Sam found the keys and unlocked the door. A woman sat tied to a chair, an IV bag attached to her arm, her sleeves ripped, her feet bare, and blood coming down from her lips.

"Are you okay?" Sam asked, coming to her side and untying her bindings.

"Yeah, why would you think…? Oh, the blood, well that's not mine." She smiled showing blood on her teeth as well, which caused Sam to stumble back a step.

"Did you bite that guy out there?"

She chuckled again, and Sam had to remind himself that she was one of the good guys. "Yeah, playing the part of la chica loca makes them think twice about messing with me. When I first got here, after they killed my partners, I did everything I could to drag my feet on the project, but they beat me. They broke me. But even then, I knew they couldn't have what I was making. So, when I broke, I added a psychotic shift, and they haven't touched me since."

"Well, I'm Sam, and I promise I'm here to rescue you."

"You're cute. I'm Susan. How did you know I'd be here?"

Sam brushed her matted brown hair out of her eyes. "Rick sent us."

"They told me Rick was dead."

"No. He's sick, but he's not dead." Sam reached over and unhooked the IV. "Can you walk?"

"That's a good question." Susan wiggled her toes. She stood up but immediately fell back in the chair. "Something's wrong." She pinched her hand. "Yep, dehydrated. And I don't think I've eaten in quite some time."

"Don't worry. I'll get you out." Sam stepped back out in the main cavern for a second, surveying the number of people as well as anything he might use. There was no way he was getting out of there with the girl without being seen.

He stepped back in the room. Looping his arm around her shoulder, he half-supported- half-drug her out.

Five steps into the main cavern, the entire place turned red followed by a loud boom and falling rocks.

"Clever boy," Susan muttered, grabbing tight to Sam's shoulder. "He figured out my trap."

"That may be well and good, but aren't we currently in that trap?"

"That we are."

They made their way forward with as much speed as Susan could stand. If anyone spotted them, they had other things on their minds.

Gunshots rang out behind them, but Sam was too focused on getting them out than shooting back.

They made it out of the cavern and into the bright light of the midday sun and an empty runway.

Max waited behind the crates for the men to come back. His bag with the tools he would need was still securely slung over his shoulder. He just hoped Rick was a good instructor.

A couple of minutes later, he heard the shuffling of feet as they brought the heavy crate in. He listened as they set it on the floor and the door of the plane closed. The men were still there.

Looking through his bag, Max pulled out the crowbar and waited for a couple of breaths. The element of surprise would only last for a few seconds, and he had to use it well.

Max let out one last breath and leapt over the crates. The crowbar came down hard on the first guy's skull with a cringe-worthy thud and the guy went down.

Bringing the momentum sideways, Max aimed for the second guy's head, but he ducked, causing the bar to go over. The momentum pulled Max out of optimal position. The man's fist met Max's diaphragm, knocking all the wind out of him.

Max brought his crowbar around to hit the man's knee, causing him to stumble.

Surprisingly, the man regained his balance and caught Max's sternum with a roundhouse kick.

Several crates broke against Max's fall. The crowbar dropped from his grip and slid under a crate.

Max struggled to his feet in time to duck a punch. He answered with an uppercut to the man's jaw, but the man still stayed on his feet. What was it going to take to down this guy?

The man stepped forward to strike, and Max stepped in, placing his foot behind his ankle. He pulled up and toward himself while throwing a left hook. The man finally went down.

Placing his knee against the man's sternum, Max punched the man's neck rendering him unconscious.

With the two men out of the way, Max could return to the task at hand: defusing the bomb. His legs hurt with every step as he retrieved his bag from where he left it behind the crates at the front and crouched down to retrieve the crowbar.

He glanced at the closed door and slowly let out his breath. At least he could do this without prying eyes and no one would know he took out the guards.

A loud whine came from the engines as the propeller began turning. But he had to trust that Collin wouldn't let the plane fly away with him still on it.

It took him a minute to get the crate open and crack the casing of the bomb. The inside looked like someone turned a rainbow into spaghetti and mixed it with LED lights. Like many times that week, Max wished he had studied to be an electrician instead of an architect, but he put that aside and replayed what Rick had told him.

Sweat poured down his back despite the coolness in the air as he finally reached the final step. There were several simpler ways he could have defused it, but he couldn't leave the uranium with the Shifting Shadows.

He put on his gloves and flipped the two clips aside, pulling out the sphere containing the uranium core.

A pounding sounded at the front, but Max assumed it was Collin trying to stop the plane.

With a shaky breath but steady hands, he set the uranium core in the lead-lined case he brought with him. His mission finished, he took a final look at the bomb and found a piece of paper stuffed between the wires in the back. The handwriting was small and hastily written with only two words and a string of numbers.

Pulling his phone out of his pocket, Max dialed the number which answered with a distant explosion. What had he just blown up?

Max got to the window to see the inside of the cave on fire, but a second more pressing problem arose. The plane was moving.

The unmistakable feeling of his stomach dropping as they lifted off told Max he was now in the air. His hand hovered over the button to open the back door, but he didn't have the guts to jump out of an airplane with a nuclear substance and without a parachute.

This was not good.

Collin inspected the plane as the men loaded up the bomb and closed the door. He mentally ran through the pre-flight checklist he did. A failure in any of those would lead him to ground the plane and do a closer inspection.

The most common reasons for a failed takeoff were engine malfunction, fire, or weather. Last he checked, he couldn't control the weather, and messing with fire while there was a nuclear bomb on board was not the best idea. That left engine malfunction.

Out of the hundreds of trips he had flown in the last years, he could count on one hand the number of times he had to put down because of his engine. Once, a bird had flown into it while flying, ripping up the propeller. Another time, the fuel line had a tear in it after so many years of use. He hadn't noticed until he was in the air over farm country and had to use an old dirt road as a runway. And the latest time had been a computer short sending all his systems on the fritz.

Imitating his bird problem seemed like the best solution at the moment. Collin picked up a handful of rocks and ran for the nearest propeller. He got two solid hits in before a familiar sound caused him to run back. The engines were turning and if he didn't stay out of their way, he would end up like that guy on Indiana Jones.

Well, if he couldn't stop it from taking off from the ground, that meant he had to stop it on board. He climbed up to the side door and tried to open it, but it was locked from the inside. He pounded on it repeatedly, hoping someone would hear him, hopefully Max.

The whine of the engines changed and the plane began to crawl forward.

Collin looked for any other way in, but this was it. Even if he could break the windows, they were too high for him to get to. The door didn't have any outside bolts that he could beat off. And the only way in once the engines were started was if someone opened the door from the inside.

"Max! Open up! Open up!"

He watched as the ground sped by father and faster and farther and farther away.

"Max! Open! This! Door!"

The door flew open, and Collin leapt inside and slammed against a box. Max hit a button again, resealing the door.

"Great job stopping the plane."

Collin rolled his eyes. "I'm not done yet. Did you take care of the bomb?"

"And some." Max motioned to the men on the floor.

"Yeah, well, I bet there's some rope around here. Tie them up. I have something I need to finish taking care of."

"Here," Max tossed Collin the crowbar, "you might find this useful."

Collin made his way to the cockpit and opened the door. The pilot sat staring ahead. No one occupied the co-pilot seat. Collin waited until the pilot straightened out and hit the auto-pilot. No use trying to fight when someone really needed to be flying this thing.

"Beautiful day for flying, isn't it?" Collin said.

The pilot nodded without looking back. "Finally seeing the sun again after the weeks cooped up in that cave. Never thought I'd miss it so much."

Collin stood at the door, wondering when this guy would realize his plane was about to be hijacked. "Where are we headin' again?"

That caused the pilot to turn. "You don't re-"

The crowbar came down on the man's skull and he was out. "Ooh, that's gotta hurt." He then yelled back at Max that there was another one to tie up in there.

After Collin settled into the pilot's seat and Max tied up all the Shadows, their watches went off with Sam's voice. "I have the girl. Where are you?"

Collin chuckled as he looked over the ocean below them. "We are on our way back to base with a stolen plane."

"And what about us?"

"Don't worry. I left the keys with Juan. Meet up with Michael. I'll let you do the explaining."

"Copy. You take care of yourselves. It's a long flight back to the States."

"Will do."

They flew in silence for a few minutes before Max asked the question Collin had been mulling over. "When we get back to base, what are you going to tell Felix?"

"The truth. What else would I tell him? Besides we got the bomb, and we got the girl. All he did was threaten to make me fly cargo again if we interfered. And it looks like I've already got a good start on that."

CHAPTER 33
SPINNING THE TRUTH

Los Angeles

Looking around her, Nichole saw the courthouse lawn was filled with protestors, many of whom held signs. Stay Home. Murderers. Send Them Back.

The rally hadn't even started, but she could feel the anger rising. She tried to spot Hunter in the crowd. He wouldn't allow a situation this delicate to be left to chance. There he was, standing next to Matias, giving him final pointers.

Nichole checked her phone again, hoping Ryan had sent everything she needed to the studio. It was a dangerous game they were playing, trying to double cross Radenie, but she knew if he won over the hearts of men it would be worse than all of his previous attacks combined.

No new messages. She would just have to trust he would steal the video, edit it, send the digital copy, and make it back before Radenie noticed it was missing.

She turned back to her cameraman, on loan to her from the news agency who gave her the contract to cover this. He appeared tired and bored.

Nichole cleared her throat and signaled for him to begin. "*Bonsoir*, I am Nichole Thomas coming to you live from the courthouse in Los Angeles, California. We are live at a protest organized by Matias

Gonzales to bring awareness of what the U.S. military is doing in other countries."

She then began interviewing random people in the crowd, making her way toward Hunter. The people were there for different reasons, some out of outrage, some out of curiosity, but none with any idea they were being played.

"And what brings you here?" Nichole held the microphone up to Hunter.

A look of confusion flashed across his face as he looked at her, but it changed to a smile as he spotted the camera. "I'm just a friend of Matias."

"And how did you meet?"

He hesitated and looked toward the stage. "Some other time. It looks like we're about to begin."

Nichole turned her attention to the stage, where Matias was making introductions.

Flock Headquarters

Tonya stood in the operation room on the Light floor in front of nine flatscreens, all working together to show her Nichole. All she could do was watch, wait, and pray that everything worked out smoothly.

Hunter's face filled the screen for half a minute, giving Tonya enough time to do a screenshot. It was the most recent photo of the new Radenie the Flock had. He hadn't changed much in the last year since he held her prisoner, but there was an unmistakable authority to him. There was no doubting he now carried the title of Radenie.

The screen changed to an unfamiliar face of Hispanic descent. He started with a lighthearted story of his wife and sons, pulling on people's heartstrings and showing them common ground. Then he spoke of soldiers, of fire, and of death, raising his hands to show the scars.

A slideshow of pictures flashed across the screen. Matias holding a little boy of no more than two. He and his wife dancing. A village burned to the ground.

"Are these the actions of your military protecting you? Because of them I lost everyone I ever cared for."

"If that was so," Tonya mumbled, "then why did you move to this country you hate?"

"Months after that my benefactor found me and brought me here to you. There is no way my country can take on your military without inciting a war, but if you the people decided to step up and be bold, things can be done. Tell your military enough is enough. Demand oversight. And demand that they leave Argentina alone."

The crowd roared in response. Tonya felt her heart sink to her stomach. They had been too late. The crowd was now under his control.

"Some of you may wonder if what I say is really true. Let me assure you, we have proof." A projector lit up the side of the courthouse with a video of a man tied to a chair.

"Your name is Colonel Brice Fulton, is that correct?" The voice coming from offscreen was unmistakably Hunter's.

The man hesitated a moment before nodding. "What do you want from me?"

"Admit the involvement of the US military in Argentina."

"I haven't done anything wrong or illegal."

"Oh, that doesn't matter. It's all about what the people see."

Hunter stepped out of the shadows with the end of a jumper cable in his hand.

The colonel did his best to pull away. "I had nothing to do with Argentina."

"Then you admit there is something happening there."

The scene fuzzed out and came back in focus. "Ah, but it's not just Argentina," Hunter continued. "You see, the American military has a presence all over the globe. If we convince them what happened in Argentina is true, we plant doubt in their minds. What are your forces doing in the middle east, in the eastern European block, or anywhere else in the world?" Hunter leaned down and attached one end of the cable to the leg of the chair. "If we make the world see that even one unit is evil, then they will begin to doubt it as a whole. And when doubt is planted, rebellion isn't far behind. The people will rise against you, and you can't fight the people."

The projector went dark, once against showing just the outline of the courthouse. The camera panned to Hunter arguing with someone in the crowd. Tonya smiled. Ryan had succeeded. He stole the film, edited it, and swapped it back again without Hunter noticing.

"This just in." Nichole's voice came through, but the screen showed a picture of the speaker wearing a suit and tie. "Matias Gonzales's real name is Pedro Ramon. Born and raised in Albuquerque, New Mexico, he was convicted of manslaughter and is wanted for fraud in four different states. Let's see if we can trust anything he says."

A picture of a quaint village in Argentina showed next. "What you're seeing is a picture of the village Pedro claimed was burned to the ground by military forces. This photo was taken three weeks ago.

"I also have from a reliable source that this entire protest was arranged by this man." A picture of Hunter's face filled the screen. "The purpose of this was to create a riot, which would then be attacked to unify the people. He would use violence against the very people that came to support him. His name, or one of his names, is Hunter Drake. He is the head of an international organized crime ring, and is responsible for the attacks that made the headlines in Chicago and Houston. He also has an arrest warrant in Texas for first-degree murder."

The scene came back to the protest with hundreds of people gathered in groups looking at their phones. Pedro tried to continue speaking, but the uproar of the crowd drowned him out.

Tonya gripped the edge of the chair in front of her. The point was to defuse a riot, not create one.

Los Angeles

Before the protest started, Emily melded with the crowd, going from person to person asking for a phone number or email address to keep them updated on future events and the status of any developments.

People believe whatever they hear if they think it's from a reliable source. Or even if they don't know where it's from, most people will believe anything they hear.

Pedro stepped onto the platform, and Emily made her way to the projector. Where was Ryan?

Someone brushed against her, pressing something small in her palm.

There he was.

Opening the laptop, she plugged in the cords to connect it to the projector, inserted the SD card, and selected the video.

Pulling up a duplicate screen, she dragged the video over to the projector and waited for Pedro to give her the cue. She then opened the messaging app and entered all the phone numbers and email addresses the crowd had given her.

"Some of you may wonder if what I say is really true. Let me assure you, we have proof."

That was the cue. She started the projector, and everyone's attention turned to the film.

Typing as quickly as she could, she finished the list as the projector turned itself off. Hunter was furious and heading her way. She dragged the second file on the card to the message and hit send, closing out just as he came within range.

"What is going on?"

"I don't know. This is the card you gave me."

"Someone tampered with it, and I've about had it with you ruining my plans."

"Me?"

"You and your husband. Everything went smoothly until you two got involved. He let the patsy go, and you did this." He motioned to the people around him now on their phones. A vast majority of them were walking out, while another group was clearly in an outrage.

"I've been by your side all day. When would I have had the time to edit that video?"

That stopped him for a moment, but he shook his head. "I don't know how you did it, but we are done."

Hunter reached behind him, and Emily's heart skyrocketed. "Are you going to shoot me like your aunt did? In front of all these witnesses?"

"No." He shoved something against her side. "Not in front of all these witnesses."

The loud crack of electricity raced through her body and the world turned black.

The crowd was thicker than Lukas expected or liked. He was working security, looking for anyone who might start escalating the situation. Hunter wanted the scene to escalate, but he couldn't keep his eyes on the entire crowd.

Ryan slipped by him with a wink. He had successfully handed off the edited tape to Emily and was now on lookout for threats with Lukas. It was good to have a team watching each other's backs.

The crowd was too big for one person to watch, but something didn't seem right. Lukas caught sight of Zane's smug face, but he was wearing a uniform. A police uniform.

The attack was going down tonight, and the Shadows had instigators among the crowd and officers to ensure a riot would take place, which would mean injuries or even deaths.

Pedro got up on the stage, and Lukas took his place behind the platform. The expressions on the people's faces ranged from compassion to disgust to anger to outrage. At this rate there would be too many threats to stop.

Everyone turned to watch the video play on the projector, and Lukas kept a close eye on Hunter and his minions. The anger written across the faces even before the film was finished meant that it was about to go down.

There were too many to stop. All he could do was hope Ryan had pulled off the switch in time, Nichole said the right words, and Emily made sure everyone heard them.

The projector switched off and the people turned back to the stage. A majority of them looked down at their phones as Emily sent out the truth Nichole would be reporting. Lukas let out a breath as many of the audience decided to turn around and leave. Less people there meant less people would be hurt if he couldn't stop this from turning violent.

Movement toward the projector caught his attention. There were too many people in the way to see what happened. By the time he got there, no one was in the vicinity. But something was off.

The lawn had been watered recently, leaving the ground below it soft. Footprints covered the entire area, but it also looked like someone had recently fallen.

"What happened here?" he asked the people standing around.

"Some girl had a seizure," a larger man with a blue mohawk answered.

"Girl?" Emily was supposed to be there running the projector. "Describe her."

"Cute in that exotic chic way. Short black hair in a red sundress." The man went on describing her, but Lukas was already gone. What had happened to Emily?

He ran toward the road, working on the assumption that whoever had taken her wouldn't bring her deeper into the crowd.

The slam of a car door made Lukas turn, and his eyes met Hunter's. They stood there for a moment, both locked in invisible combat.

Hunter broke first and raced around the front of the car. Lukas leaped for the passenger door, but the Honda Accord squealed off before he could get hold of the handle.

Nearby a middle-aged couple was getting into a Pontiac Grand Prix.

"Stop!" Lukas called, running up to them. "That man just kidnapped my wife. I need your car!"

The man hesitated, trying to figure out if this was genuine or just a carjacking.

"Now!"

The man tossed the keys. Lukas grabbed them and sped away. The Grand Prix was an older car but he didn't need anything flashy to catch Hunter. Under its hood was 260 horsepower, giving it a slight advantage over the Accord he was chasing. And he would take any advantage he could get.

Car chases in the city have less to do with top speed and more to do with acceleration and stopping power. The quicker you can slow down to round a corner, the more time the car has to gain ground.

Lukas pressed the pedal to the floor and heard the whine of the supercharger kick in. He feathered the gas causing the automatic to shift gears. Even in the intensity of the chase, he smiled. When given an opportunity, cars sang beautifully.

Weaving through traffic, Lukas chased after Hunter. The light turned yellow, and the car in front of him came to a stop. He tried to switch lanes but knew there was already a car in his blind spot. But the sidewalk was free of pedestrians.

His car hopped on the sidewalk and took off. He couldn't go as fast as he wanted to for risk of someone stepping out of a shop, but Hunter was still in view.

As soon as he passed the light, he urged the Grand Prix back onto the road. The low front end bit the asphalt, and the car rocked.

Back on the road, Lukas tromped the accelerator again, trying to get Hunter within range. This stretch of the road was mostly clear, giving him plenty of room to accelerate.

A truck pulled onto the road between them, taking its sweet time. By the time it got fully on the road, Hunter's Accord was nowhere in sight.

Lukas knew it was dangerous to drive distracted, but he needed the help of his team to get Emily out safe. He pulled out his phone but remembered his watch. It took seconds to turn back on, which in the middle of a chase, was an eternity. He slipped off the watch and held the transmission button, that way he could hold it with one hand and drive with the other.

"Eagle, I need eyes in the sky!"

Instead of Collin, Tonya answered. "Falcon, we have your position on GPS. It will take us a minute to get a live feed."

"Then do it by GPS. Where's Emily?"

Lukas braked hard for a turn, taking a right on the second street after the truck. It seemed the most logical place Hunter could have disappeared.

"I'm sorry, but her GPS is currently offline. You're running blind."

"This is Hawk," Ryan's voice came through. "I'll make a couple of calls with LAPD and see if we can get you some backup."

The light ahead was red, but the traffic was light enough Lukas could weave his way through. Slowing considerably, Lukas looked both ways and pressed the accelerator. He made it through with a cacophony of horns behind him.

He scanned the area ahead of him, but it was getting harder to see. The streetlamps switched on, indicating evening was giving way to night. Hunter could have turned down any of those streets in the minute he was out of sight. Where was he?

"Nightingale's GPS just came on," Tonya's voice came over his watch. "Pull a U. She's travelling east-bound on the road to your… right."

Lukas braked hard and spun the wheel to the right, making the turn into an alley. A man walked out with the garbage. Lukas released the accelerator and laid on his horn. The man turned, startled, and yelled insults at him as he passed. Or at least that's what Lukas assumed he was doing, the song of the engine and the road drowned out any other noise.

Pulling right again, he swerved to avoid an oncoming car. He let out a shaky breath and got back in the flow of traffic.

"She should be about three blocks ahead of you."

"I see her."

From that distance, Lukas couldn't make out the make and

model, but he could see the right taillight flickering with a Morse code SOS. That meant three things: he was following the right car, Emily was in the trunk, and she was unhurt enough to signal him.

"Emily," he spoke into his watch, "if you hear me, I'm coming for you, love. This is going to get rough. I need you to stay to the right as much as possible and hang on."

There was no reply over his watch but the light pattern changed then went dark. Three long followed by long short long. OK.

Lukas took a deep breath and focused on closing distance.

Two blocks. The car in front of him switched lanes, causing him to break and slide through the new opening created a few seconds later.

One block. Someone got out of a car on the side of the road causing Lukas to swerve.

Four car lengths. Red and blue lights filled Lukas's rearview mirror. Hopefully this was the cavalry.

Three car lengths. Only one car left between them.

Two car lengths. It was just Lukas and Hunter on the road.

One car length. Lukas double checked his rearview mirror, making sure they were far enough ahead of traffic to pull off this maneuver safely. Thankfully, the police were keeping the rest of the cars back.

Lukas eased his nose up against the side of Hunter's rear quarter-panel. The last time he'd tried this move it had not ended well. But that was not an option tonight.

The leather of the steering wheel moved smoothly through Lukas's hands as he pulled hard to the right. But Hunter seemed to have anticipated the move and broke right.

Lukas overshot and ended up on the other side. But he had told Emily to move to the right. It would be dangerous enough for her there, let alone on the side he was going to hit.

He broke and pulled back to the left of Hunter's car. This had to work.

Turning on his brights, Lukas slid his nose behind the rear tire and pushed. Hunter's car spun 180 degrees and stopped. Two police cars blocked his escape, while Lukas pulled around to stop him from backing up.

"Everyone out of your vehicles! Hands on your head!"

Ryan had probably saved Lukas by getting the police involved, but the fact they were there now meant Lukas had to play by the rules. He stepped out of the car and raised his hands. Thankfully, Hunter also stepped out and was now the problem of the LAPD.

A police officer approached Lukas with handcuffs. "You are under arrest for-"

"Wait. Please. Open his trunk."

"That won't change my-"

"Please." Lukas's hands had started shaking with fear for Emily. "Get her out of there."

"Her?" The officer turned to the two patting down Hunter and asked for the keys.

The trunk clicked open and Lukas ran for it. "Wait!" The officer got in front of him. "Let me check."

He nodded and waited as the officer slowly opened the trunk.

Emily lay on her side, her eyes closed, and an ugly gash to her temple, but her breathing appeared normal.

Lukas's fingers shook as he brushed her hair out of her eyes. "I am sorry. I am so sorry."

Her eyes fluttered and her lips parted in a soft smile. "You did say hang on."

He lifted her out of the trunk and held her. She was alive. She was safe. And she would be okay.

Reluctantly, he let go and examined the wound on her head. The bleeding had already stopped, and although it looked bad, it wasn't deep.

She let out a short laugh. "I'm glad this day ended with a crash instead of a bullet. I'm not sure I could take one of those again."

"He was going to shoot you!" Lukas looked for Hunter who was already in a police car. "I'll rip him apart."

"Not if I get to him first."

Someone cleared his throat, bringing Lukas back to their current problem. “Leave him to the justice system. You’ve done enough hero work for one night.” The police officer stood beside them with his arms crossed.

“What about Lukas?” Emily asked, still holding tight to him. “Are you going to arrest my rescuer?”

The officer smiled softly at her. “I received a call from my boss saying the two of you were deep cover on loan to the LAPD to bring down this man and his organization. And from what I can tell, no one was harmed in this chase of yours. You are free to go. I got to figure the paperwork for this will be a nightmare, but let it be tomorrow’s nightmare. For now, go home and be thankful both of you are alive.”

“Thank you.” Lukas led Emily back to his car and paused. “What about the courthouse?”

“What about it? The protestors went home for the night. I have a feeling they won’t be coming back.”

Lukas nodded and got in the car. He looked over at Emily in the glow of the red and blue lights. With Hunter out of the way, their days of playing spies were over. But that also meant they were no longer Mr. and Mrs. Keller. He took her hand and rubbed his thumb over her ring. He would need to get her a real one soon, if she would have him.

She lifted her hands to his cheeks and kissed him. He had always thought candlelight set the most romantic atmosphere, but knowing she was safe in the red and blue glow, there was nowhere else he would rather be.

EPILOGUE

Chile – Eight Hours Earlier

Michael put on his helmet and checked his gear one last time. The warehouse they were entering was large enough to hold too many surprises. Max had warned him this might be an ambush, and his gut told him the same.

"Okay, men. All three teams breach on my mark and be on your guard. Happy hunting."

The teams split off, and Michael watched the seconds tic by on his watch. He touched the speaker on his throat mic. "Three, two, one, go."

The door flew open, and Michael was the first one through. The shuffle of boots echoed through the empty warehouse. Nothing was there. A thick layer of dust lay over the floor and the stairs. No one had been there for months.

He led his team up the stairs to check the rooms up there for anything that might have been left behind.

The third room they entered had thumbtacks in the wall, with torn pieces of paper hanging from it. Upon closer inspection, tiny holes speckled the wall, map pins marking locations of something.

Michael got out his phone to take a picture when a scream pierced the air. His team made it out the door before it slammed and the unmistakable sound of an electronic lock clicked.

Gunshots filled the air with mixed shouts from his men.

"Find cover!"

"They're everywhere!"

"Get down! Get down!"

"Get him!"

"I'm hit!"

Michael used his gun to pound against the hinges of the door to no avail. The door was thick metal. But the walls weren't.

He beat against the sheetrock with the butt of his rifle until he got a hole large enough for him to see through. Nothing. No one in sight.

He tore down the rest of the wall to get through, but the shooting had stopped. "Carlson, Manning, Newburg, report."

Silence.

"Carter, Hogan, Hinders, report!"

Silence.

"Anyone?"

Silence.

Michael made his way to the banister and looked down at the bodies of his comrades. "Anyone?" he asked again.

"Only the devil," a voice said behind him, and the scene went black.

ABOUT THE AUTHOR

Hi, friends! I'm so glad you chose to share another adventure with me. It's thrilling to get to share my stories with you and steal you away from your real life for a while.

I've been telling stories as long as I can remember. Whether playing with my sister in the backyard pioneering across America in covered wagons or fighting rogue pirates with friends after school, imagination has always filled my free time.

I started writing as an escape, but just the act of writing has become so much more, and I recommend it to anyone, whether you write stories, poems, music, or books. It helps me see things from other people's point of view, which has helped me become a better therapist. It also helps me increase my trust in God. Psalm 139:15 says, "Your eyes saw my unformed body; all the days ordained for me were written in Your book before one of them came to be." As I write, I am reminded that God writes my story. No matter what my characters go through, they will be stronger for what is next. I can trust the same about my life – that whatever I am going through God will use for my good and His glory.

The Rising Flock series was inspired through my experience in college with a group of friends. I attended West Texas A&M University for a degree in music therapy and was part of a campus ministry called the Navigators. In 2015, a group of us from the surrounding states spent the summer in Missouri in a summer training program, where we would spend the mornings in what I called Bible Boot Camp and the afternoons working at Silver Dollar

City. It was so great being a part of a tight-knit team, whose members had diverse strengths and backgrounds.

When I'm not writing, I get to do music therapy (I am a board-certified music therapist) and lead worship at my church. I've learned over nine hundred songs I can play for both professions on guitar and piano, ranging from Bing Crosby and Disney to hymns and Irish drinking songs. I am constantly adding to my collection of instruments – keyboard, guitar, dulcimer, ukulele, Native American flute, ocarina, Q-chord, my turtle (thumb piano), and my newest addition mandolin.

For more about me, check out my website at www.katebaileystories.com and follow me on Facebook @KateBaileyStories and Instagram @kate.bailey.stories.

Have a blessed day, and follow wherever your dreams are taking you.

DISCUSSION QUESTIONS

Chapter 1: The Chase

1. In the opening chase, Lukas and Collin need Nichole's eyes in the skies to give them perspective and the right way to go when they can't see everything that is going on. Who is someone in your life that is your "eyes in the skies" that helps give you perspective when you are too focused on your situation to see everything?
2. After defeated the Shifting Shadows in the previous book, Lukas and Collin feel that they have to live up to their reputation. Was there ever a time where you have to prove yourself or live up to an expectation?

Chapter 2: Back to HQ

1. Brooke introduces her friends, not by how they look but by their personalities and what they mean to her. How would you describe a few of your best friends?
2. Out of the five different divisions in the Flock, which would you prefer? (Formula: the team that designs and builds new technology, weapons, and other gadgets, and are also responsible for building projects in disaster torn regions of the globe. Light: the team that gathers and monitors intelligence. Omega: the team that devises strategies, leads to individual teams, and holds the organization together. Coordinate: the

team that works with other groups (FBI, INTERPOL, local police) as well as disaster relief agencies and working press releases. Or Knight: the team that runs operations)

Chapter 3: Threat of War

1. Emily is not a morning person, but she agreed to go on a morning run with Lukas every morning. What is your morning routine?
2. Collin tells Emily that respect is the key to a successful relationship. What do you think is the key to a successful relationship?

Chapter 4: Always Be Prepared

1. Tatiana's first step in getting the team ready for the field was teaching them first-aid. What do you think is the most important thing for people to learn in their field? What is the most important thing you learned for your job or stage of life you are in?
2. Ryan chose to find his own path through life chasing after his acting career instead of following his father in business. Do you value stability in a job and knowing you have a steady paycheck, or going after a dream and valuing adventure?

Chapter 5: Pride Before Fall

1. Michael and Tatiana disagree on how to teach the team a new skill. When you learn something new, do you break it down into smaller parts or just learn it as a whole?
2. What would you consider an unnecessary risk? Should safety always come first, or should you push yourself to the breaking point so you can grow?

Chapter 6: Strike One

1. Attacks like those Ryan saw on the tv are becoming more common. What is your first reaction when you see something like that?
2. The Shifting Shadows plan to start a war using guns, people, medicine, and propaganda. Which do you think is the most powerful?

Chapter 7: Well Laid Plans

1. Lukas and Emily changed their appearance and their personalities to go undercover and fit in with the Shifting Shadows. Have you ever changed your appearance or personality to fit in with a group (good or bad)?
2. Victor was in a life-or-death situation with stolen information, and his nerves showed through his endless chatter and pacing. What specific signs indicate you are nervous?

Chapter 8: The Hated Plan C

1. When things go wrong, do you like to improvise like Ryan or have contingency plans like Emily?
2. It took the whole team to successfully pull off the deal. Whose job do you think was the hardest, or the one you would have volunteered for? (Haggling with the enemy, being shot at, being oversight, or ensuring plan C went off as planned)

Chapter 9: Counting the Cost

1. Every action has a consequence, whether good or bad. Some people say the ends justify the means, but is that true? And if so, to what extent?

2. Brooke found comfort being surrounded by books in a library. Where is a place that gives you comfort, that you go to when you are feeling stressed? When Tonya didn't believe in herself, Collin did. Who is someone you can go to who will always believe in you?

Chapter 10: Promises

1. Ryan challenged Nichole to a duel. What are you good enough at that someone would challenge you?
2. Emily's fears nearly caused her to destroy her relationships with Lukas and her friends. What is a fear that attacks your life? And how do you overcome it?

Chapter 11: House of Death

1. Nichole, Lukas, and Collin all take different approaches to defending the house, with ambushes, traps, and decoys. Which would be your defense of choice?
2. No one knows us better than our team, our friends, or our family. They are the ones who know our weaknesses and our strengths and can help us become better. In what ways have those closest to you challenged you to make you better?

Chapter 12: You Need Us

1. Is it better to ask permission or forgiveness?
2. There are many righteous causes to stand behind and defend, like human trafficking, that have marathons, walks, banquets, protests, etc. What is one cause that you think is worth standing up for, and how do you do so?

Chapter 13: The Walk

1. Emily's response to the attack was to go after the bad guys. Brooke went for supplies to help those wounded. And Tonya

tried to keep everyone from panicking. Everyone's response was different, but that was what made them a good team. What would be your first thought in a situation like this?

2. For Emily and Tonya, having a sense of purpose and confidence in their training helped them put their fear aside to help others. What gives you a sense of purpose where you feel confidence in your element?

Chapter 14: Falling Apart

1. Working with other people and departments was the only way the Flock could help their people in Houston, but when working with others complications ensue. What has been your experience, good and bad, working with a group?
2. After Brooke was shot, Emily was stuck in her head. Lukas was the one she called to help her get her bearings again. Who is the person you talk with to help you get your perspective back?

Chapter 15: Setbacks

1. In order to combat the lies that Brooke's accident was her fault, Tonya recites truth to herself. When her anxious thoughts threaten to overwhelm her, she focuses on what she knows is true and what she can do. What are some truths that help you combat the anxieties of life?
2. Tonya's passion is for her family, and Brooke's family traveled seven hours to visit her in the hospital. Family is important. Take some time and discuss your family.

Chapter 16: Connect the Dots

1. When trying to see the pattern of attacks by the Shifting Shadows, Sam writes everything out on a white board (writing/reading), assigning them each different colors

(visual), then he talks it out with Max (auditory), and before this he would train with Max (kinesthetic). Which is your preferred learning style?

2. Brooke is supposed to be resting but she goes against Tonya and calls Sam to talk about work. Do you have a tendency to think about work when you are on vacation or supposed to be resting? What do you do to keep yourself from working on your days off?

Chapter 17: Interrogation

1. The Flock is not officially law enforcement and do not stay within the lines of legality with their prisoners. In these scenes alone they use intimidation, physical pain, and sleep deprivation to get the location of the Shifting Shadows' next attack. Do you think there is a line that should not be crossed, or do the ends always justify the means when it comes to saving lives?
2. Reaper's reputation is a feared interrogator, though that is not who he really is. For him, maintaining his reputation is important for his job. What do you believe is the importance of a reputation?

Chapter 18: Balance of Life

1. Brooke was having trouble thinking and even walking like she did before the shooting. The truth was her body needed time and energy to rest, but in order to do that, she needed to give herself grace to not be up to her own standard. Is it easier to give others grace or yourself?
2. Benji tells Tonya to stay with her own kind. In that warning, he tells her to avoid toxic people and to value time with people who value her and her skills. Take a minute to evaluate who you spend your time with and how they affect your life.

Chapter 19: Coloring Outside the Lines

1. Collin lied on his official paperwork to protect his team, namely Brooke. Even when faced with the termination of his job, Collin keeps to his lie because he believes it is the right thing. Have you ever been in a similar situation where you did something to protect someone that was not looked at favorably?
2. Sam claims to be a man from another era. Do you find yourself comfortable with 21st century technology, or do you use more traditional methods?

Chapter 20: Room 22B

1. Emily doesn't want Lukas to go undercover alone because he is her weakness. Who is your weakness? In other words, who would you sacrifice the mission or your own safety to protect?
2. When Lukas was preparing his plan B, he carefully designed rooms 22A and 22B. Location was as important, if not more so, than the actual interrogation. Think of a time when location helped make or break a plan you had.

Chapter 21: Clues

1. Brooke wrote her mantra along the top of the bathroom mirror. *You are a daughter of the King: a princess worthy of a storybook. The weight of the world was never meant for you. So, look up, take a breath, and smile.* What would be your life mantra/ saying or a truth you need to remind yourself?
2. Max, who lives behind a computer, is suspicious of any electronic communication. Nowadays our phones are constantly with us and a lot of us communicate more via technology than face-to-face. Do you think hacking and eavesdropping is a threat? And if it is, what do you do to combat it?

Chapter 22: Escape

1. As Lukas is waking up from being knocked unconscious, he identifies voices by his feelings associated with them before he recognizes who they are. Our emotions tie everything in our brain together, especially our senses like smell and sound. That is why smells bring back memories and music brings back feelings. When was a time when you smelled or heard something or someone and it brought back memories?
2. Lukas's goal was to gain Zane's trust so that when they escaped, he could lead them to the Shifting Shadows headquarters. What are ways that you build trust?

Chapter 23: Running Intel

1. Max and Sam thought in much the same way and worked together constantly to find the clues. It took Tonya coming in and looking at the human aspect for them to make a break in the case. When was a time you could only figure out a problem with the help of someone who thought differently than you?
2. Tonya knew she was emotionally compromised and that talking it through with someone would help. What helps you when your emotions get out of hand?

Chapter 24: Tick, Tick

1. Ryan despises red tape. Most organizations, especially government, have a system of checks and balances or red tape. Do you think they are a good thing to help people from abusing their authority, or are they a hassle to stop people from getting what they need, or is it somewhere in between?
2. While talking to Agent Smith, Nichole admits that her job is making coverups. What are your thoughts about coverups? Should the people know the whole truth all of the time? Why or why not?

Chapter 25: Power

1. Rick worked with radioactive materials to try to create an alternative power source. Even though he took safety precautions, he still ended up with radiation poisoning. That was an occupational hazard for him. Injury and death were an occupational hazard for the team. What is an occupational hazard for you (carpal tunnel, being yelled at by kids, sore feet, strained eyes)? And what are you doing to prevent or slow that?
2. Max has a short time to learn how to defuse Rick's reactor. Have you ever been faced with too much information to learn in one setting but had to learn it for a project to succeed, or to pass a class?

Chapter 26: Hearts of Men

1. Hunter plans to steal the hearts of men by using an attack to unite the people against a common enemy. In your experience, what is the best way to unite people?
2. One of the main segments of population Hunter tries to recruit is young people at the university. Are young adults more easily persuaded or more compassionate than their older counterparts?

Chapter 27: Into the Fire

1. Tonya points out that during a mission, Collin leads with a plan, Sam charges in without one, Max looks after logistics, and she takes care of them after. Are you more of a charge in without a plan, one that keeps your eye on logistics, or takes care of the people rather than the task?
2. Max, who was usually the logical one, ran into a building on fire on the chance that Rick's team might be in there. What is something or someone you would run into a burning building to save?

Chapter 28: The Star-Gem

1. Tonya gets a call from her mom with good news for once. It's amazing what a call or a text from a friend just to let you know they're thinking of you will do. Who is someone you can reach out to and encourage today?
2. Sam describes Max's face as "classic Max". Double furrows dug between his eyebrows, and an expression of concentration, indistinguishable from a scowl, focused on his laptop. If your friend would describe your most common expression, what would it be?

Chapter 29: Risky Maneuvers

1. Emily says "nothing good happens after dark." Do you agree? Why or why not?
2. Ryan bases his undercover persona on adventurer/inventor Orville Wright and playboy/genius Tonya Stark. Who would be two people (historical or fictional) that you would mix to make the ideal person?

Chapter 30: Lighting the Fuse

1. When Hunter tortures Brice for information, Lukas faces a dilemma of calling the cops then and risking Hunter's plan going on without him, or letting Hunter torture Brice and stopping Hunter and his entire team before the attack. Have you ever been in a dilemma where you had to choose between the lesser of the bad options?
2. Nichole saw her training as a journalist as an opportunity to help take down the Shifting Shadows. Usually, groups like that are taken out with police or military, not media. How does your experience and your training shape how you see opportunities around you?

Chapter 31: Travel Plans

1. As a leader, one of the hardest things Collin had to do was let his team go without him. In this case, he found an excuse to go with them. Relinquishing responsibility is hard for anyone. What is something that you would rather do yourself than have others do for you?
2. Collin's team was unlike any of the other teams at the Flock since they all had different backgrounds and had different skills besides operational knowledge. Do you ever feel like you or your group are not like the rest? If so, how?

Chapter 32: Fortress of DARKNESS

1. The Fortress of DARKNESS was concealed in a mountain. If you were to set up a safe-house that you didn't want anyone to find, where would you hide it?
2. Collin had to stop the plane. Max had to defuse the bomb. And Sam had to rescue the girl. Which do you think you would volunteer for?

Chapter 33: Spinning the Truth

1. Hunter's plan depended on people believing Pedro/Matias's story long enough for his other team to come in as police and break up the ensuing "riot". Nichole's plan depended on people believing the truth. The real root of the matter was from what source people believed truth. Would you be more likely to believe a story someone told you in person, or the media showed you pictures of?
2. With Hunter in custody, Lukas can finally think about the future. Are you thinking of your future and following your dreams? Or do you still have things on your checklist to do before you plan for the future (like finishing school, landing a stable job, getting married)?